THE WORKS OF

CHARLES PAUL DE KOCK

⚜

Gustave

⚜

TRANSLATED INTO ENGLISH BY
ARTHUR S. MARTIN

The C. T. Brainard
Publishing Co.
Boston   New York

LOUIS E. CROSSCUP
Printer
Boston, Mass., U. S. A.

CONTENTS

VOLUME I

CONTENTS

CHAPTER I

Lucas and Zephyr. Fright and Disaster

"Hey-up! Zephyr; courage, old fellow! trot only one league more and we shall be at home. Ah! there you go; that's fine! I see you can smell your stable already. You shall have a fine supper when we get there."

Thus old Lucas talked to his horse on the road that runs between Louvres and Ermenonville and endeavored by words, often accompanied by expressive gestures, to encourage Zephyr, who did not trot any faster for all that, but who, on the contrary, seemed to be perfectly satisfied with the amount of travelling he had already done that day.

Suddenly a fresh weight falling on his crupper made the poor beast jump and then start off at full gallop, a thing which did not happen more than twice a year, but the violence of the shock seemed to have given him wings. Poor Lucas, who was very frightened tried to cry out, but he was encircled and strongly pressed by two vigorous arms. Struck with terror, the poor villager thought the devil was on the crupper behind him ; he lost all power of speech, abandoned himself to his fate, let go the reins and shut his eyes so as not to see his travelling companion.

Zephyr, however, possessed neither the strength nor the inclination to gallop far; moreover, the ground was becoming sandy and that lessened his vigor; so he resumed his usual pace. The arms around Lucas relaxed their hold and allowed him to breathe more freely; and the poor peasant heard a burst of laughter behind him. He began to recover his senses, regained courage and, reflecting that something other than an evil spirit might well have leaped upon Zephyr's crupper, he slightly turned his head, risked a glance, and instead of Beelzebub or Asmodeus, saw a young man with a pleasant face, whose dress was somewhat disordered; but, notwithstanding that, there was nothing terrifying about him.

" God! monsieur, I must confess you've given me a bad scare."

" Didn't I, old fellow! And so you rode almost a quarter of a league without stirring, and I believe even without breathing."

" That makes you laugh, monsieur; in my opinion there's nothing to laugh at. What would my wife have said if she'd seen me come back home dead ? "

" She'd soon have consoled herself."

" That's quite possible, but I should not have consoled myself; and my daughter, my little Suzon, who loves her papa Lucas so dearly ! "

" Come, come, papa Lucas, you're not dead ;
and I hope you've got over your fright, so let us
say no more about that. You see that I am neither
a devil nor a thief."

" I'm not quite sure about that yet. A man
who falls upon me like a thunderbolt ! "

" I was calling you for some time, but you didn't
hear, so I took a run and, having taken lessons
from Franconi, I mounted without stopping you."

" Oh, you're active enough, that's true ; but do
you think I'm going to carry you far like this ? "

" To your home, I think."

" My home ! And what for ? "

" For lodgings tonight."

" Lodgings for you ! A man fallen from the
clouds ! "

" What does it matter where I've fallen from so
long as I pay you well ? Daddy Lucas, do you
love money ? "

"Certainly ! That is, when it's honestly earned."

" Very well ! Since there is no harm in giving a
traveller supper and a bed, you will entertain me
tonight. Take these twenty francs in advance for
my expenses. Now, stick in your knees, spur up
Zephyr, and let us make haste to reassure Madame
Lucas."

The young man's tone was so persuasive and
decided and his manner so frank and gay that the
peasant saw no objection to his proposition. Moreover, Lucas loved money, and twenty francs is

quite a sum in the village! So he shook up the horse into a trot.

On the road, Lucas questioned his companion further.

" I see that you were out without a hat, so you live in the neighborhood?"

" Parbleu! I didn't have time to get it; I was lucky to be able to put on my coat and trousers."

" The devil! Were you bathing on forbidden land?"

" Not exactly, but the fact is I had no right to be where I was."

" I see how it is! You were hunting without permission."

" Just so, Daddy Lucas, the land did not belong to me."

"There you are! These young people care for nothing. So you were hunting without your coat!"

" Yes, it renders it much easier to catch the game."

" Really! Get up, Zephyr! That's a queer way of hunting; I never heard of it; you must teach me."

" But Daddy Lucas, it seems to me that Zephyr has come to a halt!"

"Well, he's not accustomed to carry two loads."

"I'm famished! where do you live?"

" At Ermenonville."

" Is that the village in sight?"

"No! that is only Morfontaine, we have still a league and a half to go."

As our travellers finished this conversation they heard horses behind them. The sound grew nearer till the riders were close to our travellers. All at once Lucas's young companion seemed seized with a sudden fear.

"My God!" he cried, "it's me they're after! Quick, my good fellow, we must escape them!"

The youth prodded, pinched and punched the poor horse till he forced him into a gallop. In vain Lucas laments, swears and cries that his mount will be foundered; his companion listens to nothing. Zephyr can stand it no longer; not being used to such treatment, he gives way to a noble fury. He rears, breaks his bridle and carries his riders towards a pond wherein a dozen ducks are tranquilly feeding. Lucas shouts "Stop! stop!" Behind our travellers come cries of "Stop! stop!" At last Zephyr reaches the pond, he is bemired and falls on his side; his riders do the same, rolling on the ducks and crushing four; they are all drenched and muddy, shouting and almost out of their wits.

CHAPTER II

UNCLE AND NEPHEW. AUNT AND NIECE. A GAME OF BILLIARDS

"CURSES and damnation! forever fresh follies! another note of six hundred francs that I must pay for my young gentleman!" exclaimed Colonel Moranval, regarding his nephew with an expression of extreme irritation and annoyance.

"But it is a debt of honor, uncle," replied Gustave, deprecatingly.

"Indeed! monsieur, all debts are sacred engagements, but there is no need for you to make any when I am able to provide for all your needs. Do you know, nephew, that you are regarded as a very bad lot? You will surely be brought up short some day."

"I, my dear uncle? I don't see how I deserve this?"

"Ah! you don't see; very well, I am about to make you see. Sit down there, Gustave, in front of me; be quiet, if you can, and don't dare to interrupt me."

"My dear uncle, I know too well all I owe to you."

"Silence! Hortense Moranval, your mother

and my sister, was a good woman, amiable, sedate, economical —"

. "She had all the good qualities."

"Hold your tongue, monsieur, I know what my sister was ; I also know that, blinded by her love for her dear son, she could not see that he was passionate, uncontrollable, a liar, a gambler."

"Oh, uncle ! "

"Now, will you be silent ? Your father was a man of intellect ; his talents, his merit and his amiable character made him sought after in every circle of society. He would have made a great name for himself in the legal profession which he practised with so much honor, but death took him suddenly from his wife and friends. You were too young to appreciate that loss, you cannot remember that dear Saint-Réal."

"At least, uncle, I shall always cherish and revere his memory."

"If you did reverence it, monsieur, you would never be guilty of so many follies. But to return ; I spent part of my life in the army ; on the rare occasions when I came to Paris and went to visit my sister, you took my sword and used it in place of the spit, my plume became the cat's prey, my hat changed its form, my epaulettes lost their fringe, and I found pellets of Gruyère cheese in my pistols and ashes substituted for powder. All this was a mere bagatelle ; but I noticed that you were not learning anything. Your mother had

provided masters whom you would not listen to;
you danced with your Latin and history teacher, you
fired crackers in the face of your violin professor,
you filled your drawing-master's pockets with can-
dle-ends — in fact, you played the devil. I told
my sister to correct you, but she believed that time
would ripen your reason. Poor Hortense, she
thought you charming."

"Ah, uncle, all the women shared her opinion."

"Indeed! then that's the reason why you love
them all alike!"

"That's from gratitude, uncle."

"Is it also from gratitude that you deceive them,
that you lead maidens astray, debauch honest
women and cuckold their husbands? But let us
continue: your mother, my poor sister, died; you
were greatly distressed at her loss, I acknowledge
that you loved your mother; that is quite natural,
in grieving for her you only did your duty. On
her death-bed Hortense recommended her son to
me; I swore to watch over you, and God alone
knows the trouble you have given me so far. I
sent you to school at the age of twelve. For a year
or so you were reasonable enough. They wrote
to me that you were making rapid progress, and
I was delighted. Presently I come to Paris; you
had just turned sixteen; I come to your school,
making a holiday of it to see my dear nephew;
I ask for Saint-Réal. People's jaws drop, their
faces look black and they stammer. I grow impa-

tient, I raise my voice and become angry. At last
I am informed that my fine fellow disappeared a
week ago, also a girl of fifteen who did the fine
starching for the young gentlemen at the school,
and who lived opposite!"

"Ah! Uncle, is it my fault if love —"

"Blood and bullets, monsieur, an elopement at
sixteen."

"Lise was so pretty, so sparkling."

"And you so libertine! Well, I tracked
M. Gustave and his Dulcinea to a little room on
the fourth floor in the Rue de Fauconnier. I sent
the young person back to her mother — I know
not in what condition, but that's the business of
the parents, who did not know how to look after
their daughter. As for you, since that time you
have not allowed me a moment's breathing space."

"Oh, uncle, for a few trifling follies —"

"If I leave you in town, you frequent the balls,
you associate with bad characters, you bring them
to my house, you drink my best wines, you leave
my horses broken in wind, you wreck my cabriolet and, what is worse, you contract debts. If I
make you stay in my country-house, you devastate
my garden, you kill my rabbits, you wound my
hunting-dogs, you fight with the peasants and get
their wives into trouble. What the devil! monsieur, there must be an end to all this. You do
not want to be a soldier, I understand that; you
don't know how to obey, and I do not insist upon

it, because in a short time I should fear to hear that you had been condemned to be executed for having disobeyed your superior officers. Besides we are now at peace, and it is not necessary that you should pass your youth in garrison. But in conclusion, you are twenty years of age; as for me, I am beginning to grow old; the work that you provide for me is too fatiguing, I am very eager for repose, but I want to force you to behave yourself, and to that end, monsieur, I am going to get you married."

"And is that to make me behave myself?"

"Do you mean to say that you could not be contented with your wife?"

"That depends, uncle; in the first place, she must please me; in the second place, she must love me."

"Do you take me for an imbecile, nephew? do you think that I have not considered all that? The young lady will please you, because a girl that is well brought up loves the husband that is destined for her; because, moreover, you are a fine fellow, and usually women have only too strong a leaning towards rascals. Finally, this marriage will afford me great pleasure, and I hope that that will count for something with you."

"Oh, uncle, my greatest desire is to prove my attachment to you."

"In that case, Gustave, you will set out for the seat of M. de Berly, which is situated eight leagues from here, between Louvres and Senlis; there you will see his niece, the youthful Aurélie, whom I destine for you."

" But uncle, I know neither M. de Berly nor his niece."

" You will make acquaintance. De Berly is a fine frank fellow whom I knew of old, when he was commissary in the army. Besides, you are expected; on my word you will be well received."

" But what about you, uncle? "

" Me! you can see very well that I can't stir now; my cursed gout keeps me in Paris; but as soon as it gives me a little peace, I shall set out and rejoin you. In the meanwhile, you can get along without me; you will amuse yourselves and you will hunt, for De Berly is mad about hunting."

" Very well, uncle; since you wish it I will go and see this young lady, Aurélie."

" You will not be sorry, you deceiver. Here, since you are becoming reasonable I am willing to forget your past follies; there are a hundred louis for your journey and amusement at the Château de Berly."

" Oh, my dear uncle, how good of you! "

" But, nephew, no more of your rogueries, duels, elopements, or disguises. Break entirely with all the dressmakers and the opera-dancers; more particularly do not see that little Lise, the object of your first love; it is she who induces you to disobey me."

"No, no, my dear uncle; oh, I swear."

"Lastly, monsieur, be good, or I warn you that I shall be seriously angry and shall use rigorous means to effect an alteration."

"That's all over, uncle: I see the error of my ways."

"Take my gray horse. It is ten o'clock; you will arrive at the château before dinner. I have told Benoit to pack your portmanteau. He shall be your valet instead of that rascal of a Dubois, whom I have just discharged."

"What, uncle, your porter's son? Why, he is a perfect goose!"

"So much the better, for you will not be able to use him for intrigues. Now get along, and do as I have told you."

Gustave embraced his uncle, and, followed by Benoit, set out for M. de Berly's country-house.

While passing through La Villette, Le Bourget and Vauderland, a road, by the way, that does not afford much to interest the traveller, Gustave made the following reflection: before marrying, people ought to know one another and find out whether they are suited (and for such a scatter-brained fellow this was a very sage observation). He made up his mind that he would not have Mademoiselle Aurélie unless she was pretty, amiable, gentle, modest, sensible and loyal — in short, such a woman as he had not yet met; for at twenty Gustave had had all the experience of a man of mature years, because he had begun his follies at a very early age. This has its good and bad sides; good, because it gives one some knowledge of the female heart; bad, because one thinks one knows it completely, and is often deceived because one cannot imagine such a thing possible.

Gustave possessed an inexhaustible fund of gayety; and when, in addition to this, his purse was well-filled, everything appeared to him rose-colored. In this happy frame of mind, our hero—for you now see, reader, that Gustave is the bad lot with whom we have to deal — our hero, I say, passed through Louvres and turned towards Senlis, from which De Berly's estate was not far distant.   The nearer he approached, however, the more curious he became to know this M. de Berly and his niece. He did not remember having seen them at his uncle's, which was not very extraordinary, for he was accustomed to be away most of the time, and in order to escape Colonel Moranval's sermons, he rarely went into society with him.

Remembering that his new servant, Benoit, who was the porter's son and was sometimes required to wait at table, might know the person to whose house he was going, he decided to question Benoit. Gustave's new lackey was a boy of eighteen, tall as a bean pole, strong as a Turk, fresh as a rose, red as a cherry, awkward as a peasant woman from Champagne, and stupid and stubborn as an ass. Gustave burst out laughing as he looked at Benoit,

whom he had completely forgotten along the way.
The lackey's appearance was indeed calculated to
provoke mirth. Benoit had never ridden a horse
before, but not having dared to tell this to Colonel
Moranval, whom he dreaded like fire, he had made
up his mind to do it, and bestrode the smallest of
the horses, on which he sat as stiff and as serious
as a Swiss.

Gustave stopped his horse to let Benoit over-
take him; but the new valet, who had got his
father to give him a detailed lesson and had sworn
never to deviate from his teaching, remembered
that he should always keep at a respectful distance
from M. Gustave. Firm to his principles, he
stopped as soon as he saw his master do so.

"Come on!" cried Gustave, impatiently.

"No, monsieur, I am not so stupid."

"What do you mean by that? Come on, I tell
you!"

"I know my duty too well, monsieur, I will do
nothing of the kind."

"But, you idiot, I order you!"

"That makes no difference, monsieur, I know
the respect a valet owes to his master, and I will
not come any nearer."

"Cursed fool! I suppose I shall have to come
to you!"

Gustave spurred his horse and rode up to Benoit, whose frightened mount gave a sudden jump
aside and threw its rider into the brook. The big

fellow picked himself up, crying and greatly dissatisfied with the result of his respect for his duty.
Gustave pulled his ear to make him mount his
horse again and compelled him to stay beside him.

"Well, Benoit, you will listen to me now?"

"Yes, monsieur, yes, hi! hi! hi!"

"Why, you big booby, you are actually crying."

"Well, monsieur, I think I am hurt."

"Where?"

"Well, monsieur, it is — it is —"

"But where?"

"Well, monsieur, somewhere around the bottom of my back and the top of my thighs."

"Idiot, can't you say it's your stern?"

"Well, monsieur, I hope I know my respect
and duty."

"The rascal will make me swear with his con-
tinual 'respect and duty!' You can bathe the
place when we arrive at the house to which we are
going; but now, answer me, do you know this
M. de Berly? Did you ever see him at my
uncle's?"

"Yes, monsieur."

"What kind of a man is he?"

"Well, monsieur, he's neither tall nor short,
neither handsome nor ugly."

"How old is he?"

"Neither old nor young."

"I am well instructed; and his niece, how old
is she? What does she look like?"

" Well, monsieur, as to that, I don't remember
ever having seen the niece."

" Come along, I see you are good for nothing.
I see a handsome house; that ought to be M. de
Berly's. Let us go on."

The travellers had in reality reached the end of
their journey. Gustave made inquiries of a villager, and finding that he was not mistaken, he
entered a large courtyard with Benoit, and asked
for M. de Berly. The porter invited him into the
gardens, where he would find his master, unless he
should prefer to wait for him in the parlor. Being
impatient to see his host, Gustave chose the former, recommending Benoit to the care of the porter. He crossed a terrace and entered the gardens.
Our youth walked along several paths of lilac and
honeysuckle, admiring the plan of the garden and
the taste with which it was laid out. Thick shrub-
beries, the entrance to which was almost hidden
by rose-bushes, seemed to invite to repose or love.
Statues adorned these charming spots, but they
were not sorrowful Danaides, the unfortunate Tantalus, the frightful Polyphemus, the hideous Cen-
taur, nor the revolting Philocetes that came into
view; they were Venus unloosing her girdle, Love
sharpening his arrows, the Graces fluttering around
Cupid; and, if in the background of a grotto
Vulcan was to be seen, the image of the poor, lame
god suggested nothing disagreeable to the imagination.

Gustave was admiring everything, thinking that the master of the house must be a man of taste and intellect, when, at the turn of a walk, he perceived a young woman seated under a little clump of trees. Never doubting for a moment that it was M. de Berly's niece, Aurélie, the young lady who was intended for him, he stopped to look at her. Happy Gustave! With what pleasure did he admire a charming mouth, a well-shaped nose, a good brow shaded with beautiful light hair, a trim waist, curved and rounded outlines of form, a small foot that seemed scarcely to touch the ground, and a bosom whose every movement made our hero's heart beat violently. He could not see her eyes, for they were fastened upon her book, but he could guess what they were like and imagine their soft and voluptuously languorous expression. Not being able to restrain his agitation any longer, Gustave advanced towards her. On hearing him, the young lady looked up from her book straight at him.

" I was sure of it," thought Gustave, " the loveliest eyes in the world ! "

" What do you want, monsieur," said a voice that went straight to the heart of the youth (whose heart, as you know, was very inflammable).

" Pardon me ! mademoiselle — I wanted —. I came — but, indeed, I want nothing now that I have found you."

The young lady, who had smiled on hearing

herself addressed as mademoiselle, seemed flattered at the effect she had evidently produced on
the handsome youth, who notwithstanding his emotion, appeared neither awkward nor shy. No matter what people say, the heart, good qualities and
character are the essential things, although a handsome face, an agreeable appearance and a graceful
bearing are not to be despised. Ask maidens and
even married women whether that is not what pri-
marily attracts them. I am quite aware that a man
who possesses nothing but physical advantages
soon ceases to please; that should be so, and it is
a great compensation for those who are nice but are
lacking in good looks.

" May I ask you, monsieur, if you happen to be
the young gentleman whom we are expecting —
M. Gustave Saint-Réal ? "

" That is my name, and I suppose that you are
Mademoiselle Aurélie, M. de Berly's niece."

" No, monsieur, I am that gentleman's wife."

" His wife ? — What ? M. de Berly is married,
and you are — "

" His wife. Yes, monsieur ! "

Gustave could not get over it ; he did not know
that M. de Berly was married, and, moreover,
married to a woman who was not yet twenty. Then
this beautiful young person was the aunt of Mademoiselle Aurélie ! How could any niece have
power to please by the side of such an aunt as
Madame de Berly ?

"Well," said Gustave to himself, "let us wait before deciding. This house seems to be the home of the Graces; undoubtedly I shall soon see another marvel."

Madame de Berly proposed that she should take Gustave to her husband, who was impatiently awaiting his arrival.

"He will be delighted to see you," she said, "and so will my niece, Mademoiselle Aurélie."

These last words were uttered with a smile; she regarded Gustave with an arch look, and he also tried to read the eyes of his charming guide. Thus they strolled along for a few moments; both seemed preoccupied; they exchanged glances, sighed and remained silent.

The words, "Here is my husband," roused Gustave from his thoughts.

"Let us see this husband," said he to himself, "this happy mortal who is the possessor of so many charms. By heavens! he must possess great merits indeed, much intellect and many natural advantages in order to have captivated such a lovely woman."

Gustave raised his eyes and found himself in front of a little man of fifty years, fat, red and pimply, with small, dull eyes and a mouth reaching from ear to ear.

"Another surprise!" said our youth to himself, with difficulty suppressing a burst of laughter which the sight of M. de Berly had excited. The last surprise, although not so agreeable as the first, caused him, however, a secret joy, the reason for which will be easily guessed by the intelligent reader.

"My dear," said the young lady, "here is M. Gustave de Saint-Réal, whom I introduce to you."

"Ah! young man, so you have come at last! I am delighted to see you; let us embrace! Your uncle is my friend, he has often spoken to me of you; he says that you are a bad lot. Ah! well, by heavens! I was one myself. When one is young, one has passions; one is guilty of follies. That is perfectly natural. My friend, this is my wife, and I flatter myself she is as good as any of them; you must become acquainted."

Gustave allowed himself to be shaken by the hand, embraced and made much of. He had not yet found time, however, to respond to M. de Berly's politeness; he had not had time, either, to get a word in edgewise with this gentleman when once he had begun to talk (which very often happened). Seeing this, Gustave had to be satisfied with bowing and smiling and gazing upon madame, who also smiled.

"Tell me, wife, has anyone told Aurélie of our young man's arrival?"

"My dear, I really do not know."

"Good, good! she does not know anything about it; so much the better, we will surprise her;

she does not expect to see you today. Peste ! she will be delighted. I should not be astonished if you had been going the pace in Paris ; I did the same myself. I went it pretty strong ! I was the darling of the beauties, but now I am virtuous ; ask my wife ! Do you hunt ? I am very fond of the chase myself. Oh, that is also a passion with me. I spend many days in the forest tracking a deer or a hare ; then I shoot. Ah ! I am a good shot ; ask my wife if it is not so ! "

"Monsieur, I only hunt."

"You hunt? bravo ! we shall have some famous sport. You will admire my woods ; they are full of game. I have excellent hounds, and guns that never miss fire. But I think it must be dinner time ; my stomach never deceives me. Let us go to the table, and there we can make each other's acquaintance and chat as we pass the wine ; that's the best way. I see you are a clever youth ; I shall take great pleasure in talking with you."

They reached the house. While M. de Berly gave orders to his servants, and, according to his custom, went into the kitchen to have a look over things, Gustave gave his hand to madame and was led into the parlor. A young lady was at the piano.

"There is Mademoiselle Aurélie," said Madame de Berly.

Heavens ! what a difference between the aunt and the niece. Gustave's eyes soon betrayed to

Madame de Berly what his heart already felt. She pretended not to notice his silent avowal; but the young man remarked that she did not seem at all displeased at his preference.

Mademoiselle Aurélie was tall, upright and heavy; her face was not ugly, but neither was there anything agreeable in it; her eyes were large, but seemed to be starting out of her head; she had pursed lips, a long and aquiline nose, and a skin rather yellow than white, and a general air of prudery about her whole personality gave to Mademoiselle Aurélie's manners a kind of stiffness that inspired neither love nor friendship.

The young lady rose on hearing the voice of Madame de Berly, bowed gravely to Gustave and resumed her place at the piano.

Gustave said to himself, "So that's the lady that they want me to marry! Really, my dear uncle is too kind! Nevertheless, I am delighted to have come into this house; certainly, I will not marry the niece; but, in case the aunt is open to sentiment —"

Madame de Berly begged Gustave to regard the house as his own home. She said, "You see that my husband is an unconventional man; be good enough to follow his example; I will try to render your stay here as little wearisome as possible."

"Ah! madame, near you, anybody would find it charming!"

And the young man, who had taken the young aunt's hand in his own, pressed it with great warmth,

while the niece was running hers over the keys
of the piano. The aunt quickly withdrew her
hand; but the look that she darted at Gustave
did not express extreme anger.

"Come to dinner! come to dinner!" called
M. de Berly, entering the parlor. "What the
dickens are you all doing here instead of coming
into the dining-room? Ah! I understand, the
young people are scrutinizing and criticising one
another! Ah! ah! wife, isn't it true that they are
already sighing for each other?"

"My dear, I can hardly tell."

"Yes, yes, that's all right!—you don't want to
talk about that — you who have such a cold and
severe heart that you can't imagine that anybody
can fall in love in a moment. Well, well! Gustave, my wife is very peculiar; she laughs and jests
when I tell her of the passions I inspired in former
days. But, come along; dinner is getting cold.
Give your arm to Aurélie, my young friend, and
you, niece, suppose you try to smile a little! Oh!
the fact is she is extremely shy (aside to Gustave),
innocence itself — but the devil loses nothing by
that!"

They went into the dining-room; Gustave was
placed between Madame de Berly and Mademoiselle Aurélie. "At least," he said to himself, "if
the left hand bores me, the right will make
amends."

During the first course, M. de Berly, who was

almost as great an eater as he was a sportsman, gave his listeners a little repose. His wife was then able to talk to Gustave, who was enchanted with her cleverness, gayety and amiability. The niece spoke little, but whenever she did say anything, it was with a primness, an affectation and an attempt at disguise that revealed pretentiousness concealed under the veil of a false modesty.

"By the way," said M. de Berly, as his wife was carving a fine fowl, "I suppose that tall young lout I saw picking sorrel just inside the vegetable garden belongs to you?"

"Yes, monsieur, I forget to mention him to you; indeed, I am astonished that he should have taken the liberty ——"

"Oh, the devil! there's no harm in gathering sorrel. I hope my servants will give him everything he wants."

"I fear, monsieur, lest he may be guilty of some foolishness; he is a very stupid boy whom my uncle has taken into favor."

"Good! good! he will soon rub the rust off; all my servants here are clever, and then as people say, 'Like master, like man.'"

Gustave laughed to himself at M. de Berly's awkwardness. The latter did not notice that while thinking he was paying Gustave a compliment he had been guilty of a rude remark. He had already made up his mind to find everything that his host might do or say quite perfect. He had stretched out first a foot and then a knee. At first the foot and knee that he had encountered had shrunk away, then the lady was obliged to yield to necessity ; and, though she did not look at Gustave any more, she seemed greatly agitated ; her heart beat violently, though there was nothing in her manner that expressed either indifference or anger.

"What!" perhaps you exclaim, "bold enterprises already! Knees, feet and hands at work already! These gay young dogs don't lose much time!" And can they be blamed? Why not find out quickly whether one pleases, or is even loved? But you will say, "Ought modesty to be outraged thus?" Oh, you are right, modesty should be respected. But please note that all this occurred under the table, and could not be seen. Ah, reader, if one day or one evening you could slip in under a table at which pretty women and nice men are sitting, you would see very funny things. Then poke your head out and look at those downcast eyes, that candid brow and that ingenuous air. So you clearly see that what is hidden does not alarm modesty.

The dessert set M. de Berly going again ; the others had to listen to his recital of yesterday's hunt, when he killed a roebuck that he had wounded a week ago, and of the courage he had displayed in firing almost point blank at a blind wolf that had been devastating the neighborhood for several days.

They rose from the table and went into the

drawing-room. Soon afterwards some of the people who lived in the vicinity and formed part of M. de Berly's circle dropped in. The latter was very fond of tric-trac and considered himself a master at the game. Madame de Berly sang with exquisite taste, and accompanied herself very gracefully; Mademoiselle Aurélie pounded the keys like a horse on the pavement, and her uncle exclaimed as he played his game, " Do you hear my niece? The devil! what fire, what vigor; if she isn't a 'first-class performer, I don't know who is!' "

They broke up early. Madame de Berly had acquainted Gustave with the habits of the house; he was again entreated not to stand on ceremony, but to consider himself at home.

Gustave could not repress a sigh on seeing Madame de Berly withdraw with her husband; and the recollection of the statues that adorned the garden forcing itself upon him made him feel certain that Madame de Berly had presided at the selection of the gods. This idea gave him a secret hope; and he made a low bow to the superb Aurélie and followed a valet who conducted him to his apartment.

On the way, our hero met Benoit, who was limping.

" Here you are at last, you idiot!' " said Gustave, " why haven't I seen you before? "

" Ah! monsieur, you see that I can hardly stand since using the specific that the cook recommended."

" Did you happen to apply sorrel to your but-tocks ? "

" Exactly, monsieur ; in the kitchen they told me it was the best thing to cure a broken skin. I went and gathered some and they chopped it up for me and I made a poultice of it, but damn it, it stings awfully, and I'm inclined to think that they've been playing a trick on me."

" Poor Benoit! I see that M. de Berly's ser-vants are very smart ; that's all the better, since your stay in this house will teach you a thing or two."

" Ah, monsieur, if they often teach me like that, I shan't survive it."

" Go to bed, you idiot, and try not to be caught another time."

" Yes, monsieur, here is my room ; if you want me, you have only to call me."

" You can go to sleep in peace ; for I certainly shall not want to consult you for the success of any of my projects."

While undressing, Gustave thought of the youth-ful aunt with whom he was deeply in love. Benoit tumbled into bed swearing at the cook and sorrel ; the master sighed with love and hope and the valet groaned and made faces. In his dreams, our hero saw Madame de Berly more lovely, more beautiful, more attractive than ever; he seemed to be with her in a bower of myrtle and roses far from curious eyes ; he pressed her slender waist and her voluptuous form ; he pressed on her rosy lips a burning kiss that brought intoxication and delirium.

Benoit dreamed that he was trying a remedy.

At dawn on the following day Gustave was already in the garden. I do not know how it chanced that Madame de Berly was also there ; they met and exchanged greetings.

" What, madame ? up already ? "

" Oh, monsieur, it's a pleasure to be up early in the morning."

" How happy I am to have run across you ! "

" It is probable that while you are here we shall often run across one another."

" Ah ! madame, if I could —"

" My husband has gone hunting. He wished to have you called, so that you could go with him ; but I said that it would be better to let you rest today at least. Perhaps I have deprived you of a pleasure ? "

" Oh ! you don't think that, madame. Could I find any where you are not ? "

" Really ! M. de Saint-Réal, you make very gallant speeches. "

" No, madame ! I am not gallant, I express what I feel."

" What nonsense ! but you are mistaken ; it is to my niece that your homage must be paid ; remember that you are to marry her ! "

" Marry her ! Never, madame ! "

"What? You won't carry out your uncle's intentions?"

"No, madame! I will never marry a woman whom I could never love."

"How can you tell? Perhaps, when you know Aurélie better, for at present your acquaintance is a very slight one, your feelings may change. M. de Berly's niece has some good qualities and virtues."

"It seems to me, madame, that you are very anxious to make me adore her!"

"Why, monsieur, I ought to. This wedding would satisfy an uncle who loves you."

"And my own happiness, madame, does that count for nothing with you?"

"But how about yourself, M. Saint-Réal? where have you set your happiness hitherto? If I am to believe all that is said about you, inconstancy is your happiness; seduction and perfidy are your chief pastimes."

"Ah! madame!"

"I know very well that almost all men are flighty, and that young men especially are fond of change."

"I have given up all those follies."

"You are reformed — at twenty!"

"But you, yourself, madame, who are preaching so well to me — have you none of them?"

"I, monsieur, I am married!"

"Alas! yes, madame."

" So, monsieur, you are going to leave us ? "

" Why, madame ? "

" Since you don't like Aurélie, you won't care to stay here long."

" Ah ! madame, I shall only go away from you when you chase me away."

" What an idea ! we shall be delighted, monsieur, to have you here; your presence will afford pleasure to —everybody. I flatter myself, moreover, that by seeing Aurélie often — "

" Oh, madame, let us speak no more about that ! "

" Very well, so be it for today. Now, let me show you the delights of the garden ! "

Gustave offered his arm, which was accepted. They walked through all the windings of a garden covering more than three acres. They visited a little grove shady with thick foliage, which the sun's rays never penetrated ; they entered a grotto carpeted with moss, whither Madame de Berly resorted almost every day to read or to work; they climbed to the top of a rock that afforded a view of an extensive stretch of country ; and then they passed along the front of some thick hedges.

" Madame, " Gustave asked, " what is this place that we are not visiting ? "

" Oh ! that's a labyrinth."

" A labyrinth ! Oh, I am so fond of those places in which people can lose themselves ! "

" But, monsieur, I don't know whether I ought — Come along, since you wish it ! "

The young woman reflected that a refusal to enter the maze would be an exhibition of fear and that fear is a proof of weakness. Not wishing to let Gustave see what, perhaps, she was unwilling to acknowledge to herself, she yielded to his wish. Besides, this young man had said nothing more to her than the sort of thing that is said to all women; he had made no sort of avowal that could alarm her. To be sure, his eyes were very expressive and constantly gazed into her own; they were tender, ardent and eloquent, but perhaps M. Saint-Réal's eyes were always like that, and then this young man had only arrived the day before and she might seem to be already fearing his attempts. Come along; decidedly, it is necessary to take him into the maze!

Reader, don't think that anything happened there that I dare not relate. No, they walked about, and that is all. Gustave seized a hand and tried to kiss it, but it was very quickly withdrawn. He tried to lose himself, but he was always brought back into the right path; and he had to leave the maze just as deeply in love, but no farther advanced.

"By the way," said Madame de Berly, "I nearly forgot to show you our billiard-room. As we spend only the summer here, we play in the garden."

This room was close to the parlor on the ground-floor, being separated from it by a few trees only. Enclosed by hedges of honeysuckle and lilac, it

was lighted only from above. The interior was
decorated with handsome shrubs; banks of turf all
around it made it look like a natural bower.

"What a delightful spot!" said Gustave.

"Do you play billiards, monsieur?"

"Yes, madame."

"In that case, I count on your kindness to teach
me the game. My husband plays it very little;
he cares for nothing but his tric-trac. Besides, a
husband very rarely has time to teach his wife
anything."

"Madame, I shall be delighted to be able to be
of any service to you; if you like, we can begin
now."

"No, it is too late now. This evening I will
remind you of your promise."

They left the billiard-room and went into the
house. How delightful it is to be with a pretty
woman whose husband is fond of hunting! one is
alone with her the whole day. "Oh, my dear
uncle," said Gustave to himself, "how good it was
of you to send me to keep company with Madame
de Berly."

The better to deceive Colonel Moranval, he
wrote to him that he was enjoying himself hugely
at Madame de Berly's; that everybody there was
delightful; and that he would remain there as long
as they would keep him.

Although he had said nothing explicit with regard
to Aurélie, his letter enchanted the colonel, who no

longer doubted his nephew's love for the lady he had picked out for him. Reassured on Gustave's account, the colonel wrote a letter to M. de Berly, in which he told him that everything was progressing in accordance with their desires, and sent his nephew, who seemed disposed to comply with his uncle's wishes, a fresh sum of money as a reward.

While this correspondence was going on the nephew was furthering his own affairs. Julie (that was Madame de Berly's name), could not help finding Gustave exceedingly amiable. In the country, the cold and formal tone of the town is banished and confidential relations are more easily established. In the course of conversation, our youth learned that Julie, married off by harsh parents who had not even condescended to consult her taste, had not seen her future husband till the moment the contract was signed. As a matter of fact, she did not complain of M. de Berly, who was complaisant and left his wife free to do as she pleased ; but could love be born from so disproportioned a union ? M. de Berly was more than twice as old as his wife; he was silly and garrulous, while Julie was tender and intellectual. He was ugly and she was charming ; he called love the need of the senses, while Julie had a heart capable of knowing all the delicacy of that sentiment ; in all good faith, she could nothing more than esteem her husband. Thus do parents who give their daughter to a husband whom she cannot love condemn her never to give herself up to Nature's sweetest sentiment. Poor women! strong virtue is indeed needed; and it is the weakest sex, the one that is ceaselessly the object of our homage and seduction, that must exhibit the most strength, insensibility and firmness. In truth, all this is very badly arranged, and those gentlemen who drew up the "Code civil" might well have given more study to the code of Nature.

It was that bad lot of a Gustave who indulged in all these reflections while watching Julie sitting before her embroidery frame and Mademoiselle Aurélie strummed to them on the piano the air from Beniouski, which she sang like a cathedral chorister. After dinner, they would go to billiards, in which Julie took lessons from Gustave; what a pleasure it is to educate a charming scholar in this game! The young man always placed the balls in the middle of the cloth, so as to oblige Madame de Berly to lean over the table. Then he could admire ravishing contours that a light muslin robe covered without concealing. To guide his pupil's hand, he would put his arm around a shapely figure; sometimes he grazed an alabaster neck, and then his eyes would wander over a breast that he burned to kiss. Julie complained that he often made her try the same shot over again, but Gustave taught her with such sweetness that she could not be annoyed.

Mademoiselle Aurélie did not play billiards, she

would have considered her dignity compromised by learning an exercise which she regarded as too masculine. Her eyes expressed astonishment mingled with annoyance every time Julie and Gustave went into the garden, but she did not dare allow herself to make any remarks about what to herself she called her aunt's folly.

M. de Berly wanted to take Gustave out shooting with him every morning, but the latter, on the excuse of having hurt his knee and being slightly lame, had hitherto escaped his host's company. Colonel Moranval's letter had given great pleasure to M. de Berly, who, not being much of a connoisseur in matters of love and gallantry, was persuaded that Gustave adored his niece. To this passion and the desire of staying beside Aurélie, he even attributed the young man's refusals to accompany him in hunting hares.

A certain M. Desjardins had arrived at M. de Berly's three days after Gustave. He was a tall, dried-up man about fifty years of age, a great eater, a great player, and a great liar. Possessing only a modest income, he found a way of not touching his own money by habitually living at other people's houses. He possessed the qualities necessary for a parasite; he was complaisant, a flatterer and a backbiter when it was pleasing to his hosts. He could do a little of everything: he played the violin well enough to accompany a Pleyel sonata; he drew fairly well and made silhouette portraits;

he danced when it was necessary and played all
games. Every evening M. de Berly and he sat
down to tric-trac, and while they were so engaged
M. Desjardins seized the opportunity to address
his compliments to Madame de Berly, praising
Mademoiselle Aurélie's singing, caressing the cat,
and feeding the dog with biscuits.

For a fortnight now Gustave had been beside
Madame de Berly, becoming ever deeper in love,
but not obtaining any favors from Julie. He had
made the confession of his love, which had been
listened to jestingly; the lady was entirely willing
to please, but was not willing to fail in her duty.
However, the billiard lessons continued and were
becoming very dangerous. The couple were always
alone; the thick hedges that surrounded the spot
prevented anyone seeing them from outside. The
teacher was tender, amiable and enterprising; and
the scholar, only too accessible to sentiment, felt
her courage failing, so she refused to continue taking lessons.

"Well! she does not care for me," said Gustave,
"decidedly she is nothing more than a coquette
who wants to amuse herself with my torments;
I am a fool to sigh after her. But this is the end
of it; I won't talk with her any more; I don't
want even to look at her again!"

Having formed this resolution, Gustave attempted to make love to Aurélie, but the task was
too painful. The daytime was now quite different;

Madame de Berly, anchored to her embroidery-frame, did not leave the parlor, and in the evening she watched them playing tric-trac or listened to the singing of the indefatigable Aurélie. She was sad and dreamy, but always gentle and obliging towards those who came to see her husband. She did not seem to notice Gustave's ill-humor, nor his affected devotion to the tall niece, nor his epigrams on female coquetry. The youth flew into a rage; he did not know what to do. In his despair he went out hunting with M. de Berly; he shot at the dogs instead of the hares and mistook magpies for woodcocks and a fat hog for a wild boar. In the evening he must needs play tric-trac and made false moves time after time, cast the dice on the floor and kept dropping his box. He tried to sing, and found he had no voice; then he attempted to play the violin, but his hand trembled and he could play neither in time nor tune; he did not know what he was doing. M. de Berly chaffed him; Desjardins laughed; Mademoiselle Aurélie opened her big eyes, and Julie sighed.

"Aha!" thought M. de Berly to himself, "the youth is madly in love with my niece, I hope that's evident to everybody!"

The dear uncle talked about it to Desjardins, who always shared his opinion on principle, and to his wife, who contented herself with the response that she wished it might be so.

"Wife! look at Gustave, sitting over there all

alone in a corner ; do you notice his gloomy air, his careworn and melancholy brow? Well, it is love that causes all that. Oh, I know all about it. Moreover, during the first days of his stay here he was quite different; he laughed and played and sang, and played a thousand tricks, and now he never opens his mouth except to sigh ; he casts up his eyes, and if you could only see what an idiot he makes of himself out hunting you would die with laughter. Upon my word, he's got it badly. I am going to write to his uncle for him to conclude the matter, for we must not let the poor lad wither away. Isn't that so, Desjardins?"

"You are perfectly right, for—"

"As for my niece, she does not say anything, but I am sure that the little sly-boots does not think the less. Ah ! if only the colonel were not troubled with his cursed gout, he would have already been here ; how it keeps me from showing him his converted nephew."

"But, my friend, are you quite certain?"

"Yes, madame, yes, I am certain that this marriage will be as happy as ours. But, by the way, why do you no longer play billiards?"

"Because—"

"It amused our lover. The devil! we must give him a little fun ; he will have time enough to indulge his reflections after marriage. Gustave, my wife is complaining that you won't give her any more billiard lessons."

"I ? I did not say so !"

"Hush ! let me alone !"

"Whenever madame likes," said Gustave, rising, "I am always at her orders."

"That's right ! Come out of your reveries for a little, young man, I am going to have a game of tric-trac with Desjardins ; have the billiard room lit up ; you will have time to play before supper. Come, Madame de Berly, go along ; don't you see that the gentleman is waiting for you ? "

There was no means of refusing ; M. de Berly wished it. Gustave offered his hand to Julie and felt that the one she gave him was trembling greatly ; a vague feeling of hope and pleasure sprang up in his heart.

They went into the billiard-room ; after lighting up, the servant went away, leaving them alone.

Madame de Berly was silent, but she seemed agitated. Gustave looked so sad that it would have been a hard heart indeed that would not take pity on him.

At last Madame de Berly asked in faint tones, "What has been the matter with you for several days past, you don't condescend to speak ? "

"The matter with me ? Ah! madame, is there any need to tell you again ? I adore you, and you detest me ? "

"I detest you ! What an injustice ! If that were true, should I be afraid to listen to your protestations and talk ? "

Julie had said too much. Gustave seized her
hand and laid it over his heart.

"Let me alone!" said Madame de Berly, "you
will bring me misfortune. Ah! Gustave, do not
abuse my weakness!"

But a lover who learns that he is loved listens
to nothing but his own ardor. Gustave pressed
her to his breast and with kisses dried the tears
she was shedding.

"Wife, wife!" cried M. de Berly, who, as we
know, was separated from the billiard room only
by a few trees and a hedge which prevented people
from seeing but not from hearing one another,
"I have just made 'grande brédouille'; it is the first
time I ever got it. How are you two getting
along?"

"Very well, monsieur," replied Gustave, for his
companion had lost the power of speech, "we are
getting along very well this evening; Madame
de Berly is making remarkable progress."

"So much the better, so much the better! She'll
be a stronger player when she and I have a game
together; but be sure to teach her the doublé, it's
the prettiest shot of all."

"That's just what I am now doing, monsieur."

It was evidently a long game, for Gustave and
Julie did not return to the parlor till just as it was
time to sit down to supper. Madame de Berly's
eyes were very red, but Gustave was radiant; his
face shone with pleasure and happiness.

"Well!" said M. de Berly, "were you well matched? Who won the most games?"

" I think madame did."

" Bah! get out, you let her win out of politeness. She can't be a match for you, who are almost as good a player as I am.   Isn't it true, dear, that I can play a good game when I try?"

" Yes, but you can't play as well as M. Gustave."

" Go along! you want to flatter your teacher. But you look tired.   In truth, billiards is a very fatiguing game — standing the whole time and walking backwards and forwards."

" Well! as for me," said Desjardins, " I once played for three days at a stretch ; we were mad over it; even our meals had to be brought to us, and —"

But the company was already in the dining-room, and M. Desjardins had to defer his anecdote to another occasion.

During supper Madame de Berly spoke little and constantly kept her eyes lowered. Mademoiselle Aurélie did not take her own off Gustave and her aunt ; these prudes are sometimes very clear-sighted ! M. Desjardins contented himself with eating and applauding the talk of everybody without distinction.   M. de Berly never ceased talking of his skill at billiards and the wonderful shots he could make. As for Gustave he was gay, amiable and extremely agreeable to M. de Berly, praising his skill in hunting, his amiability towards the ladies, and his undaunted courage in the face of danger.

The poor husband was enchanted with the youth; on rising from table, he warmly shook his hand and promised that his uncle should be informed of his good conduct.

After that, who says that people have presentiments?

CHAPTER III

A Catastrophe. The Devil and the Black Cow

Madame de Berly's tears were very soon dried. A woman's love invariably increases with the sacrifices which she makes for her lover; the more she gives, the more devoted and attached she becomes. With men it is different; they tire of pleasure and weary of a continuity of happiness. Notwithstanding the fact that desire inflames them, enjoyment cools them and indulgence in delight undoes the knots tied by love.

What is to be done then, my dear readers? Live together according to the decrees of Plato's doctrine? Oh, then, love of that description would last much longer, but it would also end by growing tired of waiting. Moreover, that style of loving would prove fatal to population and cause the ruin of governments; and then, again, it is neither in Nature nor in the Scriptures, since we are instructed by the latter to "Be fruitful and multiply."

Therefore, we must take things as they are, philosophically; and it is in love especially that it is good to be philosophical. Must we be driven to despair because a mistress deceives us, or when a lover is faithless? At first, it is an evil that cannot be remedied; and then, why should infidelity be a proof of indifference? One may have a moment of forgetfulness. "Errare humanum est."

If one were to make a frank confession of his weaknesses, then confidence would bring back love, jealousy would torture the heart less and Discord would cease waving her torches and serpents over the slaves of Love and Hymen.

But I don't know why I have said all this, nor what relation it has to the love affairs of Gustave and Madame de Berly. So, reader, kindly consider that I have not said anything.

By the power of love, Gustave had calmed the fears, sighs, tears and remorse of Julie. Every day they played billiards; they played morning and evening, and I think they played even in the little grove, in the grotto and in the maze.

It is no crime to play billiards; but if you want to do it in secret you must take proper precautions; and this is precisely what they neglected.

> Love, love, when thou hold'st us true,
> We may well say, "Prudence adieu!"

One evening, when the game of tric-trac had come to an end earlier than usual, M. de Berly went into the garden to see his wife and Gustave at billiards, whither they had gone.

The dear husband approached the hedges, but he was surprised at seeing no lights. "It would

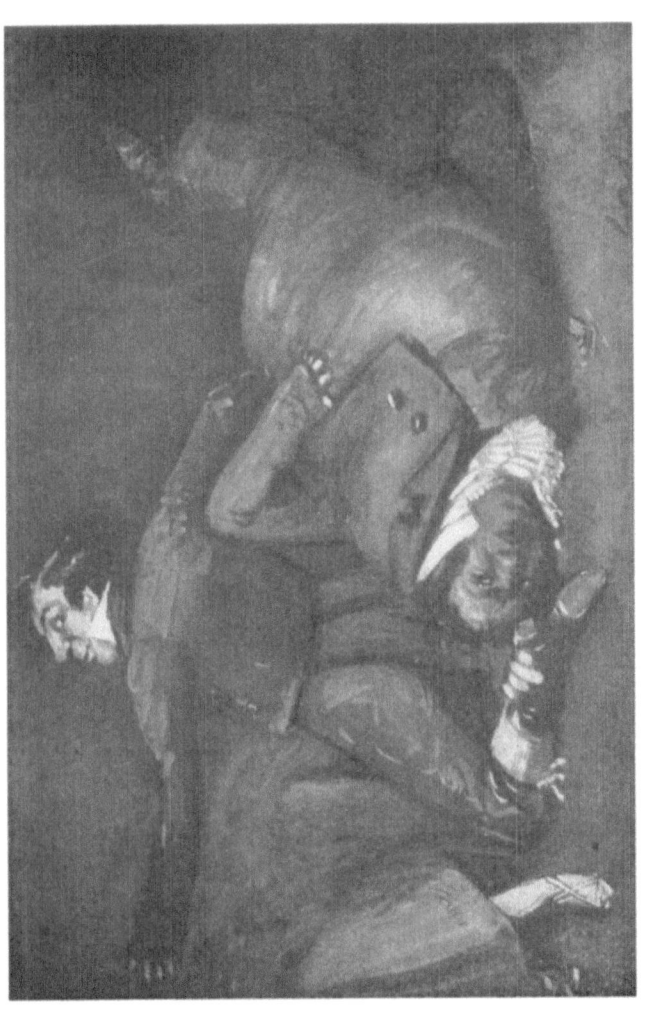

seem that they have changed their minds," he said to himself. "Doubtless they are in the music-room!"

He was about to turn back when a well-known voice uttered these words, "Ah! how happy I am! what a delight —"

"Why! upon my word! that's my wife," said the gentleman; and he went into the room, where it was too dark to see anything.

"What the devil! are you playing without any lights?" The dear husband could not see anything; his feet caught in something, he fell down and rolled over and found himself on top of Gustave who, for some reason or other, was kneeling down beside a grassy bank.

"What! is it you, monsieur? I was walking in front of you.   Allow me to assist you to rise."

"Hallo! is that you, dear?" exclaimed Madame de Berly, as she moved quickly away from the turf bank.

"Certainly, it is I! To the devil with your idea of playing in the dark! I believe I have raised a bump on my forehead."

"But, monsieur, it has only just got dark; we were just going to have it lit up."

"Upon my word, you are very clever to be able to play under such conditions.   You surely can't find the pockets."

"Pardon me, monsieur."

"If it hadn't been for hearing my wife's voice,

I should not have come in; but I heard her utter a joyful exclamation."

"Yes, madame had just put down — "

"Come on; I'm going to see your skill. Wife, tell them to light up. I will play the two of you."

Madame de Berly had the lamps lit and they played. M. de Berly beat the pair, as he had wanted to; Gustave took care to play a poor game, and Julie's hand was shaky ; so the husband won every game and was delighted. There is always some compensation.

Mademoiselle Aurélie did not share her uncle's joy. Gustave's conduct towards Julie seemed to her one of shocking familiarity ; and the young man's coldness to herself when she sang, " My heart sighs," appeared very extraordinary to her. She did not dare to say anything to her uncle, but she began to spy upon Julie and Gustave, and without exactly knowing why she had the desire to discover something.

Benoit's buttocks had healed, but the poor lad was none the smarter for that ; however, in order to escape any similar experience in his future travels, he practiced horseback riding every morning, and began to manage it a little better.

M. de Berly had written to Colonel Moranval a long letter in which he detailed to him the edifying manner in which his nephew behaved himself, his virtuous love for Mademoiselle Aurélie, his kindness to Madame de Berly and her liking for him.

Colonel Moranval replied to M. de Berly that he was delighted to hear that Gustave had reformed; that his gout gave him a little peace now and so he was about to join them all and conclude the marriage; but he did not want anything said about it to his nephew, because he wished to surprise him.

Matters were in this condition when one morning M. de Berly was informed that the tracks of a wolf had been seen about three leagues away, towards Montaigny. This news pricked the self-love of our hunter. What glory for him if he were to kill a beast that might devastate the neighborhood! Nevertheless, he did not appear decided to match his prowess against a wolf, but Gustave encouraged and excited him, hailing him in advance as the deliverer of the country side. Desjardins also boasted of having once killed four in one day. "In that case," said M. de Berly, "you shall accompany me on this occasion; I should like to see if you are still able to kill one."

Desjardins had gone too far to venture to withdraw; so he armed himself from head to heel. As for Gustave, he had had a nasty fall the day before when running in the little grove with madame, and his side was still very painful; so that he was in no condition to follow the other gentlemen. Besides he recognized that he was too poor a hunter to match himself with them.

"But," said M. de Berly "it is quite possible that today we shall not be able even to discover the lair of the animal; I don't want to go so far for nothing. It so happens that I have a small farm near Montaigny, so we will sleep there tonight, Desjardins and I; by this means, tomorrow at daybreak we shall be on the spot. I promise you, wife, that I won't come back without bringing you some trophy of the beast."

Madame de Berly applauded this idea of her husband's; and Gustave recognized a noble and heroic devotion in the plan. It was therefore settled that M. de Berly would not come home to sleep; that suited everybody.

Our hunters are armed from head to foot; the dogs are let loose; the horses are saddled; the guns are loaded and the farewells taken.

Happy at being left alone together, Gustave and Julie determine to make the most of it. Mademoiselle Aurélie is not feeling well and keeps her room, which circumstance adds to the security. Madame de Berly declares that she does not feel very well either, and goes and shuts herself up in her apartment, leaving orders with the servants that anybody who calls is to be sent away.

Matters being thus arranged, about six o'clock in the evening madame retires to her bedroom, all admission to which is prohibited to the profane. As for Gustave, doubtless he also was indisposed; for he forbade Benoit to disturb him in his room.

It was the season when the summer days are longest, when night does not fall till nearly nine o'clock. It was only eight when a stranger presented himself at M. de Berly's door. The servants informed him that there was nobody at home who could receive him; that the mistress was ill and the master had gone away for two days' hunting.

"Well, upon my word!" exclaimed Colonel Moranval, for it was no other, "I did not come merely to go away again; if M. de Berly isn't at home, I will wait for him; I will instal myself in the house without any ceremony."

The colonel's tone was one that admitted no reply; the servants let him in and he saw Benoit in the courtyard.

"Hallo! why, there is — colonel, it's you, monsieur!"

"Yes, my lad! Was I not expected?"

"On my word, no, monsieur."

"Where is my nephew?"

"He is not well, monsieur; he told me so this morning; he is in his room, where he is doubtless asleep, for he told me not to come and disturb him."

"And Madame de Berly."

"She is indisposed; she has also given orders that no one is to go to her room."

"But Mademoiselle Aurélie? it is to be hoped that I can see her; I suppose that she is neither away hunting nor ill?"

"On the contrary, monsieur, she is feverish and has been lying down since the morning."

"Good heavens! this house is a regular hospital. Never mind! I will wait alone, since it must be so."

As the colonel uttered these words horses' hoofs were heard, and the servants ran to see who had arrived. They found M. de Berly and Desjardins, who had already brought their hunting to a close.

The colonel embraced his friend.

"Hallo! there you are; your people told me that you would be away for two days."

"I thought so myself, colonel, but Fate decided otherwise. I had been told of a wolf whose tracks had been discovered; but when Desjardins and I arrived the brute had just been killed. I was terribly put out, because I felt such courage, such ardor! Well! have you seen your nephew?"

"No, I have only this moment arrived. But everybody in your house is ill; both your wife and my nephew have gone to lie down."

"Bah! there were no signs of it this morning! it won't amount to anything. My friend, I must compliment you on your nephew; he is a charming fellow. Think of it! you wrote to me that I should find him a bad lot! On the contrary, he is a very good and very well-behaved fellow. His whole pleasure seems to consist in playing billiards with my wife; he never leaves the house; he is so obliging, so gentle!"

" Really ! the air of this district works wonders. I am impatient to embrace him."

" Go and find him ; he will be astonished to see you ; he doesn't expect you. Oh ! I didn't say a word ; I am discretion itself."

" Come, Benoit, lead me to your master's room."

" But, monsieur, he forbade me to —"

" Devil take you : there's no prohibition against an uncle, idiot ! Go on, lead the way."

The colonel followed Benoit, who led the way with trembling knees. For his part, M. de Berly prepared to surprise his wife, who did not expect him till the next day. They told him that madame was lying down and that she was ill, but nothing deterred him ; when he had anything in his mind, he could never be turned aside from it, and now, persuaded that he was going to give his wife an agreeable surprise, he quickly mounted the stairs to her apartment.

Madame de Berly's bedroom was on the first floor and looked into the garden. M. de Berly entered the anteroom to it. A door locked from within barred farther progress ; but M. de Berly, who did not share his wife's room, had a duplicate key to enable him at night, when love kept him awake, to seek the society of his wife.

A duplicate key is a terrible thing ; it lays one open to all kinds of danger. There was a bolt to the door ; but no one had taken the trouble to shoot it; their minds were tranquil, they thought the husband so far away. Fatal lack of foresight.

M. de Berly went straight to his wife's bedside; he drew aside the curtain, and instead of kissing his wife's neck, as he intended, he kissed Gustave on the back. The head of Medusa Euryale, or Scylla, the eyes of the basilisk or the sphynx, the teeth of Cerberus, or the claws of Ashtaroth would have produced less effect on the poor husband than Gustave's back. He stood rooted to the spot with fixed eyes, open mouth and arms extended. Julie huddled herself up in the bedclothes; but Gustave, who did not lose his head, got up, made a random snatch at a few of his clothes, opened the window and jumped out into the garden. He fell right on top of his uncle, who, after vainly seeking him in his room, was going through the gardens with Benoit with the hope of coming across him there.

The colonel fell on his face; Gustave recognized his uncle, and only ran the faster. His uncle recognized him, got up and ran after him, while Benoit stood still in stupefaction at the sight of his master clad only in his shirt. The latter soon distanced his pursuer, slipped on his coat and trousers; and then, jumping over walls, hedges and ditches, reached the country road, where he caught sight of Lucas and Zephyr as I have had the pleasure of relating to you at the beginning of this volume.

"Hallo! is that you, Benoit?" said Gustave, raising his head out of the pond and looking at the rider who had been pursuing him for some time and finally had caught up to him whilst Zephyr was stuck fast in the mud.

"Why! certainly, monsieur; I am the one who has been galloping after you with this other horse that I brought along for the sake of precaution. Ah! damn it! it is not very pleasant yonder — your uncle is in such a rage — he is cursing and swearing worse than ever — when I heard him —"

"All right; you can tell me all about it another time; first you can help me get away from these cursed ducks, and rescue this good man, whom I hope is not hurt."

Father Lucas was more frightened than hurt. It was with the greatest difficulty that Gustave persuaded him that no bones were broken. They set him on Zephyr, whose fire was cooled. The young man mounted the horse that Benoit was leading and they set out again on the road.

Gustave laughed for a time at what Benoit had done, for he had taken him for his uncle. However, when he looked back at the events of the evening, and when he thought of Julie, whom he had left in such a critical situation, he became serious and pensive. What did she do? This was the thought that pursued him ceaselessly. He felt sure that women, who always have presence of mind, know how to get out of the worst kind

of scrapes; but there are some cases where even
a woman's wit is of no avail; and Madame de
Berly was precisely in one of those unhappy pre-
dicaments.

However, since our hero was not of a nature
to distress himself about anything for very long,
he soon stopped worrying; and, reflecting that
sighs could never mend matters, he left it to his
good star to set everything right.

They arrived at Ermenonville at last; after
crossing several little bridges — there is a great deal
of water in this country — they stopped in front of
a village house, a thing that in Paris would be
called a hovel. Lucas recovered his speech on
seeing his home, and Zephyr his legs on nearing
his stable.

" Here we are, thank Heaven! We didn't get
here any too easily."

" All right, Father Lucas, now we will wake
everybody up!"

They dismounted; Gustave and Benoit knocked
unmercifully, while Lucas called out at the top of
his voice, " Marie-Jeanne! Suzon! Nicholas
Toupet!"

" And your wife," said Gustave, " aren't you
going to call her?"

" Oh! I'm not such a fool as that! I don't
want to wake her up; she would be savage with
me. Hallo! Marie-Jeanne! Nicholas!"

At last a little dormer window under the roof

was opened. "Is it you?" asked a thick, harsh voice.

"Yes, Nicholas; come down, my boy, and open the door; but be careful not to wake my wife up."

In about ten minutes — for peasants are about as brisk as wet hens — Nicholas opened the door into the yard. He uttered a loud exclamation when he caught sight of Gustave and Benoit.

"These are some people from town whom we shall have to take in," said Father Lucas, as he led Zephyr to the stable; "you give them the room Cousin Pierre Ledru sleeps in when he comes here; and tomorrow my wife will tell us if it is all right or not."

Nicholas was disposed to obey; Gustave stopped him.

"And do you imagine that you can send us to bed without any supper, Father Lucas? Why, I haven't had anything to eat since three o'clock this afternoon, and I am awfully hungry; I warn you if you don't give me at least an omelette, I'll turn the house upside down!"

Father Lucas was extremely embarrassed; for his wife had the keys of the sideboard and the larder. But while he was trying to decide what to do, a terrible racket was heard upstairs; the good man, recognizing his wife's voice, crept behind some old casks, Nicholas went into the stable, and Benoit, who wasn't any too calm, went and hid in the shed. Gustave alone remained to face the storm.

A fat, little red-faced woman, whose eyes were flashing with anger, came flying down the stairs at the back. "What does all this noise mean in the middle of the night? Does that fool of a Lucas think that I will submit to this sort of thing? Why didn't he stay at Louvres all night? The drunken idiot, to wake me up like this! he has been guilty of some silly prank I suppose."

Just as Madame Lucas ended, she saw Gustave, who was standing calmly in the middle of the yard, waiting till her anger had cooled a little. Frightened at the sight of a stranger whose looks were decidedly suspicious, for Gustave's clothes were covered with the slime of the pond and his face was bleeding from the scratches that the ducks had administered with feet and bills, Madame Lucas had not the slightest doubt that thieves has broken into the house; she gave a few piercing screams and threw a pitchfork, a spade and a broom at Gustave; and while the latter jumped aside to avoid being struck, she ran across the yard and through the village, screaming with all her might and main, "Thieves! Murder!"

Peasants are heavy sleepers; and therefore the Ermenonville people did not respond to Madame Lucas' cries. Then she decided to throw stones at the windows and to cry "Fire!" At the word fire, which alarms everybody, for a village is soon burned, the peasants woke and ran into the street, which shows how true it is that we always hear what interests us personally, but for the troubles of others — but let us make no reflections ; Madame Lucas is in the streets of Ermenonville in her night-gown; and we cannot leave her like that.

"Where is the fire? Where is the fire?" the villagers asked Madame Lucas.

"Well, my friends, I think it is a great deal worse than that. I believe the Cossacks are in town."

"The Cossacks?"

"Yes, indeed; they have already entered my house — and, perhaps, by now, my little Suzon and Marie-Jeanne are already —"

"We must go to their assistance," cried all the gossips, who did not fear the risks of war. The men, however, were not in such a hurry. They suggested that they should barricade themselves in their own houses, and await the enemy there. One of the sharpest of them all observed that there had been no talk of war for a long time, and Madame Lucas certainly could not have seen any Cossacks.

"Then they certainly must be thieves," the peasant replied, "for they made an infernal noise and forced my door open; at first I thought it was my husband returning from Louvres, and I went downstairs to give him a good scolding, but

I found myself face to face with a great red and black man."

" Merciful Heavens! It must have been the devil himself!" the terrified women exclaimed, shuddering.

" Did you see his claws and tail?"

" I cannot say for certain about his tail, although I am quite sure he must have had one. But, as for his eyes, they flashed and burned like coals of fire."

"We'd like to see that," said the men, who did not seem to fear the devil as much as they did the Cossacks.

" We had better wake up the priest," said some of the women, "so that he can come and chase the demon away."

The villagers armed themselves with pitchforks, pickaxes, spades and shovels, in short, they had seized anything they could find, and formed themselves into a very compact battalion. Madame Lucas placed herself in the centre, and the other women brought up in the rear, and in this manner they marched forward to encounter the devil, who had disturbed the repose of the inhabitants of Ermenonville.

In the mean time, Gustave, after escaping the fusilade from the handle of Madame Lucas' broom, decided to go into the house and help himself to something to eat without taking any more notice of the peasant-woman's cries, or of the alarm of the poor husband, who did not dare come out from behind the casks.

Benoit remained in the shed, where he had been milking a cow while the whole village was alarmed. As for Nicholas, the cries of his mistress had filled him with alarm; and being satisfied that the house was full of thieves, he did not dare come out of the stable, and so he lay down flat on his stomach by the side of Zephyr.

Our young hero mounted the stairs at the back, going up two flights; he listens and hears a sound. He opens a door which was scarcely shut and someone utters a cry. Gustave recognizes a woman's accents, so he advances and finds a bed; he gropes about and satisfies himself that someone is lying there. This someone is a peasant, doubtless; but this peasant has firm flesh and rounded forms and she yields so complacently to the touch. "Upon my word," said Gustave, "I'm going to try to get her to take pity on me; perhaps, presently, I can induce her to make me an omelette."

The armed peasants arrived before the house of papa Lucas at the very moment when he had made up his mind to quit his casks; the good man, terrified by the noise he heard, jumped into the middle of the crowd. "There's one of them already; fall upon him; don't you see that he is black and red?"

In fact, Lucas, who was black with the mud he had gathered from the pond, had rubbed against

the casks that had just been emptied and were
still red with wine lees: the poor fellow was unrecognizable.   They fell upon him and beat him
with sticks ; he cried aloud and ran away.   While
he was being pursued, his wife entered the yard at
the head of the boldest men of the neighborhood;
she calls Suzon, papa Lucas's daughter, whom her
mother fears the devil may have already carried
away.

Suzon opened her window and asked the cause
of all this row ; she was informed that the Evil
Spirit had found his way into the house of her
parents.

The young girl was unwilling to stay in her
room alone ; she imagined she already saw Satan
on her bed.   As her window was not far from the
ground, she put out first one leg and then the
other and let herself down ; but a nail caught in
her nightgown and pretty Suzon found herself
like a fruit tree nailed against a wall.

"Shut your eyes!" cried Mother Lucas.   The
rustics, on the contrary, raised their torches so as
to see things better.

"Ah! mother," cried Suzon, "I am sure it is
the devil that has hold of my chemise.   The
schoolmaster says that that's always where he gets
a grip on the girls."

"Wait a moment, my child ; there's a ladder
in the stable.   I'll go and unhook you.   Father
Thomas, let us go and find it!"

Thomas advanced towards the stable, the door of which was shut; he opened it and immediately a black cow darted out, upset Thomas and dashed furiously among the villagers with terrifying bellowings.

It must be remembered that Benoit had taken refuge in the stable, and that, being very fond of new-drawn milk, he had occupied his time with trying to milk a cow that could not yield any at that time, since Marie-Jeanne was accustomed to milk her every evening. In his anxiety to quench his thirst, Benoit stroked the udders of the poor beast as hard as he could till it finally grew tired of his manipulations. Deep lowings soon announced the impatience and anger of the animal. Benoit, in ignorance of which cow it was that made the noise, continued his attempt, and was about to become the victim of his greediness, when Thomas, opening the stable door, changed the course of events.

The peasants, who were terrified to see in their midst a maddened cow at the very moment when they were looking for a devil, had not the slightest doubt that the poor beast was possessed by a demon. Moreover, it was a black cow; and of course you know, or you don't know, that the evil spirits affect that color. Demons, hobgoblins and imps are conjured with a black fowl. In truth, Marshal D'Ancre was burned to death at Paris for having killed a white cock under the full moon; but nobody doubts that if the cock had been black the devils would have been able to save the marshal.

Poets have adopted this hue in order to get the devil in them, for Voltaire has said that it is necessary to be bedevilled in order to write good stuff; he even calls dramatic works "works of the devil."

Doctors dress in black: some jesters say that they wear mourning for their patients. I think, on the contrary, that it is in order to gain the favor of the devil and induce him to teach them how to cure the plague, mange, leprosy, dropsy, epilepsy, phthisis, madness and other nice ailments that certainly can come only from hell.

Finally, magicians wear long black robes. Perhaps you are about to ask me what magicians are. I will reply that they are people who pretend to overthrow the laws of Nature, that is to say, do impossible things. In truth, I have never seen a sorcerer; but they certainly must have existed, since in former times there was a jurisprudence established concerning magic, just as today we have one regarding theft and murder; and the common people could not help believing in magicians since the magistracy believed in them.

It seems that sorcerers liked to get themselves burned, because just as soon as they were burned they were seen to spring up in every direction. Now that the authorities content themselves with putting them in madhouses, we no longer see

either sorcerers or magicians. We have a few
ladies who tell fortunes by cards and in other
ways, but that's all; and the industry is falling off
from day to day.

The villagers push and crowd upon one another,
knocking each other down and dropping their
torches. The maddened cow escapes from the
yard and goes careering through the village. Suzon
climbs back and sits astride her window-sill, hesi-
tating between her fear of the devil within and the
black cow without.

The peasants now cannot see anything distinctly
and this increases their terror. Mother Lucas,
however, reanimates their spirits, assuring them
that the cow has departed, and that the devil has
taken flight in the body of the animal, and that all
that remains is to restore peace in the house.

To this end, the first thing is to have light; so
they go up to the room of Marie-Jeanne, who has
a flint and tinder. It was Madame Lucas again,
at the head of the least cowardly, who undertook
to go up to the garret.

They reached Marie-Jeanne's door; inside, they
heard ejaculations, sighs and stifled sounds. " By
the Lord!" cried Madame Lucas, "the devil has
entered into Marie-Jeanne."

The peasants did not dare to open the door;
they huddled close together.

"Say, Marie-Jeanne," cried old mother Lucas,
"has the devil got into your room?"

"Yes, yes! But let me alone; I can easily manage him single-handed."

" Take care that you are not possessed with him ! He assumes all sorts of forms ; be careful to hold your breath."

The peasants, who expected to see Satan come out of the room and spring upon them with teeth and claws, scuttled down the stairs and reached the yard more frightened than ever, only to find another scare in store for them. The women who had remained behind beside the stable, being persuaded that the devil had just made his escape in the form of a cow, in order to assure themselves of the truth of the matter, tried to look in and see if the black cow had really gone: dawn was beginning to break, but it was still difficult to distinguish objects. Some of the peasants made a mistake and went into the stable, while others went into the cow-shed. They walked on without watching their steps and the former encountered Benoit's head, while the latter stumbled upon Nicholas' legs. These gentlemen were both lying asleep on the manure heaps. They uttered loud cries on feeling themselves trampled on.

The peasants ran away with still louder cries ; thinking they had stepped upon goblins. Just at that moment the male peasants, frightened by Marie-Jeanne's words, came tumbling down the stairs pell-mell. " The house is full of sorcerers!" cried the women. " Marie-Jeanne is possessed with the devil," exclaimed the men. "Don't let us stay here; let's get out; let's get out!" such was the general cry.

Suzon put both legs outside the window; she jumped, and this time reached the ground; she pushed Thomas, who pushed Mother Lucas, who pushed the cooper, and he pushed the green-grocer, who pushed the grocer, and so on.

Pushing one another forward in this manner, they arrived in front of the château, and there they left off pushing; and they did well, for otherwise they would have fallen into the moat that surrounded it.

CHAPTER IV

Ermenonville. Marie-Jeanne. Suzon

If people would only reason before giving way to panic and excitement, if they would listen to what others have to say before arguing a question, if they would reflect on all the consequences before being guilty of a folly, if they would get well acquainted with the temperament and habits of thought of one another before marriage; then children would no longer be in terror of the bogey man, girls would not fear to go down alone into the cellar, at night peasants would pass a graveyard without huddling together and shutting their eyes, in the evenings pretty women would read the romances of Lord Byron and Anne Radcliffe without shuddering; the Sarmatians, Hungarians and Moldavians would no longer believe in the existence of vampires, nor the Scotch in second sight, nor nurses in were-wolves, and weak-minded people in general would no longer worry about ghosts, phantoms, witches and apparitions.

Then we should see fewer wars, because sovereigns would appoint ambassadors who would not try to pass ahead of one another when out of doors, which of old was often the cause of much blood-

letting, and if that did happen, they would try
to hold their coachmen responsible, and not an
entire population, which is forced to take up arms
just because one horse has passed another. People
who have dined and spent the evening together
would not suddenly resemble fighting-cocks because
politics had become the subject of conversation;
two youths would not go out to cut each other's
throats or blow out one another's brains because
one had trodden on the other's toe; then, also, a
youth would not try to seduce an honest girl whom
he had no intention of marrying; a married man
would have nothing to do with ladies of easy virtue;
people would not run to roulette to compromise
their honor, and empty their purse for the benefit
of the keepers of gambling-houses; nor would
they buy lottery-tickets for the purpose of pleasing the government; nor frequent large assemblies
where they are lavish with punch, ices and sorbets
to induce you to play ecarté at a hundred francs a
hand. Then an old man would not marry a young
girl, nor a jealous one wed a coquette, nor a sensitive woman a libertine, nor a respectable woman
a drunkard, nor would an amiable woman marry
a fool, nor a man of intellect a devotee. Then
there would be a few happy households, and the
children would not so often resemble the friends
of the family.

In short, if Madame Lucas had come downstairs
quietly, her husband would not have had to hide

behind the casks, nor Benoit in the stable, nor Nicholas in the shed; and if she had not mistaken Gustave for a thief, all the inhabitants of Ermenonville would have spent the night in their beds.

When the peasants had gone away, Gustave went downstairs with Marie-Jeanne, whom he had let know very clearly what he was, and who was not at all afraid of him. In the yard he found Benoit and Nicholas, who were coming out of their bedrooms. They each related what they had seen. Big Marie-Jeanne laughed heartily about her mistress' fright, Gustave washed his face, while Benoit cleaned his clothes, Nicholas Toupet was very much worried about his master and Mademoiselle Suzon. Soon loud cries were heard in the street from the villagers who were coming back; but as it was now broad daylight and Marie-Jeanne had assured Gustave that he was too good-looking to cause the retreat of the gossips of the place, our hero calmly awaited the arrival of those he had frightened so terribly.

Day brought courage to the villagers; they decided to revisit the bewitched house; but as they turned into the wide street they saw a peasant leading a black cow.

"There is the black beast!" cried the peasant women.

"Why, that's my husband!" exclaimed Madame Lucas.

It was indeed papa Lucas, who, having washed

himself in one of the château moats, so that he
might not be taken for a thief again, was returning
home with his black cow that he had found wandering about the streets of Ermenonville all alone.

They met and explained everything. Father
Lucas complained of the blows that he had received, and told his wife of his meeting with the
young stranger, their tumble into the mud, and their
arrival in the middle of the night. They all began
to see that the devil had nothing to do with the
matter. Mother Lucas scolded her husband for
having brought home a young man who had disturbed everybody; but when she learned that this
young man was rich, and had a valet and two horses,
and heard, moreover, that he seemed to be gener-
ous and inclined to pay his host liberally, her anger
cooled; she even recovered her good-humor, and,
in order to atone for the blows he had received,
she even permitted her husband to kiss her.

They now came to the house — the scene of the
events of the night. Gustave's face, attitude, and
manners succeeded in cheering Madame Lucas up,
for our young man had plenty of cash; Benoit
had brought along some of his master's clothes,
and one of the waistcoats fortunately contained the
purse with the two hundred louis that the uncle
had sent the nephew, and which the latter had had
no way of spending while he was at Madame de
Berly's.

Our hero, seeing that the first thing to do was

to please Madame Lucas, slipped a louis into her hand, so as to make her forget the fright that he had involuntarily caused her.

Suddenly the whole house was in a fever of anxiety to pay attentions to the man whom they had tried to kill with shovel and broom. They gave him the best room, they brought breakfast to him, and told Benoit that he might milk the cows and drink the milk from morning to night if he pleased.

There was only one thing that still rather troubled the peasant women and even Madame Lucas; what could Marie-Jeanne have meant by saying that she had suffered the assaults of the devil? Something very extraordinary must have happened in the house. So they sent for the servant and questioned her. "Good heavens!" replied Marie-Jeanne, "I remember now that I was having bad dreams and finally had the nightmare, which was suffocating me when you came upstairs and woke me up suddenly; and, finally, I suppose that I told you of my dream."

The villagers laughed at their scare till they held their sides; at the dream of Marie-Jeanne, who laughed also at what she had said, and, perhaps, at what she had done. Finally, calm was re-established, and everybody returned to his daily work.

After breakfast, Gustave retired to his room with Benoit, and ordered his servant to tell him as well as he could what had happened at Madame de Berly's after his flight.

" Well, monsieur," replied Benoit, " I'll tell you
what I saw and heard.   First your uncle, whom
you had knocked down in jumping out of the window, got up to run after you ; but you ran so fast
that he very soon saw that he couldn't catch you.
Then he returned to me and asked how long it was
since you had gone insane ; for, seeing you clearing the hedges and ditches with flying shirt-tails
made him think that you had lost your reason.
At that moment, M. de Berly came running up to
us, looking as if he had taken leave of his senses ;
and, as soon as he caught sight of your uncle, he
cried, ' Your nephew has cuckolded me ; I have
just found him in bed with my wife.'   Colonel
Moranval immediately replied, ' I was sure of it ;
I was willing to bet that the rascal was making fools
of us, you, your niece and myself! '   And then your
uncle began to swear. My God! how he can swear
when he's angry ! M. de Berly also used fearful language, in which he joined his wife, the marriage and
the billiard-room.   As for me, I was going back to
the house when I met the cook ; you remember,
monsieur, she was the one who made me put sorrel
upon my — injury ; she is a good sort of woman at
bottom and has a great liking for you, monsieur, for,
as soon as she saw me, she said, ' Well, you idiot,
are you going to let your master run about the
country without his clothes ? Go up to his room
immediately and get his effects and money, and
then go to the stable, mount your own horse and

lead your master's, and gallop after him ; you will easily find out what road he has taken; a naked man attracts attention.' I did as the cook told me, monsieur, and you know where I caught you."

"Very good, Benoit, now leave me; but, as long as we stay in this house, don't ever try to milk a cow without my permission."

"Make your mind easy about that, monsieur, I have had too bad a scare. I would not even try to milk a ewe!"

On being left alone, Gustave set his mind to work to decide what he should do. He had no means of entering into correspondence with Julie, who, moreover, would be very closely watched. However, he was burning to tell her that he would adore her forever; this assurance would be some consolation to one who had sacrificed her peace of mind and reputation for him. "I must write to her," said Gustave; "perhaps, by the services of that good cook, I may find some means of getting a letter to her. But I dare not trust Benoit with this commission; he is too stupid, he certainly will make a mess of it—peasants never know how to carry on an intrigue. Eh! Upon my word! I must go myself, but I will take the precaution to disguise myself. But I had better wait until the excitement is over; then the husband's vigilance will have relaxed, and I shall succeed more easily. But to spend a week at Ermenonville—a whole week! poor Julie. It's an awfully long time, but

I suppose I've got to do it. In a week's time, my uncle will have returned to Paris, and there won't be the slightest danger of meeting him."

This plan being settled, he began to wonder what he should do with himself in the village for a whole week. But, after all, this village is Ermenonville, whose name alone is sufficient to recall touching memories, and whose enchanting situation would charm even a man who cared nothing for the country. Joseph II dined in a cottage here; Gustave III visited the spot; Jean-Jacques Rousseau spent the last years of his life here — and, therefore, I think M. de Saint-Réal ought to be able to amuse himself here for a few days. And then, there is a certain Marie-Jeanne, who fights very well indeed with the devil; and a little Suzon, whose pretty face is quite sufficient to distract his thoughts from an unfortunate love affair. Very well then, our young man need not be bored at Ermenonville.

"Suppose I begin to have a look around the country," said Gustave.

He found Madame Lucas plucking pigeons, while her husband was feeding the chickens.

"Madame Lucas! I should like to have a look around the village and the country."

"Why, don't you know this place, monsieur?"

"No, Madame Lucas; I came here to become familiar with it. I prefer to stay in a quiet house than at an inn, where one is often uncomfortable."

"You are right, monsieur. Oh! you can stay with us as long as you please; you won't put us out at all — on the contrary —"

"Thank you very much, Madame Lucas!"

"You will be delighted with the country—oh, indeed! you will see some beautiful things."

"What I have already seen here seemed good enough!"

"Bah! you arrived at night, you could not have seen anything. The park of the château is very beautiful."

"Can I go in?"

"Certainly! my daughter will go with you. There is nobody at the château just now but the porter — Suzon, Suzon!"

"I'll take the gentleman there!" said Marie-Jeanne, stepping forward.

"No, no! you must stay and make the butter and cheese. Suzon will go with him."

Marie-Jeanne was not at all pleased with the preference given to Suzon; and so she went back to work at her cheese-making in a very bad temper.

The young girl put on her pretty cap and her Sunday apron, and got ready to take the handsome gentlemen very gladly; but the mother, who thought that she might please her guest by accompanying him, told her husband to pluck the pigeons and see about dinner, and got ready to follow her daughter. Perhaps her little girl was not exactly safe with this young gentleman from Paris, who seemed to be honest enough, but who had a very animated air by the side of a pretty girl; and, then, what would Nicholas Toupet say on returning from the fields when he learned that Suzon had gone out for a walk with a stranger? And you must know that Nicholas Toupet was the accepted husband of Mademoiselle Lucas.

And so they had to put up with the mother's company. Suzon, without knowing exactly why, would have preferred to be alone with the young man; but Marie-Jeanne, on the contrary, was very much pleased with the new arrangement. As for Gustave, he looked at Suzon, who was only sixteen, with blue eyes, pretty teeth, a sweet mouth and very black hair.

He sighed as he saw Madame Lucas putting on her apron; he would have sighed still more if he had seen Suzon the night before with charms by the side of which Marie-Jeanne's would have paled.

They set off, and went through part of the village; and on the way Gustave noticed that all the inhabitants had fine teeth; which may be attributed to the purity of the water.

They entered the park of the château. What a delightful place! leafy shade, beautiful lawns, winding and interlacing brooks, cascades, lonely grottoes, meadows bespangled with flowers, a lake that bathed the walls of the château and on whose banks there rose an ancient tower covered with ivy and honeysuckle. From the tower, called the Tower of

Gabrielle, there is a beautiful view; an old suit of armor was hanging at the entrance; and everything here reminded one of the days of chivalry and tournaments. What a pity that such an old building should be crumbling away!

At the base of the tower, a ferry-boat attached to two ropes, running over rollers, allows you to cross by pulling at one of the ropes. In that part called the desert, you can see Jean-Jacques Rousseau's cottage, situated on an eminence, from which there is a full view of the surrounding landscape.

In a grotto encircled by a brook, Gustave copied the following verses,—

> O limpid fountain, fountain dear!
> May silly vanity
> Ne'er dwell among thy flowers here!
> And may thy paths from cares be free,
> That render life so drear : —
> Ambition, Envy, Fear,
> Deceit and Jealousy.
> So still a spot, so fresh a grove
> Should harbor merely thoughts of love;
> Each bough so sweetly interlaces
> To veil this haunt of Loves and Graces!
> The mirror of this crystal wave
> Should offer to the sight,
> The best that Nature's grace e'er gave
> And visions of delight!

"If only Julie were with me," thought Gustave, "I should have nothing more to do with Suzon or her mother. I should sit down on this mossy

bank, where so many others have been happy —
judging, at least, from the inscriptions with which
the walls are covered. Lovers are very indiscreet!
Is it at all necessary for everybody who is taking
a stroll to know that strangers and, indeed, that Mr.
and Mrs. So-and-So have come here to make love?
At least, put down only your baptismal names."

They left the park and went to the other side
of the château; that is where the Isle of Poplars
is, where Jean-Jacques rests. To reach this part
of the lake, it is necessary to pass through an old
building that was formerly a watermill, and which
now is uninhabitable. You find yourself on a road
bordered with willows and surrounded on all sides
by water; facing the isle, you find a little boat that
enables you to cross and visit the tomb of the "man
of nature," this, at least, is the name given to him
on the simple monument that contains his ashes.
A small placard fixed to a post invites you not to
write anything on the tomb of Jean-Jacques. This
inscription has not been respected in the slightest
degree, for the mania of writing one's name on
curious monuments becomes a necessary and, indeed, indispensable matter; people take good care
to take a knife or penknife with them when they go
to visit the Catacombs, the Augustins, or the tombs
of St. Denis, etc.   Let us say nothing about grottoes and groves; but what charm can one find in
reading Philip, Francis and Justin by the side of
Jean-Jacques Rousseau?

In Germany, Switzerland and England there are, in the inns situated near any noteworthy spot, pads on which travellers may write down their thoughts in prose or verse; these pads, on which you are invited to write something, are seldom renewed; the reason is that it is easier to write one's name than a thought.

After having rowed about on the water for some time, Gustave and his guides took the road back to the house, where a good dinner awaited them. They sat down to table, where there was no ceremony, etiquette, or constraint. Suzon, her parents, Gustave, Marie-Jeanne and Nicholas Toupet all sat at the same table. As for Benoit, always penetrated with a sense of his duty, he wanted to stand behind his master's chair to serve him, and it was only with the greatest difficulty that Gustave induced him to consent to sit in a corner, at one end of the table, where his dinner was served to him.

Madame Lucas, who was a bit of a backbiter, related to Gustave during the repast all the doings of the countryside, and the stories of her neighbors' lives; she broke off her tale only to order her husband to fill the glasses and Suzon to sit up straight. The maiden was placed beside the gentleman, who smiled upon her, which brought a blush to her cheeks; for in the country people are less accustomed to that kind of thing than in town.

Madame Lucas was telling the story of the cabi-

net-maker's wife who had set up her daughter in
Paris, in order to make a great lady of her. "To
finish the story, monsieur," she said, after filling
Gustave's plate, when he had already eaten to re-
pletion, "you must know that this girl found her
nest lined in Paris.— Drink up, monsieur! To your
health, if you will permit me!— Without anyone
knowing exactly how she managed it, she had a carriage and a pair of horses.— Lucas, fill the glasses,
instead of sitting there idle.   You are not eating,
monsieur.— But, to tell you the end of it, what is
stranger still is that this handsome girl—Lift up
your head, Suzon!— Well! it was that she came
down into the country in a coach to pay a visit —
Pour it out, Lucas! Another slice, monsieur?—and
would you believe it? she did not lodge at her parents' house! It's a fact! she had the airs of a
princess.— You are not eating, monsieur! Lucas,
what are you doing, instead of giving the gentleman something to drink?—So that when the neighborhood saw that, it made fun of the parents who
wanted to make a lady of their daughter.—To your
good health, and to that of your good mother
and father, and friends and acquaintances.— And
you must acknowledge that they were justified,
for, as the saying is, ' He who tries to jump higher
than the moon — ' "

The old woman was here interrupted by Nicholas, who uttered a loud cry and swore a great oath
that somebody had trodden on his bunion.   Old

Lucas, who was just about to pour out, let the bottle fall upon the table, and the wine ran into a dish of rabbit stew. Marie-Jeanne bit her tongue to keep from laughing, and Benoit swallowed a piece the wrong way.

They rose from the table; Madame scolded Lucas for his awkwardness, Gustave conversed with Suzon, but Marie-Jeanne did not lose sight of them. A peasant has passions just like a city lady; sometimes the passions give wit to fools and make intellectual people very stupid.

After dinner Gustave went for a walk alone in the wood; he thought about Julie and the means he should employ to get a letter delivered to her. The sight of the shade and the carpet of verdure recalled the pretty billiard-room and the sweet lessons that his pupil took so aptly. He heartily cursed his lack of caution. Ah! if he had only shot the bolt!

On his way back to the village he thought of Suzon, her air of timidity and her innocent ways. "Come, come!" he said, "it was wrong of me to touch her foot and press her knee. The little one is modesty itself, and I shall put ideas into her head! I make her blush; that's bad! I love women, that's all right; I am inconstant! that's not my fault; I make a cuckold of a husband; if I didn't do it, some one else would. It's doing husbands a great service to put their wives to the test; the woman who is good only for lack of opportunity possesses no great merit; but one should not lead an innocent girl astray and run the risk of wrecking her whole life. Although they call me a bad lot, I cannot reproach myself with anything like that. As for those girls who ask nothing better than to be seduced, and who, when the time comes for them to leave the convent, possess in theory what they lack in practice, it is permissible to attack them. They know what a lover wants and what they have to do."

So Gustave returned to Lucas' house with the firm resolve of not making Suzon blush, which, moreover, might give umbrage to Nicholas Toupet; it was already enough to have stamped on his foot.

They were waiting supper for the young gentleman. During the week, peasants know only three things; working, eating and sleeping. Gustave ate, he had nothing better to do ; and then he went up to his room to repair with sleep the fatigue of the preceding days.

Marie-Jeanne watched him mount the stairs to his room; she tried to read his eyes, but the young man, who was greatly in need of repose, paid no attention to her ogling; he went and shut himself in.

Benoit was sent up to a room under the eaves, close to the one occupied by Nicholas Toupet; and all the others sought the sleep which the events of the preceding night had not permitted them to enjoy.

Marie-Jeanne had no desire to sleep; nevertheless she retired, but she listened and waited and hoped. The big girl was strong enough to withstand the devil every night; however, she had not, as Gustave had, ridden some leagues on horseback, jumped out of a window, fallen into a pond, etc.

But the night passed on, and nobody came. You know, reader, "A woman's desire is a devouring flame."

Marie-Jeanne at length jumped out of bed. So, merely slipping on a skirt, she opened her door and went down; she did not need any light, as she knew every nook of the house.

The big girl reached the door of the room in which the young stranger was sleeping; she knocked softly at first, then louder. At last Gustave awoke.

"Who is there?" he called, without getting out of bed.

"It's I, monsieur!"

"Who are you?"

"You know very well!"

"Oh, it's you, Marie-Jeanne! what the devil do you want?"

"On my word, what a question! I — I came because — because you did not come."

"Ah! my dear girl, the devil does not spread his net of temptation every night; demons are not made of iron, and one who was doing the devil's work yesterday has need of sleep today. Goodnight, Marie-Jeanne!"

The poor girl stood transfixed in amazement before the door that wouldn't open to her. Her heart was torn with grief and anger, and jealousy soon intervened; one idea gave rise to another. She remembered how Gustave had looked at Suzon, his service and attentions to her, the young girl's blushes, and the stamp on the bunion that Nicholas had received under the table. "Come!" she said to herself, "they are in love, they understand one another; and the reason why he does not want to open the door to me is because— But what a horrible suspicion! Suppose she is with him now! Ah, the devil! I must find out where she is!"

Marie-Jeanne applied her ear to the keyhole, and knelt down to look under the door; she fancied she heard talking, moving and sighings. In order to be perfectly sure of her facts, she determined to go and knock at Suzon's door; if the young girl should not reply, that would leave no room for doubt that she was in the gentleman's room; in that case Marie-Jeanne was fully determined to wake up the whole house, and Nicholas Toupet first of all.

She crosses a little passage and knocks at Suzon's door; there is no answer; so she knocks again, and is about to raise a rumpus.

"Who's there?" asks a gentle, little voice.

Marie-Jeanne recognizes Suzon's voice; she was mistaken. She is about to go away when she receives a vigorous thump on the back; the servant screams and takes to her heels.

Nicholas Toupet was in love with Mademoiselle
Suzon, who was to be given to him in marriage,
because he was a good workman and the heir of a
rich uncle. He also had become jealous; the city
gentleman was such a handsome fellow, he had such
insinuating ways with the women; and then Mademoiselle Suzon blushed and cast her eyes down.
All this had disquieted Nicholas; and, suspecting
some project that would be detrimental to his love
affairs, he could not get to sleep. He had heard
steps upon the stairs, for the big girl made a noise
even when she went as softly as she could, so he
had gone down and hidden near Suzon's door;
he had heard some one come along, and then that
somebody had knocked at the maiden's door; that
could only be a lover! Anger and jealousy recognize no distinctions of rank; Nicholas punched
Marie-Jeanne with all his might in the back, thinking that he was hitting his rival.

As Marie-Jeanne mounted her rickety stairs, she
made a false step and fell. Nicholas was pursuing
her; he reached her and caught hold of her.
"Hallo! this it not the gentleman!" he exclaimed
in surprise.

"What, is that you, Nicholas?" cried the servant, as she got up.

"Why, it's Marie-Jeanne! If I had known that
I should not have hit so hard; I took you for a
robber. But what were you doing at Suzon's door?"

"Why! I went downstairs because I thought

I heard the mistress call me ; and how about your-·
self, Nicholas ? "

" Me ? Oh ! I heard a noise and went down to
see — but since it's nothing I'm going back to bed.
Good-night, Marie-Jeanne."

" Good-night, Nicholas."

They both went to their own rooms, entirely
satisfied. Nicholas knew that Suzon was in her
own room, and Marie-Jeanne was convinced that
the handsome gentleman was alone in his room ;
both went to bed, pleased at having deceived each
other.

Poor jealous simpletons, you were the active
cause of the very event you dreaded, which, perhaps, without your agency would never have occurred !

Suzon, as you know, had been awakened by the
second knock at her door ; she inquired, " Who's
there?" and nobody replied ; and then there was a
scream — the young girl recognized Marie-Jeanne's
voice. Suzon got up, being uneasy as to what might
be the matter and fearing that her parents or the
young gentleman might be ill.

On his side, Gustave, after being awakened, found
it difficult to go to sleep again, and reflected that
he had been hard-hearted in sending away this poor
girl who had come to seek him and that at least
he owed her some slight consolation. Marie-
Jeanne was not so pretty as Suzon, but she had
her value ; and, as he wanted to spend some days

with these villagers, it would be wise to humor her.

Our hero yielded to the temptation, or chance, or destiny, or whatever you like to call it. He got up, opened his door, took a few steps down the passage, and found himself face to face with Suzon, whom he took for Marie-Jeanne. He drew her into his room, she not making any resistance; then he kissed her, and she submitted to his kisses; for she found such pleasure in them that she lost all power of speech.

When she found her voice, Gustave exclaimed, " Good Heavens! this is not Marie-Jeanne."

" No, monsieur! it is I."

" Suzon! then it is written that I am always to be guilty of some fresh folly. This time, however, it is not my fault, for Heaven is my witness that I did not mean to lead her astray; but since fate throws her into my arms let me give thanks to my lucky star!"

Gustave, who had been too tired to entertain Marie-Jeanne, recovered all his ardor with Suzon in his arms. Our hero took a seat beside Suzon and they began a mutual explanation.

" My dearest, how did I happen to meet you in the passage in your night-robes in the middle of the night?"

" Because somebody knocked at my door, and that woke me, so I got up to see who it was; I feared that you might be ill!"

" Poor little one! so you were thinking of me?"

" Oh, yes, monsieur! Are you annoyed at what has happened?"

" Well, I am both annoyed and pleased."

" But as for yourself, I see very plainly that you mistook me for Marie-Jeanne; and you scarcely gave a thought to me."

" On the contrary, Suzon, I was thinking of you a great deal; I loved you, but did not dare to tell you, I had too much respect for your innocence; and even now, when you have made me the happiest man in the world, I should curse my happiness if it were to cause you any grief."

" What's the use of crying over spilled milk?"

" But how about Nicholas Toupet?"

" He'll never know!"

" Do you love him!"

" Oh, no; I never did care much for him, and now I don't like him at all."

" But you are to marry him?"

" Marry him! oh, no, monsieur; I don't want to marry anybody."

" Why, dear?"

" Because I could not love my husband, since you are the one I love now."

" Suzon, darling, I love you with all my heart, but I can't marry you."

" Oh, I know that very well, monsieur."

" You said just now that Nicholas would never know about to-night."

" Certainly, but I should know ! ''

" But what would your parents say if you refused to marry ? "

" I am sure I don't know."

" So you see that it is necessary to be reasonable."

" Yes, monsieur ; but I will never marry."

" Oho ! this is a girl of strong character ; I shall
never succeed in making her listen to reason today ; but when I have gone away, she will marry
that fool of a Nicholas."

And Gustave, having moralized sufficiently with
the little one, who was in tears because he no longer
embraced her and wanted her to get married, took
her in his arms and pressed her to his heart and
consoled her with all the eloquence of which he
was master. Suzon timidly asked Gustave if she
might come to his room and pay him a future visit.
On his assurance that nothing could give him
greater delight, she went away fully satisfied with
her happiness and already sighing for its renewal.

As for Gustave he went back to bed with the
intention of sleeping all day, since in papa Lucas'
house the nights were so well spent.

On coming down about the middle of the morning, Gustave met Marie-Jeanne on the stairs and
said to her in severe tones, " My good friend, I
advise you henceforth to stay in your own room at
night and not come knocking at my door. In consequence of a mistake, I had a moment of weak-

ness ; but henceforth I am going to be good and so deserve to live in the house of honest people. Remember that if you are ever again guilty of last night's folly, I shall be forced to leave this house immediately."

Marie-Jean, in great confusion, stammered a few excuses ; and went away in great anger with young city gentlemen, from whom you never know what to expect.

Suzon impatiently awaited the appearance of him who had made her so happy during the night, and with whom she was to be again so happy. At sixteen, the heart becomes attached very quickly ; but the little peasant was too open to sentiment to be fortunate.

Nicholas, cured of his suspicions, no longer worried about his future. Marie-Jeanne, shamefaced in Gustave's presence, kept out of his way whenever she saw him. The confiding and unsuspicious parents did not watch over their daughter, besides Benoit provided them with quite enough to occupy their minds, for, since they had set him at his ease, forgetting the fright the cow had given him, he amused himself all day in riding the asses to death or in setting the cocks fighting or in birdsnesting, climbing the trees and breaking the branches; eating the hen's eggs, milking the cows and upsetting the milk in his attempts to make butter, chasing the chickens and shutting the ducks up with the pigeons.

While the peasants were repairing M. Benoit's blunders, Gustave was out walking and wandering in the meadows with Suzon; night found them together again; and when it was time to part, she constantly repeated, "Ah! I will never marry Nicholas!"

A fortnight had elapsed. Gustave had intended to stay only a week at Ermenonville; but Suzon's rustic grace had made him forget his vows to Julie. However, on the sixteenth day, Gustave, who had again fruitlessly tried to induce Suzon to marry Nicholas, comprehended that it was not by staying at her side that he could succeed in curing her of her love for him. He reproached himself also for the indifference with which he repaid Madame de Berly's affection; and, as one of our hero's distinguishing qualities was to execute promptly what he had made up his mind to do, he immediately bought a suit of peasant's clothes and ordered Benoit to saddle the horses, lavishly paid Madame Lucas, tenderly embraced Suzon, slipped a louis into Marie-Jeanne's palm, and announced to the peasants his departure for Paris.

Suzon, who was not prepared for this departure, which, however, she had secretly dreaded for some time, but which she flattered herself was a long way off, because her heart could not entertain the idea of living without Gustave, gave a scream and fell at her mother's feet. Our hero grew pale and trembled, uncertain whether he ought to stay any longer. The peasants, who attributed their daughter's fainting to a simple indisposition, hastened to carry her out into the open air. She revived, and looked at Gustave without saying a word ; but he, feeling his courage fail, hastened to mount, and left the village without daring to look back, fearing to meet Suzon's supplicating gaze again.

CHAPTER V

A Clever Woman can Make a Man Believe in Miracles. A Wedding

When Gustave had ridden about a league from Ermenonville he dismounted and entered a thicket and ordered Benoit to keep a good watch on the road in both directions, because anyone might imagine he was some man who was being pursued by the gendarmes. Gustave had not wanted to put on his new clothes before leaving the village house, for fear of arousing the curiosity of the villagers and having to answer their questions as to his actions.

He put on a pair of wide gray trousers, a blue vest, and covered his head with a large round hat and then approached Benoit, who nearly ran away, not recognizing his master in his unique make-up. Gustave then ordered his valet to go to Paris and wait for him at the house of his friend, Olivier, whose friendship for him had never failed and where he would be certain to find shelter so long as his uncle's anger should last.

"How about the horses, monsieur?" asked Benoit. "You must know that they belong to your uncle!"

"Idiot! Does not anything that belongs to the
uncle also belong to the nephew? Besides, hasn't
the colonel given them to me?"

"Shall I take them also to M. Olivier's?"

"The devil! That's a difficulty! Olivier has
no stables."

"If he had a little room on the groundfloor?"

"Stupid! what are you talking about? Ah! tell
Olivier to sell them; indeed, I shall have need of
money in a short time, and that will set me right."

"What, monsieur, must I follow you on foot?"

"Are you going to make a big fuss about that?"

"What a pity! I am beginning to ride so well.
If only one were sold, monsieur, you could keep
the other for both of us. I could hold myself very
well 'en croupe' behind you."

"You are awfully stupid, my poor Benoit, I
shall never make anything of you. Come! do what
I tell you. Go to Olivier's, let him sell my horses
and keep you till my arrival. Ah! Benoit, if by
any mistake you should meet my uncle as you
enter Paris, you will tell him — the devil! Ah!
you will tell him that I am ill."

"Yes, monsieur."

"But he will want to know where I am!"

"I shall tell him that you are dead!"

"Idiot! My uncle loves me in spite of his
harshness, and such news would only distress him."

"Well, since you want to soften him —"

"You will tell him that I have gone to stay with

one of my friends whose name I have not given you."

"Yes, monsieur, one of your friends whom you do not know."

" Benoit, I am certain that you will be guilty of some foolishness ! "

" On the contrary, monsieur, you will see that the colonel will be defeated."

"Once at Olivier's house, don't venture to go out; someone might meet you, follow you and find out where I was."

" But how about eating, monsieur ? "

" You will be taken care of. Get along, Benoit."

" I am off, monsieur."

Benoit started off, galloping toward Paris ; Gustave took the road that led to M. de Berly's house; and, on the way, he thought of the best means of getting a letter to Julie.

Was he sufficiently disguised not to be recognizable ? Was Julie surrounded by spies ordered to intercept her letters ? Could he trust a servant who might pity a young man that ran away in his shirt, but who, nevertheless, might not be willing to run the risk of being discharged ? Moreover, would not this be once more compromising to Madame de Berly, whose error could be judged only by what had been witnessed, and who had perhaps found means to justify herself in her husband's eyes, — á thing that seems difficult, but which is, however, not impossible, for women often have special ways of making what is evident seem doubtful, and husbands, for their own sakes, are compelled to see nothing in broad daylight.

After having reflected for some time upon what he should do, our hero decided to leave himself in the hands of Fate — a thing he often did. He walked along quickly, and finally saw the country house in which he had spent such happy hours, and which he had left so abruptly. He stopped a moment to breathe more freely and to control his emotion.

As some of the villagers passed along the road, Gustave hid himself; he imagined that everybody was watching him and that everybody knew that he was not what he pretended to be. However, as everybody went along the road without taking notice of him, he soon recovered his equanimity. He approached the house and looked through the railings into the gardens that he had walked in so often; he looked for the billiard-room, but he could not see it from this point. All the windows of the house were shut. The garden seemed like a desert. Where was everybody? Wherever had they gone? Gustave hastened his steps and arrived at the grand entrance of the courtyard. He looked about; nobody was in sight. He entered. Pulling his hat over his eyes, he approached the porter, whom he saw at the garden entrance.

"What do you want?" said the latter in a gruff voice.

" M. de Berly."

" He is in Paris."

" And — his niece ? "

" His niece also."

" And — his wife ? "

" His wife also."

" What ? Have they all gone away ? "

" Certainly! If you want to see them about anything, you will find them in Paris, Rue du Sentier."

So saying, the porter turned his back. The man was unwilling to talk, he was evidently stupid, brutal and stubborn; it was very certain that Julie had not confided in him. He would have to return without having had any news of her. As Gustave was returning towards the gate, suddenly a woman ran out from the hall on the groundfloor and came towards him. Oh, thank heavens ! it was the cook who had spoken to Benoit. Should he make himself known to her ? But before he had time to reflect, the servant had come up to him and said in a low voice,—

" I recognize you, monsieur, I have something for you ; go out, and wait for me behind the acacias on the other side of the road."

She left him and busied herself with hanging up some linen in the courtyard. Gustave hurried away and went to the acacias.

" This servant recognized me," he said, " from the interior of a hall without hearing me speak, and she had only seen me a few times, while that idiot of a porter, who saw me pass him twenty times a day, suspected nothing! Ah! woman! woman! in all classes and conditions of society, you have such tact, such vision! You see in one instant what it takes us a week to discover!"

The servant did not keep him waiting long; she ran towards Gustave.

"I have been waiting for you a long time, monsieur, I only stayed here in the country on your account, monsieur. I had to pretend to be ill, so as to keep from going to Paris with all the rest. Madame told me that she wouldn't trust anybody but me with a letter for you."

"A letter! Give it to me, my good friend."

"Madame thought that you would have come for it sooner—and as for me, I was beginning to get very tired here. Here it is; take it!"

"Will you take charge of this one for your mistress?"

"Yes, monsieur, she shall get it at once."

"Here, Marguerite, take these two louis to pay for the trouble you have had in waiting for me."

"Oh, monsieur, I don't want any money for serving madame; she is so kind."

"That's all right, Marguerite, but I want you to take it."

"Well, to oblige you, monsieur."

"Good-by, don't forget my letter, Marguerite."

"Don't be afraid, monsieur; madame shall have it this evening."

The kind servant departed.

"But for her," said Gustave, "I should have had no news of Julie. It seems that the cook is attached to the mistress, while the lady's maid, the recipient of favors from Madame de Berly, must have been capable of betraying her! Well, now, what does that prove? that benefits often create ingrates; while others can have a kind heart and love to help people, although busy chopping up parsley and fricasseeing a chicken.

"But let us read the letter,—

My Dear Friend:—I need not tell you what I am suffering apart from you; I like to think that your heart shares my grief, and feels what mine does at the sorrow of our separation. But I must tell you what has happened since you went away.

M. de Berly went out of my room very soon after you jumped out of the window; he went into the garden, but he soon came upstairs again. I had almost lost my reason. However, I wished to deceive him regarding my fault. It was not so much for my own sake as for his that I tried to make this effort, — to do him the kindness of dismissing from his mind an idea that distressed him. I am perfectly willing to lose my own peace of mind; but I could never forgive myself for having destroyed M. de Berly's. Just as M. de Berly was going to give vent to his rage, I pretended to be terribly angry myself. I reproached him for not taking vengeance upon a young man who had forced himself into my room when I was asleep, and who, in spite of my resistance, was on the point of triumphing over my virtue if he had not come in suddenly and delivered me from his insolent attempts. M. de Berly did not know what to say or to believe; he looked at me, walked up and down the room, and did not know what to make of it all. Seeing his indecision, I began to weep bitterly, and I can assure you that my tears were not feigned. M. de Berly, never having seen me weep before, threw himself at my feet and begged my pardon for his hastiness, which I willingly forgave. He was grieved at having told the colonel that things were different from what they really were. I told him to see the colonel again, and begged him to keep the affair quiet. M. de Berly swore that he would be revenged on you, but I do not fear that threat; I know that he would never attack anything but game. Therefore, peace is established again; but I shall never see you again! Oh, Gustave! this punishment is so cruel that it ought to be an expiation for my fault. My life must henceforth be spent in tears. Ah! if people only knew how cruel it is to pass one's life with somebody whom one never can love, they would consult a young girl's heart before they married her off. My parents sacrificed me. M. de Berly never tried to please me! Moreover, how could he? — our ages, our tastes, our characters are too opposed! — and yet it is criminal for me to love another! — Oh, my dear one! how much women ought to be pitied!

Good-by! be happy, but think sometimes of

JULIE.

"Dear Julie — oh, I shall see you again! Fate will smile on us," and Gustave kissed the letter of the woman whom he had already deceived. He could not help laughing at the credulity of M. de Berly, who, after finding a man in bed with his wife, still believed in her innocence.

"Certainly," he said, "it was for husbands that that passage of Scripture was written, 'Oculus habent et non videbunt.'"

"Let us go back to Paris," said Gustave, "there is nothing to keep me here. I will go to Olivier's; there I can plan how to see Julie without compromising her, if that is possible; certainly I can

succeed, because they say with perseverance anything is possible; after all, this is only half true,
because I have tried a hundred times to be good,
and I haven't succeeded. How many people spend
their lives without accomplishing their aims? Al-
chemists who are searching for gold and ruin themselves with their furnaces; stockbrokers who risk
money on the fogs of the Seine; authors who think
they will become rich; aeronauts who expect to
fly like birds; travellers who seek the ends of the
earth; mathematicians who try to square the circle;
physicians who attempt to cure the ailments of the
nerves by mean of electricity; mechanicians who
think they can run horseless carriages; loving souls,
who seek for pure friendship and faithful love, and
many other fine things besides, that I cannot enu-
merate because I can't remember them all; but all
these people run the risk of wasting their energies."

With these reflections Gustave went on his way
to Paris; but he had only reached Vauderland,
and had still five leagues to go, when he began to
feel tired. As he wished, however, to get to Paris
that evening, he tried to find a coach with a spare
seat. This time fortune did not favor him, for all
the coaches from Louvre, Senlis and Mortfontaine
were full.

"Come!" said Gustave, "courage! I shall have
to walk. But this confounded costume bothers
me! I may easily enough meet with some open
carriages in which room might be found for the

elegant Saint-Réal; but into which a peasant would never be admitted; they would look at me and laugh me to scorn; I am sure that my get-up is perfectly ridiculous!"

As Gustave was trying to console himself by walking faster, he heard a carriage approaching; he looked back; it proved to be a vehicle in which there was a good-natured looking, fat old fellow, whose joyful countenance inspired cheerfulness.

"On my word!" exclaimed our hero, "I must not lose this chance, perhaps this man won't refuse me a seat beside him; and even if we only go a league together, that will be a little lift. Come! let's accost him; but I must not forget that I am a countryman!"

Gustave ran up to the wagon and cried, "Hallo, monsieur!"

"What do you want, my friend?"

"On my life! I am as tired as the devil; I started too late from Ermenonville, I missed the coach to Mortfontaine, and I have to go to Paris; if it wouldn't put you out too much, you would oblige me very greatly by giving me a seat."

"Oh! that is easy enough. Get in, here is a place for you; we shall be comfortable enough, my wagon is large. Get in! sit down beside me."

"Many thanks! I am beginning to be very tired."

Gustave seated himself beside the fat old fellow and they entered into conversation.

"You come from Ermenonville? I know some-body there — a small farmer named Lucas."

"Why it is precisely with him that I have been staying."

"Good! In that case, you can give me news of the family. Does Mother Lucas scold as much as ever?"

"Oh, more than ever!"

"And little Suzon, is she beginning to grow up?"

"Oh, she is already grown up."

"She promised to be very pretty — but, damn it! I haven't been to Ermenonville for two years; a young girl can develop very much."

"Suzon has developed very much indeed; she is well-formed, fresh, lively — indeed, she is charming."

"Ho! ho! you talk as if you were in love. Do you happen to know her betrothed, Nicholas Toupet, of whom Lucas spoke to me, and who was expected the last time I was there?"

"I certainly do, monsieur, I am Nicholas Toupet, Mamzelle Suzon's intended."

"Indeed! M. Toupet, I am delighted to meet you. You must have heard them speak of me at Lucas'; I am their first cousin, Pierre Ledru."

"Is it possible? And so you are M. Ledru? Oh, indeed they did speak of you very often!"

"Let us embrace, M. Toupet."

"Gladly indeed, M. Ledru."

Gustave embraced the fat cousin and had great

difficulty to keep from laughing. It was no great hardship to take the name of Nicholas Toupet for a few hours. Gustave loved to amuse himself, and he saw that the cousin's mistake would furnish him with a fine opportunity.

"Well, now, M. Nicholas Toupet," said Ledru, after the first transports of acquaintanceship were over, " are you going to Paris on important business ? "

" Well, provided I get there by tomorrow — "

" Look here! I am going to make you a proposition. I am going to La Villette to attend the wedding of one of my god-daughters, who is going to marry a rich grocer of the place. I ought to have arrived there this morning for the ceremony, but my business prevented me ; but I shall get there in time for the supper, which is the best after all. Come now, you must go ; I will introduce you, and everybody will be glad to see you."

" You are very kind, M. Ledru. Do you think any of M. Lucas' relatives will be there ? "

" No, nobody but myself; but you need not be concerned, however ; only the best society will be there, all established people — the tanner, the locksmith, the master mason and the garbage contractor of La Villette. Oh, all the best people ! "

" All right ! I agree, M. Ledru, I am with you."

" Ah, that's the way to talk ! We'll have lots of fun ; we'll drink, eat, dance, and carouse."

" That's right ! You look like a high liver."

"Well, such as you see me, I am a gay dog."

"Really!"

"By God, yes! they must have told you that at Lucas'."

"That's true. They did tell me some of your escapades."

"They're good enough, eh?"

"They are pretty bad."   .

"I hope to get the bridegroom in a rage. And then the garter, I'll yield none of my rights to it."

"Is the bride pretty?"

"My god-daughter? Oh, she is passable! The bridegroom is gray-haired. Her hair is rather red and her nose quite large, but, altogether, she is a nice-looking blonde. And strong! Ah, she could pick up a man as if he were only a kite; and she can go through the musket-drill like one of the National Guard."

"Lord, what a woman!"

"Her husband will have his hands full tonight. Ah! Ah!"

Talking thus, they arrived at La Villette. Gustave was prepared for some new experiences. There was nobody there who visited Lucas, so nobody would suspect anything; and, besides, at a wedding the guests think of nothing but the festivities.

"I will go," said Gustave, "and play my part well; if these good people don't amuse me, I will pick up my hat and slip away without being noticed. Besides, I am just as well satisfied not to

arrive in Paris tonight in this costume; at least,
I shall not run the risk of seeing any of my acquaintances and being recognized."

They got out of the carriage in front of an innkeeper's and wine-merchant's.

"Here's the place," said Ledru, "the Flowery
Bushel — dining-room for a hundred people. Dear,
dear, I hear the fiddles! Have they dined? Why,
it isn't three o'clock yet!"

"No, monsieur, they haven't dined yet," replied
a kitchenmaid, "dinner is not until four o'clock;
the company is dancing while waiting for the meal."

"Well and good, my child, you have comforted
me very much. Come along, let's go upstairs,
M. Toupet!"

"I follow you, M. Ledru."

They went upstairs into a large room, and found
themselves in the midst of a dance; the gentlemen
had taken off their coats and tucked up their shirt-
sleeves so as to dance the more gracefully; the
wine was already circulating, and the more they
refreshed themselves, the redder their faces became.

At Ledru's entrance the dancing ceased; everybody surrounded him, embraced him and shook
hands with him, and there were noisy, joyful shouts.

"We were afraid you must have broken down
on the way, godfather," said the rather small, soft
voice of a tall stout woman, whom Gustave recognized as the bride from the portrait her dear godfather had drawn of her.

"Come and embrace me, Lolotte," said Ledru, opening his arms to his god-daughter. "Ah, my little girl, so this is the great day ; you are dancing this morning, you will dance this evening, and you will dance tonight ! "

"Oh, oh, my godfather is always joking ! "

"M. Ledru," said the bridegroom, coming forward with a pretentious manner, "we should have been very much annoyed if you had disappointed us today."

"I not come to your wedding, M. Détail? Why, I would come on my donkey. But, just a moment, there is something else. I want to introduce somebody to you."

So far, nobody had paid any attention to Gustave, who was standing in a corner carefully examining all the ladies at the wedding, and noticing with pleasure that among the twenty women he saw three or four that were quite nice-looking in their own way. He was interrupted in this occupation by Ledru, who took him by the hand and introduced him to the bridegroom.

"M. Détail, I want to introduce to you a friend, M. Nicholas Toupet, the future husband of the daughter of my cousin Lucas of Ermenonville. He is a very fine fellow !—I flatter myself he won't be in the way here."

"Why, certainly not, godfather, certainly not ! M. Toupet, you honor us greatly by coming to our wedding ! "

"Monsieur, the honor is entirely mine."

After this exchange of compliments, Gustave embraced the bride, her mother, her sister, her aunts, her cousins — in fact, all the ladies present; his polite manners pleased the whole company and M. Toupet was considered charming.

"Dinner is served!" the innkeeper, otherwise the wine-merchant, came in to announce.

"To table! to table!" cried everybody.

They went into a room that could accommodate a hundred covers, where the fifty persons who composed the wedding-party found some little trouble in getting seated, but finally they managed to take their places. Gustave found himself between a stout brunette and a little blonde, both of whom were quite good-looking.

"I shall have a choice," he said to himself, "if perchance these ladies are open to a little fun. While waiting, I had better eat heartily to keep up my part."

Soups, boiled beef, chitterlings and cutlets went the rounds; the second course consisted of veal, pork, rabbits and beef à la mode; they were not acquainted there with any light, epicurean dishes; they ate meat and then they ate meat again.

"Good heavens!" said Gustave to himself, "this certainly is a fortifying meal; I think the bride must have ordered it herself!"

While they were dining, three fiddlers sat themselves on a stage at the corner of the room and played with might and main, "Où peut-on être mieux!" "Gai! gai! Mariez-vous"; "Il faut des époux assortis"; "Tu n'aura pas, petit polisson"; "la marche des Tartares," and other airs which were appropriate to the occasion, or very effective. The noise that the musicians made compelled the guests to talk louder and louder; in order to hear one another they had to scream, and soon there was an infernal din. The wine began to warm them up; coarse jokes were bandied about and received with shouts of laughter loud enough to break the windows. Cousin Ledru had promised to make lots of fun, so now he began a running fire of jests that could not be taken with a double meaning, since the matter was expressed clearly in detail. Meanwhile, Gustave was trying to form a more intimate acquaintance with his neighbors. He first addressed the big brunette, who gladly responded to his pleasantries, for she loved mirth and laughter. The false Nicholas played the gallant, frequently offering the wine, which was accepted; then he took the carafe and thought he ought to offer some water.

"Oh, I never drink water, monsieur!"

"Ah! pardon me, madame; I did not know."

"My husband would make a fine fuss if I drank any!"

"Indeed! It's your husband who objects?"

"Yes, I'll tell you the reason; I'm afraid of accidents —"

"That's different; in that case, you are very wise not to drink any."

Gustave then turned towards the blonde; for Madame Ratel's confidences had not favorably impressed him.

In five minutes' conversation, Gustave learned that the little woman was a widow, a cousin of the bridegroom's, and a silk mercer in the Rue aux Ours; that she was very fond of the theatre, often attending the melodramas, and that on Sundays she played amateur comedy in the Rue du Cygne, in a little hall that was used as a theatre by kind permission of the commissaire; and that the acting there was almost as good as at the Doyen.

" Come! " said our hero to himself, " with a widow, I need neither fear to embroil a household nor yet to be accused of seduction; for a woman who plays in amateur comedy every Sunday can not pretend to be a novice in intrigue. Let's flirt with the widow, if only to pass the time; besides, a young man who wants to gain instruction ought to take a course of gallantry in every social class."

Madame Henri, as the little widow was named, listened to Gustave, opened her big eyes, and seemed somewhat astonished at his manners. A woman who plays in comedy is likely to have a little discernment; and our hero sometimes forgot that he was merely Nicholas Toupet.

Madame Ratel, much piqued at the desertion of M. Nicholas, who now talked exclusively with her neighbor, was trying to mingle in their conversation when the bride uttered a piercing cry; somebody was trying to steal her garter. The big booby who had crept under the table to get it had seized the ribbon and tugged at it with much force, thinking to carry it off cleverly; but Mademoiselle Lolotte, fearing lest her garter should be carried off before the proper time, had taken the precaution to tie it fast to her leg; afterwards, being entirely taken up with the pleasures of conversation and the sweet things that were said to her, she had forgotten to untie her garter.

The action of the best man was so vigorous that Lolotte slipped from her chair and gave a scream; while the great booby found himself tangled up in Lolotte's skirts. All the guests rose from their seats and looked at the bride in astonishment; M. Détail was not strong enough to lift his wife up, so the godfather helped him, proclaiming that it was a good joke of the best man's, M. Cadet. The bridegroom did not seem to find the joke quite to his taste; but M. Ledru observed that it was too dark under the table to see clearly, and so no harm was done. This luminous reflection reassured M. Détail. "So long as M. Cadet couldn't see," he said, "I'll say no more about it."

Lolotte took her place at the table without appearing to be disconcerted; and M. Cadet resumed his seat with a face as red as a beetroot. The famous garter was cut up into little pieces and distributed ; and the dessert, coffee and liqueurs were brought in. The gayety grew even more noisy; they sang and drank to one another till you could not have heard the firing of a cannon in the room underneath.

At last the time for the ball arrives. They get up from the table, run to get into place, go down stairs, push, crowd and fall over one another, and burst into fits of laughter ; the ladies are full of wild gayety, and the dancers may paw, pinch and press everything that they find in their arms ; on a wedding day all that kind of thing is allowable, and at La Villette people are not squeamish about a little thing like that.

A youth of the cabinet-maker's trade, from the Faubourg Saint-Antoine, had been ogling Madame Henri for some time, and darting black looks at M. Nicholas. Gustave paid no attention to the scowls of the cabinet-maker, and continued to laugh with the fair silk-mercer. He induced her to stand up with him in two country-dances, and then the ogling gentleman invited the lady for the next. She accepted ; but Gustave, who felt somewhat overcome with heat, proposed to the pretty blonde to take a stroll in the garden ; she consented, and went out with M. Nicholas Toupet, forgetting her engagement with the cabinet-maker.

They strolled about arm in arm, conversed, looked into one another's eyes, held hands and sighed. Gustave suggested that they should sit

down under a dark clump of trees, for a wine merchant's garden is illuminated only on Sundays and
Mondays. The little widow accepted; Gustave
stole a kiss, and she laughed; but when he tried
to go to greater lengths, she grew angry and repulsed him.

The little widow was virtuous; she didn't mind
laughter and jesting, but she didn't want that kind
of thing to go any further. Gustave said to himself, "Where the devil will severity take up its
abode next? They submit in the boudoirs and
parlors, and in the Tivoli groves; and here am I repulsed at La Villette in a wine-merchant's garden!"

Gustave promised to behave better; then he was
forgiven, and she sat down beside him again; he was
even allowed to kiss her, and then they talked again
of love, marriage and fidelity. Poor woman! she
wanted marriage; she had come to a fine shop for
it! Then she had forgotten that M. Nicholas was
the future husband of Mademoiselle Suzon of
Ermenonville? Not at all! but she was a pretty
woman; and M. Nicholas sighed when he looked
at her, so she might easily supplant Mademoiselle
Suzon! Where is the woman who does not count
to some extent upon the power of her charms?

The conversation became sentimental; Gustave
was doing his best to moderate the little widow's
somewhat severe principles, when suddenly the
young cabinet-maker stood before them. He was
in a great rage; his eyes glittered like those of a

cat whose tail has just been cut off; he approached
Gustave with clenched fists and head thrown back.

"M. du Toupet, it is not considered polite to
prevent a lady from dancing with the person with
whom she has made an engagement; and this lady
would now be dancing with me if you had not induced her to come into the garden — for what purpose, I don't know."

Gustave listened quietly to his rival's speech;
and then, forgetting whom he was impersonating,
he burst into a roar of laughter.

The cabinet-maker, realizing that he was being
made fun of, grew angrier still and gave Gustave
a punch on the nose; the latter rose and sprang at
him, and then these gentlemen fought and struggled, while the little blonde screamed and wept
and shouted for the other wedding guests.

First the waiters came, and then the master, the
waitresses and scullions; the excitement extended
into the ballroom. The dance was interrupted,
and the bridegroom, who was dancing with his wife
for the first time, thought that it was his duty to
make peace between the guests; so he dropped
Lolotte's hand and hastened downstairs. The
others all followed the bridegroom into the garden. Gustave had the cabinet-maker down on the
ground with his knee on his stomach, holding him
by the throat with one hand while he pulled his
ear with the other. The poor youth was choking,
and begged for mercy; but Gustave, who was

savage at having been forced to resort to fisticuffs, was no longer master of himself. Fortunately, the dancers arrived in a throng; they took hold of M. Nicholas, helped the half-dead cabinet-maker to his feet, and endeavored to make peace between the two combatants,

Gustave was perfectly satisfied, he could not demand any further satisfaction from people he devoutly hoped he would never see again; he had one black eye and his nose was slightly skinned, but he had wanted to see a wedding at La Villette, and, consequently, he had to put up with a few disagreeable incidents.

As for the cabinet-maker, he had had enough of it; he was quite willing to raise no more trouble with M. Toupet. The little silk-mercer wept bitterly and reproached herself with having been the cause of the fight by her lapse of memory; Madame Ratel made pleasant comments, and maliciously wanted to know why Madame Henri and M. Nicholas had sought the shelter of a clump of trees so far from the house. They all made their own reflections; and Gustave, who had had all the fun he could get out of it, asked monsieur where he could find his hat.

"What! M. Nicholas; you are going to leave us already?"

"Yes, monsieur. I have important business in Paris; I must go to bed so as to get up early in the morning."

"At least wait for supper!"

"Many thanks! I dined so well that I have no appetite left."

"At least, accept a glass of wine!"

"Nothing at all, thank you, M. Détail!"

"Very well! since you are immovable I will go and ask Lolotte where the hats are."

"I'll follow you!"

M. Détail went up into the ballroom, where he found nobody but the musicians, who were regaling themselves with the refreshments provided for the guests. "Where is my wife?" he cried as he went through room after room. "Where the devil is my hat?" cried Gustave, as he hunted in every corner, "in my present state of perspiration, I can't go to Paris without a hat; it's quite enough to have a black eye and a raw nose; I haven't any special desire to catch cold into the bargain!"

Passing along a passage, they noticed a small door; a waitress said the gentlemen's hats and coats were in there; but the key of the door couldn't be found. "Wait a moment!" said the servant, "my mistress has a pass-key for all the doors."

She went downstairs and returned with a bunch of keys; M. Détail unlocked the door and went in with a candle in his hand. Gustave followed him and the servant came after. The bridegroom uttered a cry and retreated a few steps. Gustave craned his neck and saw Lolotte and M. Cadet, who seemed to be taking lessons in untying her garter.

The bridegroom could not believe his own eyes; he went nearer, and big M. Cadet scuttled under the bed. Gustave was curious to see how Lolotte would extricate herself from the predicament. "It really is my wife!" exclaimed M. Détail; and, in his agitation he let the light fall. It fell upon very inflammable material, and immediately blazed up. Lolotte jumped up, uttering piercing shrieks, and ran and plunged her skirts in a tub in which the wine was being cooled for supper. Everybody came running to see what was the matter; M. Cadet took to his heels; the servant related what she had seen; and the men tried to console the bridegroom. M. Ledru tried to make him believe that it was all a joke that had been specially prepared in order to test his love for his wife; and Madame Ratel got him into a calmer frame of mind by giving him the address of a barber-surgeon who could readily repair Lolotte's injuries.

In the midst of all this disturbance, Gustave seized the first hat he could lay his hands on and left the Flowery Bushel, shamed and confused, vowing, though somewhat late, that he would not be seen there again.

CHAPTER VI

Scorn. The Patrol. The Little Laundress. Madame Dubourg

"That's the way!" soliloquized Gustave, as he went down the Faubourg Saint-Martin on his weary walk to Paris, "I always act without considering the consequences, and for that reason I am forever making a fool of myself! If I had acted with a little reflection and common sense, I should not have gone to that miserable wedding at all, where I was entirely out of place, and so I should not have set the Flowery Bushel in an uproar; Madame Ratel would not have confided in me with regard to her hydropathic weakness; the little widow would not have accompanied me into the garden to sit under the trees, but would have danced with all the others who wished; that fool of a cabinet-maker would not have got into a fight with me; I should have had neither a black eye nor a swollen nose; the bridegroom would not have gone to hunt for my hat in that little dark room where his better half had shut herself up with that great simpleton of a best man to teach him how to tie and untie a woman's garter properly; and poor Lolotte, the unfortunate bride, would not have been forced to sit

down in a tub of water in order to put out the fire
among her skirts. What was I doing there, anyhow?
What would my uncle say if he ran across me
in this costume and with this battered face? The
devil! I can imagine it; and it's almost one o'clock
in the morning. Shall I go to Olivier's lodgings
now? If it were only a question of exposing myself to his sarcastic remarks, I should be the first
to join him in laughing at my misadventures; but
there is a porter in his house, and that cursed
porter is asleep by this time, for those individuals
are the despair of young people; it would be necessary to knock and wake up the whole neighborhood; and to be seen in this condition, bruised and
muddy — that devil of a cabinet-maker knocked
me down twice — this hat, that I took when I could
not distinguish things clearly, hasn't any shape —
and my nose, and my black eye! What would
people take me for? I don't want to show myself
in this condition, so I must sleep in the street.
Curse the wedding! to the devil with La Villette
and all silk-mercers and cabinet-makers!"

Gustave had reached the Porte Saint-Martin;
there he halted, uncertain whether to turn to the
right or left, or whether he should go any farther
at all. Suddenly an idea struck him, and he was
delighted with it; so he began to run in the direction of the Rue Charlot.

The reader may, or may not, remember a certain
young lady named Lise, a fine-starcher, to whom

Colonel Moranval referred at the beginning of this work, and with whom our hero had run away at the age of sixteen and hidden in a little apartment in the Rue du Fauconnier. The colonel had caught his nephew and taken Mademoiselle Lise back to her mother; but since you can't keep a youth shut up forever, and since a clear-starcher must carry home the linen to her customers, the young people had managed to meet, at first very often and very lovingly, and then less frequently and not so ardently. At last Gustave had altogether neglected the little Lise, who, for her part, had found consolation and done very well.

Nevertheless, a woman always retains a kind feeling for a handsome fellow, who, although flighty, has pleasant manners. Also, a man likes to see again a pretty woman who has enabled him to enjoy all the sweetness of love and who inspires it once again when he runs across her. It is, in truth, merely the pleasure of the moment that we enjoy in her society; but even one moment's pleasure is something. Gustave and Lise always met with friendly feelings and managed to procure a few of those moments.

Four years had elapsed since the elopement, and many things had happened. The girl's mother had died, and she now worked on her own account. She had hired a room in another quarter than the one in which she had been born, because her escapades with M. Gustave had made considerable

noise in the Rue Saint-Antoine, and the clerks of
the Petit-Saint-Antoine would begin to snicker
when the laundress passed by the shop. Thence-
forth, Mademoiselle Lise was her own mistress,
she wanted to do what seemed good unto herself;
but she did not want to be the butt of evil tongues,
so she went and rented a room in the Rue Charlot.
There she was near the small theatres; she might
hope for the custom of some actor at the Ambigu
or the Gaîté, and that might procure her a few
tickets — you see that the young woman looked
ahead; as for the rest, she felt quite at her ease, and
conducted herself as a young woman can who earns
twenty cents a day and wants to wear swell hats.
Gustave had recollected Lise; she had given him
her address when last they met, and the young man
knew that young working girls who lived in their
own rooms never lodged in houses that had porters.

Our hero crossed the boulevards and arrived at
the Rue Charlot; but he had forgotten the number. What was he to do? Why, knock at every
door, of course; so much the worse for those people whose sleep he might disturb or who might be
ill; so much the worse for those who are dreaming that they have what they do not possess; so
much the worse for the author dreaming that he is
a success; for the dependent who sees himself sitting down to a good table; so much the worse for
the lover who gains a confession; so much the
worse for the poet who thinks that he is received

into the Academy; so much the worse for the
coquette who is driving twenty lovers to despair;
so much the worse for the old crone who thinks herself young again; so much the worse for the gambler who dreams that he has drawn the capital prize
in the lottery; so much the worse for the poor
wretch who does not know how he will manage
to get bread for his children tomorrow; so much
the better for the woman who is in the arms of
the man she adores, and so much the better for him
whose happiness is perfect and to whom full consciousness presents nothing but a rose-colored
future.   But, in the sum total, there is more so
much the worse than so much the better.

"Good! there's an alley; let's knock loudly!"

A window was opened on the second story and
a head in a white cotton nightcap was poked out
to look into the street.

"Who's there? what do you want?

"Would you be kind enough to tell me where
Mademoiselle Lise, the fine-starcher, lives?

"To the devil with you and your fine-starcher.
Did anyone ever hear of such a thing; waking up
a whole house to ask for an address at one in the
morning!

"It's a matter of great importance.'

"If the patrol were passing, I'd have you arrested."

"Indeed! and if you don't shut up, I'll throw a
stone through your window."

The gentleman retired and shut his window, heartily devoting Gustave to the devil.

Without being discouraged our hero went on a dozen paces or so, and knocked at another door.

" This time," he said to himself, " I will knock more gently, and try to wake the lodgers only by degrees."

He let the knocker fall gently on a little green door, and a window on the first floor was immediately opened.

" This time," said Gustave, " the people are not asleep, or at least they sleep very lightly."

" Is that you, dear ? " a young woman asked in soft tones.

" Oho ! another adventure ! Let's see what will come of it."

And our young rascal answered with a muffled " Yes ! "

" It's too bad to make you wait so long ; you know that my husband is on guard tonight at the Château d'Eau, and that he would not leave his post to come to bed with his wife. Wait a moment, and I'll throw down the pass-key ; for I can't come down, as I am undressed."

The little woman disappeared from the window; and Gustave scratched his ear in perplexity as to what he should do. A little woman with a sweet voice who is waiting for you in the middle of the night while her husband is standing sentinel at the Château d'Eau sounds very inviting ; but still, it

is not Gustave whom the lady is expecting, and
when she finds out her mistake she will be greatly
confused and worried ; and then if the lover should
come along later, as is very probable, there might
be complications ; it would be necessary to have
another fight and turn another house upside down.
No ! that would be mere folly ; and so the pass-
key must certainly not be accepted.

Such was the conclusion of Gustave's reflections.
I think that that was very good behavior on the
part of a youth who was accused of being a bad lot;
but, between ourselves, I am inclined to think that
our hero's self-love was partly responsible for this
good resolution. A young dandy hasn't the courage to appear for the first time before a woman in
an unbecoming costume and with a black eye and
swollen nose ; the first impression might not be
favorable to him, and when one is accustomed to
easy conquests one is not so anxious to expose one's
self to ridicule.

The little lady appeared again at the window ;
she tied a key in a handkerchief and was about
to throw it down to Gustave, when the latter spoke
in his natural voice,—

"Kindly accept my apologies, madame ; I think
we are both victims of a misunderstanding."

"Great heavens ! It isn't he !"

"Madame, I beg you not to go away without
listening to me !"

"Monsieur, you will probably think all kinds

of things. I was expecting my brother, and as he is on bad terms with my husband I had chosen this time of night to have a talk with him.

"Madame, I don't doubt that what you tell me is true, moreover, you may depend upon my discretion. You see that I am deserving of some confidence since I did not accept the key you were about to throw down if I had not made myself known."

"That's perfectly true, monsieur."

"Be good enough to tell me, therefore, where a young clear-starcher lives in this street."

"A little brunette?"

"Yes, madame."

"Slightly pitted with the smallpox?"

"Exactly, madame!"

"That must be little Lise?"

"The very same, madame; do you know her?"

"Yes, monsieur, that is to say, no, monsieur, I am one of her customers. That is to say, she does not know me, but she washes for a friend of mine."

"Good," said Gustave to himself, "the lady is afraid that I shall find out from Lise her own and her husband's name."

"Madame, could you tell me the number of her house? She is the one I am looking for; I have something of extreme importance to say to her."

"I don't know the number, but I may be able to describe the house. It's the first on the right after you pass the Rue Sainte-Foi. Good heavens! there's the patrol; it's my husband!"

At this moment the lady, who had been leaning out of the window to direct Gustave to Lise's house, precipitately withdrew into her room and shut down the window in a hurry.

Gustave turned round, and saw a patrol of the National Guard that had just turned the corner of the Rue Boucherat and was marching straight towards him. One of the soldiers in the patrol was the little woman's husband and had begged his corporal to go around by the Rue Charlot, because it is very nice to be able to say the next day to your neighbors, "I watched over you last night."

But in the distance the husband had seen his wife at the window talking with a man of suspicious appearance ; he left the ranks and ran towards Gustave, shouting, " Help, corporal, look out ! "

Gustave saw the patrol advancing and was uncertain whether he should wait for it ; the husband came up and seized him by the collar, ordering him to follow him to the bodyguard. Our hero's reply was a punch that knocked the poor fellow over against a post, and then he started to run in the other direction. The corporal ordered his men to pursue the fugitive ; but Gustave could run faster than men who had to carry a gun, sword and cartridges, and who, moreover, were not accustomed to carry such a load ; nor was our friend particularly anxious to spend the rest of the night in the guard house. In his flight he saw an open door ; he darted in, closed the door behind him and sprang up the winding stairs, four at a time, which in broad daylight he would not have mounted without carefully watching every step. In order to escape the patrol, he scaled the roofs and crept along the gutters. When we are in a state of excitement, we do things that we would not dare to attempt in cold blood.

At last Gustave came to a halt; he had reached the top of the mansard and there he had to stop, since there were no more stairs to climb. Where should he go? For his own part, he hadn't the least idea; so he ran the risk of pushing against a door in front of him. It flew open and Gustave started back and ran away, because, even when we can't see clearly, there are some places that we divine perfectly.

The patrol that followed Gustave had seen which house he had taken refuge in. They knocked at the door and summoned the tenants to open and deliver the culprit. From the sixth floor, Gustave heard the noise down in the street. He went down to the fifth floor with the intention of temporizing with the patrol at the hall door when well-known accents fell upon his ear.

"Good heavens! why, what a row they are making in the street tonight. It's impossible for anyone to sleep."

"It is she!" exclaimed Gustave, "I am saved!"

He knocked at the door behind which he had heard the voice.

" Who's knocking? "

" It is I, Lise, Gustave; let me in quickly."

" Gustave! "

The little laundress jumped out of bed and ran
to open the door. She cried out in affright at the
sight of the young man, whom she did not recognize under his disguise. The latter entered precipitately, carefully closed the door and threw
himself down on Lise's bed, exclaiming, " At last
I am safe ; here I can brave the guard and all husbands and patrols."

Lise took up her nightlight and held it close to
Gustave's face.

" It's really you! "

" Of course it is. As a matter of fact, I might
well be unrecognizable at first sight! "

" Good God! what a state you're in! A black
eye, a face stained with blood; and such clothes! "

" When you've heard all that has happened to
me! But wait a moment; can you hear them
thundering at the front door? "

" So you are the cause of all this rumpus? "

" Yes, dear ; I made trouble at La Villette, making a cub of a cabinet-maker jealous, introducing
despair into the heart of a newly-married man and
setting fire to his bride's shift."

" Good God! what a bad lot you are! So you
got into a fight? "

" Yes! and you see that, even when victorious,
one can be wounded."

"But how about these people who are knocking at the door?"

"Let them knock!"

"But what do they want?"

"To arrest me. It's the night watch that I disturbed because—Oh! by the way, tell me, do you know a married woman who lives close by on the first floor over a little green door?"

"Certainly! that's Madame Dubourg."

"Is Madame Dubourg pretty?"

"Yes, very; a neat figure and rétroussé nose."

"The devil! if I'd only known that before!— and how about her husband?"

"He's a man of about forty. He wears great frills."

"He wears something else, unless I'm mistaken."

"How's this? Do you know Madame Dubourg?"

"Not in the slightest; if I were to meet her in the street, I should not recognize her. But never mind about her; do you still hear them knocking?"

"No!"

"Finding that nobody paid any attention to them, they have gone away; I was sure they would!"

"But why were they after you?"

"I'll tell you all about it."

"Come, I must bathe your eyes and nose; you're in a fine condition!"

"You didn't expect me; did you, Lise?"

" Oh, certainly ! "

" It is very fortunate for me that you are alone."

" How alone ? Don't I live here alone ? "

" Yes, yes ! But that does not prevent — sometimes one has visitors who stay rather late."

" Oh, monsieur ! I don't receive that kind of visitor."

" Bah ! really ? "

" What is the meaning of that astonished look ? "

" So you are very good now ? "

" Haven't I always been good ? "

" Certainly ; but one can be very good and still have a little acquaintance."

" No, no ! I don't want any more little acquaintanceships ; men are too false, too perfidious for anyone to love them."

" You are quite right, my dear. Take care ! you are wetting my whole face with your brandy — "

" What a great misfortune ! Aren't you a lucky fellow to have somebody to look after you and attend to your hurts when you've got them running after other women ? Ah ! you're a bad lot ! your uncle is perfectly right to scold you."

" You think so ! Poor Lise ! so you no longer love me ? "

" I only wish I didn't ! Unfortunately, I still love you in spite of myself ; for you don't deserve that anybody should take any interest in you. Now, stop that, monsieur, leave me alone, or I'll throw all this in your face ! "

"Nonsense! My face is in no danger! You are simply charming in your nightcap. That's nice!"

"That's nice! Ah! what a demon you are, M. Gustave! I shall be very angry! So you are going to bed are you?"

"Would you like me to sit up all night, tired as I am? I should be dead tomorrow!"

"Why, he's as good as his word! and where am I to sleep?"

"Why, here, of course!"

"Upon my word, that would be a fine thing. Why, I believe he's asleep already; I must get to bed."

After the night had passed, Gustave awoke. Lise was already up; she was blowing the fire to heat the milk and get a cup of coffee for Gustave.

"My dear child, what are you doing there?"

"Can't you see that I'm making coffee for your breakfast?"

"Thank you; I'm very fond of coffee; but after a long run and after being beaten, after having had the patrol on one's heels and a pretty woman for a hostess, one needs something more of a restorative than coffee. Here, take my purse; it's in that big blue vest, and go to the cook-shop and grocer's and butcher's; send in some mutton cutlets and some veal, some fresh pork and sausages and chitterlings, some bologna sausage and ham and cheese; and above all don't forget the wine, the best you can find."

"Good heavens! what a breakfast! But while I am going my linen won't be ironed and I ought to deliver it this morning."

"So much the worse for your customers! They will have to wait one day longer."

"And how about the little embroideress who wants her cap for a dance tonight at the Colysée?"

"She'll have to dance bareheaded!"

"And that writer of melodramas who needs his frilled shirt today to go and read a piece he has composed for Franconi's horses?"

"The horses can hear his piece tomorrow!"

"And that fine young lady in French cashmere who is waiting for me to bring home her cambric chemise before she can take off the one she has been wearing for a week?"

"She can wear her dirty linen one day longer. Come, Lise, go and get me some breakfast; I'm dying with hunger!"

"Upon my word! I shall have to let him have his own way!"

Lise went out, and Gustave thought over what he had done and what he should do. In the first place, he was quite decided not to put on the blue vest and canvas trousers again; but how could he procure other clothes? Why, of course! He would send Lise to Olivier's, who would send by her, or by Benoit, whatever it was necessary for him to have to appear in the streets of Paris.

Olivier and Gustave were much of the same size,

and so one of the former's coats would fit; provided, however, that Olivier, who was not very
steady, had two coats at his disposal just now.
Yes, but then Benoit must have brought back to
Paris the coat that his master wore at Ermenonville, unless, at least, the stupid fellow had lost it
on the way. In that case, Gustave still had some
money ; and in Paris a blackguard can get himself
dressed like a marquis in twenty minutes.

Lise came back carrying a basket full of eatables.
Gustave got up, put on the first pair of trousers
he could lay his hands on and slipped into the
nightgown of an old dowager who lived in the Rue
des Trois-Pavillons, and set about helping Lise to
prepare the breakfast. They made a big fire and
a gridiron took the place of the milk-warmer. The
cutlets and sausages were laid out and the bologna
sliced while the fire burned up ; the table was laid
and covered with cheese, fruits, cakes and bottles;
in five minutes everything was ready and they sat
down; the breakfast was found to be excellent.
Lise laughed at Gustave's appetite, and while they
were eating, talking and laughing, they kissed one
another.

When at last Gustave had satisfied his appetite,
he said, " Come now, dearest, that's enough nonsense, now let's talk sense ; we must find some
means of letting me get away from here."

" Well ! What's to prevent you from going
whenever you want to ? "

"You've evidently forgotten the rustic costume in which I arrived, a costume, by the way, that did not bring me much happiness and which I would not wear again for all the gold in the world."

"That's true; I'd forgotten. You need some clothes. Do you want me to go and get some for you from your home?"

"My home! that's very easy for you to say, but at the present moment I haven't any home; you know that I live with my uncle, but he's angry with me just now. I want to allow sufficient time for his anger to cool."

"The poor colonel! what a lot of trouble you give him."

"I am doing him a good turn; a retired officer needs distraction. So you will go to Olivier's —"

"Aha! another fine fellow, who runs to balls, gaming-tables, girls and cafés. He's the one who has ruined you; he can give you nothing but the very worst advice."

"You think so! Really, Lise, you're getting quite strong on questions of morality. If my uncle could hear you, I am sure he would be willing to make up with you; he thinks you are nothing but a little gadabout."

"Aha! your uncle thinks that of me. It's a nice thing of that gouty old monkey to speak evil of others; when I see him I'll scratch his eyes out."

"A little more respect for my uncle, if you please, Mademoiselle Lise!"

" An old tailless fox! it wasn't in warfare that he got all his rheumatism."

" Mademoiselle Lise!"

" Ah! he calls me a gadabout, does he? I'll make him pay for that!"

" Will you soon have finished?"

" I won't allow anybody to reflect on my conduct."

" That's true; it would be an outrage."

" I, who am so good; who never go out, nor see anybody."

" That's true; you live like a vestal."

" And then to say that I am — "

" There you are! Now, enough of that, when you touch a woman on her tender spot, you never hear the last of it. So you will go to Olivier's for me?"

" Where does this Olivier of yours live now?"

" In the Rue des Petites-Ecuries, near the Faubourg Poissonière."

" Shall I ask him for some clothes for you?"

" Yes, you will tell him what's happened to me."

" Oh! I shan't tell him that you spent the night here; you may rest assured of that."

" No, you will tell him that I came here this morning. In fact, you can tell him anything you like; but remember that I need a hat and coat, trousers and boots."

" And I've got to carry all that?"

" If you like, you can get a messenger-boy; I

am afraid that my servant, Benoit, might be recognized and followed."

"All right; I'll carry out your commissions; but
during my absence, you must not open to anybody. It might do me harm if anybody saw a
young man in my room wearing a pair of trousers
and a nightgown belonging to customers of mine."

"Set your mind at ease, no matter what happens, I won't open the door; but what shall I do
to pass the time during your absence?"

"If you rummage in that press you will find
some books; some quite amusing ones, 'Jean
Sbogar,' 'Faublas,' 'Mon Oncle Thomas,' 'Vic-
tor,' and 'L'Enfant de ma Femme.'"

"That's good; I will look at them; but I beg
you to be as quick as you can."

"Yes, I'll make haste; don't get impatient."

Lise kissed Gustave, put the key in her pocket,
and started for the Rue des Petites-Ecuries.

Being left alone, our youth turned the leaves of
the novels and read a few pages, walked up and
down the room and looked out of the window to
see if Lise was coming back; but the window
looked out on the roof and the street could not be
seen. Gustave became impatient and found the
time long; he did not consider it was a long way
from the Rue Charlot to the Petites-Ecuries, and,
moreover, that it would take some time to get
together all the things necessary to complete the
toilet of a fashionable young man.

There was a gentle knock at the door. "Don't
let's make a noise," said Gustave to himself, "let's
remember our instructions." The knock was repeated, and a voice cried, "Open Mademoiselle
Lise; it is I — Madame Dubourg."

"Madame Dubourg!" exclaimed Gustave. "Oh,
on my word, I must make her acquaintance, I
can't let the opportunity escape!" He ran to the
door and opened it to the lady with whom he had
had the nocturnal conversation, and whose face he
was very anxious to see.

Madame Dubourg was somewhat fearful concerning the consequences that her adventure might
entail and was curious to know the identity of the
gentleman who had been sufficiently scrupulous
to refuse a young woman's pass-key, and original enough to try to find a laundress' address at
one in the morning. To find out something about
him it was only natural for her to seek the person
for whom he had asked and who happened to wash
for Madame Dubourg. Between women a thousand little things are said of which a husband should
be kept in ignorance; so she hoped to be able to
induce Mademoiselle Lise to talk and afterwards
to recommend the greatest discretion in case the
gentleman in question should have spoken of his
conversation with a lady on the first floor above
the little green door.

Madame Dubourg made a movement of surprise at the sight of Gustave, whom, however, she

did not recognize for the reason that she had not been able to distinguish his features in the dark, although there was a lamp not far from her house; but probably lamps are not made to illuminate, since only enough oil is put in them to prevent anybody from seeing at all.

Madame Dubourg could not presume that the gentleman who had wanted to speak to Mademoiselle Lise at one o'clock in the morning would still be in her room at one in the afternoon. However, she did not know whether she ought to enter; because a woman thinks twice before remaining alone with a man in a nightgown. But Gustave, with a very polite manner and disguising his voice as much as possible, invited the lady to wait, assuring her that Mademoiselle Lise would return in a moment.

Madame Dubourg entered and took a seat, and Gustave, after having set her entirely at her ease, resumed his natural voice and asked her if her husband felt any ill effects from his fall against a post, and whether her brother had kept her up long waiting for him. Madame Dubourg was evidently greatly troubled; she grew pale, stared at Gustave and then hid her face in her handkerchief.

"Ah! madame," cried Gustave, "be assured that I have no intention of causing you any distress; I myself have far too great a need of indulgence, for me to allow myself to censure the conduct of others. What must you think of a young man who knocks at night at every door, and who hides during the day at a laundress' — and in such a costume!"

These words calmed Madame Dubourg's agitation; she removed her handkerchief from her face and looked at Gustave with a smile. Notwithstanding a few marks of yesterday's fight, she found him very good-looking; she also saw, by the way he expressed himself, that he was a man of education; and a man who knows life is accustomed to adventures of gallantry and does not attach any more importance to them than they deserve.

"I see very well, monsieur," said Madame Dubourg, " that we ought to know one another. However, I did not expect to see you again so soon; I suspect that you are here in consequence of some prank that is quite excusable in a young man. I cannot form a bad opinion of you; be good enough to be persuaded, therefore, that it was my brother whom I was expecting last night."

"I don't doubt it, madame, but I think he is very happy in having so amiable a sister."

"I am sorry the patrol chased you, my husband is cruel in that regard; he sees robbers everywhere."

"All husbands are like that.'

"I was delighted to hear that you hadn't been arrested."

"I believe it."

"I thought that I ought to come here today to inquire whether you had been seen."

"Oh, make your mind easy, they won't find me again."

"I told my husband that, not feeling well, I went to the window to get some fresh air and that a stranger had asked me to direct him. I hope that Mademoiselle Lise does not know —"

"No, my dear madame, she won't know anything about it."

"Then there is no need for me to wait any longer for her; for I frankly confess that I came here expressly to warn her on this subject."

"I suspected so, madam, and that was why I wanted entirely to reassure you."

"Adieu, monsieur; if some day I can be of any service to you be good enough not to forget me."

"Forget you, madame! you need never fear that!"

Madame Dubourg bowed graciously to Gustave and was about to go out when Mademoiselle Lise came in with a bundle under her arm. She halted and looked at Gustave, who bit his lips, and at Madame Dubourg, who blushed.

"What does madame want? what does madame request?" asked the little laundress with a mocking air.

"Mademoiselle, I wanted to know whether my husband's shirts were ready."

"You know very well, madame, that I never bring them to you before five o'clock."

"That's true; but he's dining in town today,

and has only plain ones left; so I wanted to take
them with me in case you had not time to do them.
There they are, I think. Yes, these are the ones."

Madame Dubourg took up three shirts that were
lying on a table, rolled them up and put them into
her bag and hastily departed without paying any
attention to the cries of Lise, who called to her over
the banisters that she had mistaken the shirts belonging to an actor at the Café d'Apollon for those
of her husband.

"Ah! Monsieur Gustave!" she cried, as she re-
entered, "I don't know what you were doing with
that lady, but she is much confused; she does not
know what she is doing."

"How can you get such ideas into your head,
Lise?"

"On my word! it would not be very astonishing;
but I told you not to open the door."

"I thought I heard your voice."

"Liar! I would be willing to bet that you know
Madame Dubourg."

"This is the first time I ever saw her."

"How about your questions last night? Do you
think I have forgotten them. But I'll go to her
house at four o'clock, that's the time when her
husband is at home; I will see if he is dining in
town, and whether she was lying or not."

"Lise, you are always talking evil of others;
you don't behave kindly, and then you don't want
anybody to talk about you. But I warn you that

if you try to get this lady into trouble, and I believe her to be a very honest woman, I shall quarrel
with you and never speak to you again as long as
I live ! "

"What a terrible calamity that would be! One
could do without monsieur. It seems that I must
find him in my room making love to a little prude
who isn't worth two cents and that I must not say
anything about it, that would be very convenient!
I know well enough that you have mistresses of all
sizes and colors ; but I won't have them come to
make love to you in my house. Ah! these married women ; how bold they are. It seems that
everything is to be permitted to them ; they ought
to blush and die of shame at deceiving their simple
husbands. At least a girl is her own mistress, she
can go about with her head in the air."

While mademoiselle was holding forth, Gustave
was dressing, not without complaining of Olivier's
negligence and Benoit's stupidity. In fact, they
had sent a pair of evening trousers and top boots
and a cloth waistcoat — and it was the middle of
summer.

" Did Olivier select these clothes ? " Gustave at
length inquired.

" No! your friend wasn't in ; I saw only your
servant, Benoit. What a clownish air he has ! It
was he who gave me this bundle."

" Then I am not astonished at the selection."

" Ha, ha ! how funny you look ! You look

like a village bridegroom! that coat's too short
for you."　　　　　　　　　　　　　　　　.

"It seems as if the rascal had it made purposely,
I really believe he has sent me one of his own coats;
he shall pay for this ; but it is decided that I must
leave this place in disguise. Would mademoiselle
be good enough to go and get a carriage for me?"

"Yes, monsieur, and I'm going to see whether
Madame Dubourg is waiting for you at the door!"

Lise went down and soon returned with a cab.

"Good-by! Mademoiselle Lise," said Gustave.

"Good-by, you bad lot! Well, he's going away
without kissing me!"

"I thought you were angry with me. Good-by,
dearest; come and see me at Olivier's, you know
the address."

"Indeed! It's likely that I should go like that
to bachelors' apartments! nice things people would
say about me! What time shall I find you in?"

"In the morning of course! You know very
well that I get up late."

"Very well, I'll come and wake you up!"

Gustave went down the five flights, got into the
carriage that was waiting for him at the door, and
was driven to Olivier's.

CHAPTER VII

A Young Men's Dinner. Another Folly

OLIVIER was a young man of about Gustave's age. Having lost his parents rather early in life, he had found himself his own master all too soon for his own good. He was fond of gambling, wine and women; he was employed in a government office to which he went very regularly towards the end of the month, because pay-day was approaching; but when he had drawn his salary he decamped, and it was sometimes a week before he put in an appearance again. His superiors often reprimanded him for his delinquencies, which made him behave himself for twenty-four hours. Since he worked well and rapidly when he wanted to, they were very indulgent to him and overlooked many of his offences.

Olivier was at home when Gustave got out of the carriage; he saw him from the window and, noticing the peculiar arrangement of his toilet, came to meet him with roars of laughter.

"Here I am at last, my dear Olivier," said Gustave, wearily, "I was very much afraid I should never get here."

"Ha, ha, ha!"

"Well! what are you laughing at?"

"Look at yourself in the glass! On my honor, you are simply inimitable! Come as you are and take a turn in the Palais-Royal; you would be taken for one just landed. You would make an easy conquest of all the nymphs in the wooden gallery."

"It was that scoundrel of a Benoit who sent me this costume. Benoit!"

"Here I am, monsieur."

"Will you tell me why you sent me your coat instead of my own?"

"Ah! monsieur, it was a prank. When I entered Paris, I was afraid of being seen by your uncle, and I put on your coat so as to escape recognition."

"Oh, indeed! so you put on my coat. That's exceedingly pleasant for me!"

"I wanted to put on one of your pairs of trousers also, but I couldn't get into them; they were too uncomfortable."

"That's a great pity! But, Benoit, I beg that you will not play any more of such pranks; I am not at all pleased with them. My dear Olivier, you'll have to put me up for a time."

"You know very well that you can always regard this place as your own home; I have three rooms; there will be one for each of us."

"Before seeing my uncle again, I want him to have forgotten his marriage projects; I will tell you

all that has happened to me; you will be amused.
By the way, have you sold the horses?"

"Yes, immediately."

"At a good price?"

"Not bad; but we'll have an accounting later.
Dress yourself and let's go to dinner."

"I want to dine here; I don't want to go out
except at night for some time."

"So you are in great dread of your uncle!"

"Oh! he's not fond of joking; and I'd better
avoid his anger.   Benoit, go to a restaurant and
have dinner sent in.   Have you sense enough to
order dinner for two?"

"Oh, as for that, you will be satisfied, monsieur;
but suppose I were seen on the way!"

"Wear this old box-coat and pull this big hat
down over your eyes.   That's the way!   You look
like an old Jew!   Go to the best restaurant you
can find; and be quick!"

Being left alone with his friend, Gustave related
part of his adventures, gliding lightly, however,
over everything touching Madame de Berly.   Although a rattle-pate, our hero knew how to keep
the secret of an adventure when a woman's reputation was at stake.   He loved to make conquests,
but he had the right feeling not to say a word about
the successes he made.   In this he was very different from those coxcombs who like to go about
boasting to everybody of their good fortune and
the favors that are showered upon them; but one

should be suspicious of the veracity of these Love-laces; the biggest boasters are nearly always those who have the least success.

For an inconstant, Gustave was not without principle; he had never caused women any sorrow beyond that of deceiving them. He passed for a bad lot; but was he not more excusable than those who under hypocritical externals try to triumph over women and then ruin their reputations when they will not yield to their desires? Such men are all too common in the world; these are really villains. We may excuse inconstancy, fickleness and giddiness; but hypocrisy and calumny are the vices of cowardly and corrupt souls.

Benoit returned, followed by a waiter from a restaurant, an oyster-man, a pastrycook, a wine-merchant, and a dealer in mineral waters. Each carried his contribution to the dinner of these gentlemen.

"The devil!" exclaimed Gustave, "It looks as though Benoit wanted to compensate himself for Madame Lucas' somewhat simple bill of fare; come on, let's enjoy this superb dinner, but another time let's take care to write down the list of what we want!"

During dinner, Olivier told his friend that he had made acquaintance in the house with a little lady who embroidered with pearls and to whom he gave guitar lessons, because she was very fond of music and was always wanting to take him into a middle-class society where they gave amateur concerts.

"On my word!" said Gustave, "an amateur concert would just suit me; you know that I can play a sonata accompaniment on the violin at sight; I sometimes even venture on the trio of Rasetti. You shall take me with you. I must try to find some distraction from my unfortunate love-affairs."

After dinner Olivier went to pay his court to the lady of the pearls, and Gustave went out for a stroll in the Rue du Sentier. He asked for M. de Berly's house, and when it was pointed out to him he walked up and down for some time in front of the porte cochère in the hope of seeing Julie at one of the windows; but she was not visible. "If she only knew that I was walking in front of her door," he said to himself, "she would find some way of getting out to speak to me. If only I could see that good girl who gave me her note; but I cannot enter the house, as that would expose Julie to fresh unpleasantness!"

Gustave went back to Olivier's, and several days passed in the same way. Our hero only went out in the evening for a stroll in the Rue du Sentier; Olivier went in the morning to hang up his hat in the office and then came back to court his guitar pupil. These gentlemen kept a splendid table to make up for the decorum of their conduct. Money went out rapidly, but none came in. Olivier could touch only a quarter of his salary; the other three-quarters had to go to his creditors. Gustave was getting to the bottom of his purse; but he depended upon Olivier, who had the money from the sale of the horses. Besides, the colonel could not remain angry for ever: his nephew had already written to him a very humble and respectful letter in which he spoke of his love for Madame de Berly as a passion that had so far led his reason astray as to lead him to introduce himself into the chamber of that lady, who in no wise shared his guilty passion. Gustave did not flatter himself that his uncle could be duped by this lie; but he had to try to excuse Madame de Berly and support what she had said to her husband.

Gustave was beginning to find the life he was leading very monotonous, when one morning, after Olivier's departure, there was a knock at the door and Benoit opened to Mademoiselle Lise.

She was dressed in her best; she wore the rose hat, the elaborately trimmed dress and the fashionable shawl of the day, and from her mien and bearing nobody would have guessed that she was merely a clear-starcher. But in Paris, nothing is so deceptive as appearances. You are sitting in the theatre between two men who are dressed alike — their fortunes are equal then! Not at all; one is a member of the cabinet and the other is a valet — a lackey who brushes clothes in a furnished apartment. The linendraper's wife wears cashmeres; the grocer's wife wears feathers; the factory girl wears fine hats; the barber has the latest style of hat and the waiter a frilled shirt. What a pity that we cannot buy an organ of the body as we can buy a fichu, then we should never hear a hoarse voice proceeding from beneath a velvet mantle. Patience! perhaps even that will come; we have already mutual instruction to reform the Ts and Ss that too often slip into the conversation of our fashionable ladies.

"Here I am, monsieur," said the little laundress; "I have kept my word, and come to see you."

"On my word, my dear, you could not have arrived at a more favorable moment; I was engaged in melancholy reflections. Your presence will restore me to gayety."

"You in reflection! It's for the first time, then."

"Listen to me; there's a beginning to everything; I'm getting old!"

"This old man of twenty-one years of age!"

"Are you going to spend the day with me?"

"I'm quite willing to!"

"Will you dine here? You won't be afraid of Olivier?"

"I should much prefer to be alone with you; but since it's his place—"

"And I will take you home this evening? Is it an arrangement?"

"You know very well that I'll do whatever you want me to."

"You are perfectly charming; let me kiss you!"

"Now, stop! Your servant is looking. Before dinner, I must go to pay a visit to my aunt. I will go now, so as not to have to leave you later."

"Run along then; and don't be too long."

Lise went away, and Gustave called Benoit. "Benoit! today we must have a delicious, super-fine and epicurean dinner; young women are particularly fond of dainty morsels; and I also share their tastes."

"Monsieur, I don't know how you are going to get even a modest dinner."

"How is that, booby?"

"Because the caterer, who is already owed for five, says he won't serve any more without first getting paid for the others."

"Are five dinners owing?"

"Yes, monsieur; without counting the breakfasts that I have had sent in by another man."

"And why did you not tell M. Olivier that? He ought to pay for them."

"M. Olivier always sends me to you when it's a question of money."

"So he thinks that my purse is inexhaustible! He ought to be in funds; we have not yet touched the money the horses brought — But I hear him now coming down from his pearl embroideress."

In fact, Olivier was just coming down from his neighbor's room; he entered the apartment with a very joyful air.

"You have arrived just at the right time," said Gustave. "But what's the matter with you? What an air of triumph! Have you drawn a whole month's salary?"

"My month's salary! I have seen nothing of it! But listen to what pleases me; I have just left my little neighbor; she is an entirely unconventional woman, you know."

"Of course, a grisette!"

"Nonsense! a grisette indeed! she is a widow whose husband was a ship's captain."

"Yes! or down in the hold. But go on!"

"Well! her aunt, that old lady with whom she lives, has gone to spend the day at Belleville; and I have induced my neighbor to come and dine with us today."

"Well, that will suit capitally, Lise is also coming, so we will make a partie carrée."

"That's fine! what fun we shall have!"

"Yes! but, in order to have a jolly time, it is first necessary for us to give these ladies a good dinner."

"Oh! a splendid dinner! that's what I came to see you about."

"And I was about to come to your office to see you."

"What about?"

"To get the money. The caterer won't supply any more without first having the old account settled. Go and pay it and order the dinner!"

"I go and pay it! with what?"

"Haven't you the money from the horses?"

"Ah! my poor Gustave! I haven't dared to tell you yet, but—"

"What do you mean?"

"I put your horses down on the red; and by this time they are far enough away?"

"What? Have you played the money away at roulette?"

"Yes! my friend; the very day that I sold them I had a bill to pay at my tailor's; I wanted to double our money. I had invented a new martingale—"

"To the devil with all martingales! You have done a fine thing! You are incorrigible—always playing and losing!"

"Well, if I had won you would not have reproached me."

"We're in a fine mess now; my purse is empty!"

"Mine's never full! And this is only the ninth of the month; three weeks longer before I can draw my quarter!"

"And the caterer who won't serve us with any more dinners!"

"And these ladies whom we have invited!"

"Poor Lise! whom I expected to regale—"

"My neighbor! who confessed to me that she is very fond of champagne!"

"Indeed? she'll be lucky if she even gets sour wine!"

" Poor Gustave ! I feel like tearing my hair ! "

" Stop your foolishness, and try to find some way to get out of our embarrassment. Benoit ! "

" Here I am, monsieur."

" Do you happen to have any money laid by ? "

"Yes, monsieur, I have some little money."

" Really ? You are a charming fellow, Benoit ! about how much have you ? "

" Well ! monsieur, I've quite — yes, I have about two francs."

" Idiot ! and he calls that ' something.' Can we give a fine dinner on your two francs ? At least you might have genius enough to think of some happy expedient. But with a valet like you one might die of hunger."

Olivier strode up and down the room, stamping his foot and cursing fate and roulette. Gustave was racking his brains to find some way of getting a dinner ; while Benoit stood motionless before the two young men, awaiting the orders they might be pleased to give him. Suddenly, Gustave's face brightened. " My friend," he said to Olivier, " we shall dine ; in truth, I don't quite know how we shall manage to pay for our repast, but the principal thing just at present is to dine. You know that six months ago, whilst my uncle was staying in the country, I remained in Paris. At that time I sometimes went to dine in a restaurant kept by a little darling of sixty years of age, who was six feet tall and had an arm like Hercules and a joyful countenance. This amiable lady is very fond of young people; she looked upon me with approval, smiled when she spoke to me, and when I passed the desk she always offered to wait for payment till I owed for several dinners. I was then in funds, and did not profit by her obliging offers; but now I am going to put her good will to the test. I will go to see her and pretend to have just arrived from the country; I want to treat several friends, and I throw myself on her kindness to guide me on this occasion. The good lady, flattered at my confidence in her, will let me have anything I want. I shall order a charming dinner; and when we have eaten it, we will contrive some means of paying for it."

" The very thing! it is a stroke of Providence! It reminds me of a confectioner's niece with whom I have established amicable relations while writing mottoes for her uncle for his pistachios. I will go to the confectioner's shop in the certainty of having a delightful dessert of sweets."

" Come! that's fine; let's hasten to go there and order what is needed to regale the ladies. I will expose myself for their sake; I will go abroad at noontime at the risk of being seen by my uncle."

" Good! you won't run across him this morning precisely."

" I abandon myself to my fate."

The young men were about to go out when Benoit stopped them.

" Messieurs, there is still something wanting for your dinner."

" What is that ? "

" Why, you haven't any wine ! "

" Oh ! the fellow is right; that's absolutely essential ; how can we get it ? Olivier, do you know any wine-merchant's wife, or niece, or daughter ? "

" For shame ! my friend ! I have always selected my conquests in a higher class of society ! "

" That's too bad, because a little plebeian passion for a female wine-merchant would relieve us of considerable embarrassment at the present moment ; a dinner without wine — that wouldn't be a very gay affair ! "

" The coffee-house keeper opposite knows me and will let us have some beer."

" That's a fine drink to put one in good spirits !"

" We will tell the ladies that it is the Lacryma Christi vintage."

" They would not be deceived."

" We can even have a bowl of punch or two."

" People don't drink punch with fricandeau."

" We will have it cooked with wine."

" Oh, get along ! "

" Gustave, a sublime idea has just struck me ! We shall have wine after all ; both Bordeaux and champagne. Will you lend Benoit to me ? "

" Oh, you can have him ; do anything that you want with him."

Gustave ran along to the big mamma who kept

a restaurant, while Olivier stayed behind with Benoit, on whose assistance he depended to procure the wine. The big lad looked in astonishment at his master's friend as he put on a great big necktie, a very long coat, a very short waistcoat, combed his hair very straight, reddened the tip of his nose, took a hand-whip, put on gaiters and a small peaked cap and studied himself attentively in the glass, trying to assume a brutal and insolent air.

"Is monsieur going to act in a comedy?" Benoit asked at length.

"Well! almost that. Here I am made up; now it's your turn, Benoit!"

"What, monsieur! you want to disguise me also?"

"Hold your tongue and obey. Put on these old leather breeches which I used to wear when I went out for a ride in my moments of prosperity, when I had a horse of my own."

"Monsieur! I am afraid I shall never be able to get into them."

"Yes, you will; they'll stretch. Now take this red waistcoat and this nankin jacket that I wear in the morning and put this little cap on your head."

"It's far too small for me, monsieur."

"So much the better; you will look all the more like a man who has just arrived from the banks of the Thames."

"You want to run me through a 'temse,' monsieur?"

"Listen carefully, Benoit; and don't make any mistake."

"I am all ears, monsieur!"

"I am an English lord, and you are my jockey."

"What is a lord, monsieur?"

"It's an Englishman who comes to Paris to see the monuments, theatres, gambling-houses and women. They are easily recognizable in the streets by their grotesque get-up; at the theatre by their air of astonishment; at the gambling-table by their oaths; and with women by their guineas."

"Oh, yes, monsieur, I saw two the other day in the Rue de l'Echiquier shedding tears of joy as they watched two cocks fighting. They said that whenever they saw two animals tearing at one another's faces it reminded them of their own country."

"Very well, Benoit, you've got to imitate the ways of an Englishman; you will follow me to a big wine-merchant's. Remember if you are spoken to never to answer anything but 'Yes.'"

"Yes?"

"Yes — no matter what's said to you — 'Yes,' never anything but 'Yes.'"

"That's quite sufficient, monsieur! It's very easy to remember."

"That's not all; when I go away, you will remain behind till I or Gustave come for you; if you come home without permission you'll get a sound cudgelling; do you understand?"

"I won't come home, monsieur!"

"You'll get twice as much if you give our address. So now keep all that in mind! You won't come back alone?"

"No, monsieur; and always 'Yes' when I am spoken to."

"Exactly. Now, follow me, Benoit."

Olivier left the house; Benoit followed him, though he found it hard to walk in his leather breeches. He pulled his cap down over his eyes and turned over in his mind the lesson he had just received; the poor lad was worried; the promised cudgelling and his English manners greatly troubled him. Olivier had a hard struggle to keep a straight face when he looked at his jockey's expression.

When they reached a cab-stand, Olivier got into a carriage with Benoit and, speaking in broken English, ordered the driver to take them to one of the best wine-merchants in Paris. The driver whipped up his horses and they started; on the way Olivier repeated to Benoit his instructions, from which he must not deviate in the slightest. At last they stopped in front of a wine-merchant's. Olivier got out and went into the shop waddling and putting out his stomach; Benoit followed him walking with legs straddled and eyes on the ground. Our young rascal uttered a few English words, and as the merchants are very glad to do business with these foreigners, the English lord received prompt attention.

" Moi, vouloir un joli panier de vin pour régaler deux milords de mes amis, if you please."

" Wine, milord? We have it in every quality, and of all countries and ages."

" Donnez-moi du meilleur et du plus vieille, if you please. Je ne regarde point le prix."

" You shall be satisfied, milord. How many bottles?"

" Nous être trois, I will neuf bouteilles : trois bordeaux, trois beaune, trois champagne, dans un panier."

" Yes, milord! Sparkling champagne?"

" Yes, I will, que le bouchon saute au visage."

" The cork will fly up even as high as the ceiling, milord!"

" Is it good?"

" Non, milord, vous n'en perdrez pas une goutte."

They hastened to put the nine bottles of wine in a basket and take it out to the carriage; the merchant presented the bill to milord, who did not raise any difficulties about the price but did not feel in his pocket.

" Je avais laissé mon bourse à l'hôtel ; monsieur le marchand, faites venir un de vos jokeis avec moi pour toucher la petite somme, if you please! "

" Yes, milord! that's very easy. François! go

with this English lord; you will receive sixty francs
for the nine bottles.   Milord! I shall be glad of
your custom."

"I will you acheter souvent, monsieur le marchand. Good morning! Benoit-son, suivez-moi."

"Yes!"

Benoit-son followed milord without raising his
head; they got into the carriage with François, who
did not dare to sit down in front of my lord.
Olivier had told the coachman to take them in the
direction of the Champs-Élysées. When they had
driven some little way, milord struck himself on
the forehead as a man does when he has forgotten
something of great importance; then he ordered
the coachman to stop.

"Mon ami," he said to François, "j'ai oublié
l'essential; il me faut six bouteilles de vin d'Es-
pagne, allez vite me les chercher; mon jokei va
vous accompagner; vous reviendrez avec lui à
Hôtel des Milords. Benoit-son, allez avec ce jeune
marchand."

"Yes."

François did not make any objections to leaving
the wine in the carriage, as he had milord's servant
as security. He and the jokei got out and hastened back to his master for the Spanish wine.

Having got rid of the youth, Olivier had himself driven to the Porte Saint-Martin; there he
got out and paid the driver, hired a messenger
to carry the wine and went home to find Gustave,

triumphantly presenting to him the beaune, bordeaux and champagne.

"How the devil did you manage to get this basket of wine?" Gustave asked his friend. Olivier related the means he had employed and the success of his disguise. Gustave shook his head, and did not seem greatly pleased at Olivier's roguish trick.

"Do you know," he said at length, "that what you have done is not quite nice?"

"Why?"

"Disguising one's self to buy wine that one doesn't mean to pay for."

"No, indeed, I certainly do mean to pay; and the proof is, that I have left a security behind."

"That idiot of a Benoit is a fine security!"

"My friend! however much of a fool he may be, a big fellow of twenty years is well worth sixty francs."

"But he will betray us!"

"Impossible! I have taught him his lesson. Come, banish vain scruples; I promise you I will go and redeem Benoit as soon as I draw my salary."

"In that case he will remain in pawn for a long time."

"But you don't tell me what you have done!"

"Oh, we are going to have a splendid dinner; fish, roast and removes — nothing will be wanting."

"My friend! it is not quite nice to eat a dinner for which one can't pay."

"Why, what difference does that make? I had a

voluntary offer of the credit. The big mamma offered to let me have meals by the month!"

"By the month! Oh, my friend, what a find you've made there, with eleven more kind-hearted caterers, we should be assured of meals for a whole year!"

"Come, stop your nonsense and let us lay the cloth; the girls will be in in a minute! How awkward you are! you don't know how to set a plate! What will our little beauties think when they see us without a servant?"

"They will think that we have sent our servants away so as to be all the freer to give ourselves up to gayety and tenderness; they will be all the more pleased with us."

"You look at the bright side of all that; but I am afraid lest that idiot of a Benoit may be guilty of some foolishness!"

"Hush! There's a knock!"

"Look through the keyhole; is it the dinner?"

"No! it's my neighbor."

The little neighbor was introduced; she first blames herself for her thoughtlessness in coming to dine with these young men; but the gentlemen promise to be discreet and reassure her by telling her that she will not be the only lady at the dinner. In fact, it was not long before mademoiselle arrived; she made a little grimace at the sight of a woman, but her annoyance was dissipated when she saw that the neighbor had not come down on Gustave's account.

At last the caterer arrived, bending under the weight of the matelote, fricandeau and beefsteak; they hastened to relieve him of the dishes he brought, covered the table with them, and resigned themselves unreservedly to their appetites and to gayety.

While these ladies and gentlemen are at table, let us see for a moment what is happening to poor Benoit, whom Olivier had metamorphosed into Benoit-son, the English jockey.

.   François hurried along the Champs-Élyseés with his companion, who took care not to open his lips, but silently cursed Olivier, the basket of wine, and the leather breeches.

François tried to draw him into conversation, but Benoit would not reply anything but "Yes" to everything the other said, so the wine-merchant's clerk stopped a conversation which he had to carry on all by himself. At length they arrived, François quite out of breath and Benoit as red as a cock's comb, for he foresaw that the affair was going to turn out badly for him.

When he saw Benoit, the wine-merchant asked, " Is milord dissatisfied with his wine."

" Yes ! " replied Benoit.

" It isn't that, monsieur," said the clerk. " Milord has not tasted the wine yet, but on the way he remembered that he needed six bottles of Spanish wine, and we have come back to get them."

" Six bottles of Spanish wine ! but what kind ? "

" Milord didn't say."

" Monsieur jockey, do you know which kind your master prefers?—madeira, sherry, malaga?"

"Yes!" and to every question, "Yes."

"Ah! I understand, it's malaga, that's his business. Here, François, take this basket. You will collect ninety francs instead of sixty. Does milord live far from here?"

"Yes!"

"At the Hôtel des Milords," said François, picking up the basket. "Come along; lead the way, M. Benoit-son, I'll follow you."

M. Benoit-son, who did not know what to do next, since Olivier had forbidden him to give their address or to return to his master under penalty of a good thrashing, made no reply to François, but stood stock still in the middle of the yard.

" Has this jockey forgotten his way?" exclaimed the wine-merchant impatiently. " Where is the Hôtel des Milords, my friend?"

"Yes!"

" To the devil with his everlasting 'Yes'! It seems as if this jockey does not understand French. Now, how can we find out where his master lives? Ah! it is doubtless at the Hôtel Meurice, where all the great milords stay?"

"Yes!"

" Good! I was lucky to guess it! François; go quickly with M. Benoit-son to the Hôtel Meurice."

" Yes, monsieur."

François started off again ; they had to push the jockey out into the street to make him accompany the clerk ; finally he yielded and sulkily went along. On arriving at the Hôtel Meurice, François made signs to his silent companion to find out whether he recognized the hotel, and Benoit said " Yes " a dozen times. The clerk went in and asked for milord's apartment. The porter asked him to explain himself. François pushed Benoit in front of him, and said that he was inquiring for the master of this tall jockey. The porter examined Benoit and said that he had never seen him before ; and, moreover, that the dinner at that hotel was perfect, and the guests were not in the habit of sending outside for wine.

François was furious ; he looked Benoit in the eyes and asked him whether his master was staying in that hotel, or in another quarter. To every question, the jockey only answered " Yes," and the porter burst out laughing ; so François, being very tired of all this walking, pushed Benoit before him and kept a close watch on him all the way back to the shop.

The wine-merchant became very angry with Francois when he saw him return with the jockey ; he began to fear that he had been swindled by a rascally thief and to suspect milord's honesty. There are thieves in England as there are elsewhere, and this idea disquieted the merchant, who at last began to press Benoit to explain himself and tell where

his master lived. At length he thought of a means
of arriving at the truth ; he remembered that a gentleman who lived in his house understood English,
and through him the jockey could be made to reply.
François went to fetch him ; he came immediately
and began to interrogate Benoit.

But they pressed the jockey in vain with questions in English and French ; he would not go
beyond his " Yes," and they could not draw from
him any information about his master. The wine-
merchant saw that he had been duped ; but he had
to have a victim, and so Benoit was to be sent to
prison. François already had his hand on the collar of the false Benoit-son, when a military officer
entered the shop. At the sight of him, Benoit
recovered his speech ; he shouted, wept and struggled, and tried to throw his arms around Colonel
Moranval's legs.

The colonel had come to the house to visit one
of his old comrades when he heard Benoit's cries.
He asked where his nephew was. The wine-merchant came to demand his money and explain what
had happened. The colonel, who guessed part of
the truth, paid for the wine, went security for Benoit,
gave François a good tip so that he should not gossip about the affair, and went away taking Benoit
with him, hoping at length to hear some news of
Gustave.

Our young people had forgotten Benoit and their
creditors ; in their delight at being at table with two

young, amiable and pretty women, they gave themselves up to the wildest gayety, which was shared
by their partners ; they sang, and uttered whatever
came into their minds ; they were delightful without any effort, witty without pretending to be so,
and mischievous without being ill-natured. Here
and there, the gentlemen stole a kiss from their
neighbors, but nothing more ; the young women
knew how to keep the men in order when they
tried to go too far and they did well; in order for
a feast to be gay, it must not degenerate into a
debauch.

They had reached the dessert, the champagne
cork had struck the ceiling as the wine-merchant
had promised milord it would, the wine sparkled
in the glasses and the effervescing liquor had warmed
the already high spirits of the feasters, when several
loud knocks at the door interrupted Gustave in the
middle of a Bacchic couplet.

The young people looked at one another in uncertainty as to whether they ought to open or not;
the ladies looked at the gentlemen, trying to learn
from their eyes the reason of their uneasiness. The
knocking was repeated.

" Well, gentlemen ! " said Mademoiselle Lise,
" can't you hear ? "

" Of course we can hear," said Gustave, " but
we don't know whether we ought to answer ; it
may be some inopportune visitor."

" Oh, I understand ! some lady who comes to

see these gentlemen, and they fear lest she should find us here. I'm going to open the door ; I want to see this beauty whose anger is dreaded."

Mademoiselle Lise, who would not listen to what anyone said when it was a matter that piqued her curiosity, ran into the front room, and notwithstanding the prayers of Gustave and Olivier, was about to open the door, when a forcible string of oaths was distinctly heard in the hall which altered the resolution of the young woman, who returned, pale and trembling, to Gustave.

" Oh, my God! it's that old bear of a colonel!"

" Who ? My uncle ? "

" Himself! I clearly recognized his voice! "

" Good heavens! He must have seen me in the street this morning! What's to be done, Olivier ? "

" Let him knock as long as he likes, we won't open! "

" Then your uncle is a very bad man! " said the little neighbor in her turn.

" Ah! madame, he's in a rage. He's angry because I wouldn't marry a young prude he intended for me. Wait! just hear how he's knocking! "

" Blood and thunder! will you open ? " cried Colonel Moranval through the door; "if you don't open I will break the door in! "

" My God! he'll do as he threatens!" cried Lise, running into the inner room to find some nook that could hide her from the eyes of the colonel, whom she dreaded like fire.

Gustave stroked his brow and tried to think of some way of avoiding his uncle; the little neighbor trembled at the voice of this uncle who seemed to be so formidable to the others; and Olivier gulped down several glasses of wine to collect his ideas.

"Well, there's only one thing to do," said Gustave, as he removed his coat, waistcoat and cravat.

"What are you going to do?" cried the ladies.

"I'm going to bed."

"Going to bed! in our presence? what an outrage!"

"Mesdames, in urgent cases, people glide lightly over conventionalities. Besides, I will keep my trousers on, so that what you are pleased to call an outrage may not be too manifest."

"Finish this dissertation," said Olivier, "what is your plan?"

"I am in bed sick unto death since yesterday; you are taking care of me!"

"Good! I understand; but these ladies?"

"Well, we must hide them for a few minutes."

"Yes! but where? there is no wardrobe large enough. Ah! the little closet! that will easily hold two. The colonel won't go to look for you there."

"Well, I think this is a fine dessert you're giving us!" exclaimed the little neighbor.

"For my part," said Lise, "I'll go there willingly, the colonel's arrival has given me the colic."

"It won't be for long, ladies, but, for heaven's sake, let us pacify the dear uncle!"

"Come on! since there is no help for it; let us get into the closet; but at least, M. Olivier, give me your bottle of eau de cologne!"

"Here it is, madame!"

The two young women hid themselves in the little closet behind Gustave's bed; Olivier removed the four plates and the remains of the dinner as quickly as possible; and then, while Gustave pulled a cotton nightcap down over his eyes and rolled himself up in the bedclothes, with a handkerchief in his hand and his face assuming a lugubrious expression, he went to open the door to Colonel Moranval.

The colonel was growing very impatient; he was about to carry out his threat and break in the door just as Olivier appeared.

"Aha! you have decided to open at last, monsieur! Aren't you aware that it's not polite to allow a visitor to knock so long without answering the door?"

"Colonel Moranval, you were not forced to remain at the door!"

"Oh, yes! I don't doubt you hoped that I would go away. I had made myself known, monsieur, and you ought—"

"Colonel, that was the very reason why I didn't open!"

"What! you dare—"

"In consideration of your feelings—"

"My feelings! stop this fencing. Where is my nephew?"

" Hush ! "

" What do you mean ? "

" Hush ! let me implore you ! "

" What do you mean by your ' hush ' ?   I want to see my nephew ! "

" You shall see him, colonel ; be good enough to follow me into the adjoining room, and I beg you to walk on tiptoe."

" You are making fun of me, M. Olivier ? "

" Ah, monsieur !   I have no inclination to laugh. Poor Gustave ! come along ; there he is, colonel ! look at his condition."

The colonel reached the bed in which Gustave was rubbing his face with dried figs while his friend was interviewing his uncle — in order to render his complexion yellow and cadaverous.

The colonel looked at his nephew in surprise ; Olivier turned his head away so as not to burst out laughing at the sight of Gustave's smeared face.

" What's the matter with him ? " asked the uncle, examining his nephew with a somewhat incredulous air.

" What is the matter with him, colonel, is a brain fever, which shows symptoms of becoming putrid and malignant."

" Brain fever ! Since when ? "

" Since — yesterday."

" And it was to cure this fever that you went this morning, as an Englishman, to swindle a wine-merchant out of some wine ! "

" My dear colonel, that's rather a strong term; and if my friend had not been ill —"

" On my word, monsieur! I don't believe any of your tales, sick people are not restored to health with champagne."

" And that is the reason, monsieur, that I got it for myself, merely to have strength to sit up and watch over my friend."

" And for the same reason, you left his servant in pawn!"

" We had no other security to offer!"

" To expose that lad to be put in prison!"

" Colonel Moranval, Patroclus let himself be slain for Achilles; Pollux died six months in the year for Castor; Orpheus went down to Hades for his wife; St. Vincent de Paul had himself sent to the galleys for people who were not worth the trouble; so Benoit may well be imprisoned for his master's sake."

" This is not a question of Orpheus and Pollux, but of my nephew, who, thanks to you, M. Olivier, is guilty of all kinds of folly."

" Oh! Colonel Moranval, I am afraid you flatter me!"

" Has he lost all power of speech?"

" He's in a state of temporary coma, following the violent attack he has just had."

" What the devil is that on his skin?"

" Nothing; it's the effect of the fever."

" Have you sent for a doctor?"

" Not yet, colonel."

" What ? when your dear friend is ill ! "

" Colonel Moranval, we have no money to buy the medicines which he would undoubtedly order."

" What nice conduct ! no money to live on ! "

" Colonel, that happens every day to exceedingly worthy people."

" It should not happen to you, because you have a good situation. But I want to know the truth. Go and fetch me a doctor, M. Olivier ! "

" A doctor ! what for ? "

" Damnation ! what a singular question ! Go, monsieur, I want to know whether my nephew is as ill as you say he is ; in that case, I will not leave him here. What terrible disorder ! clothes on the floor ! plates under the table ! "

" I keep a cat, colonel."

" Corks ! aha ! what's this ? Is this also for your cat, M. Olivier ? this woman's reticule that you have put under this chair ? "

" Ah ! good Lord ! so I've found it at last ; that's my charwoman's bag ; she was hunting for it at least two hours this morning. Poor Fanchette ! she thought she must have lost it in the street."

" So you have a charwoman who carries a morocco bag with steel mountings ? "

" Certainly, my dear colonel ; everybody has them now ; they have become very common."

" That's very good ! Come, monsieur, don't

waste any more time. I will stay with my nephew while you go."

"Oh, don't take that trouble, my dear colonel, the portress will come up and look after him ; besides, I think he's asleep now."

"I prefer to do as I said, monsieur, and, by God ! I'll prove to you that I'm a determined character."

The colonel was angry ; there was no way of making him alter his resolution.

"My goodness !" said Olivier to himself, "Gustave and the little ladies will have to get out of the mess as best they can ; for my part, I've done all that I could, and now I'll get out."

Gustave was not at his ease during the conversation between the colonel and Olivier ; several times he had nearly burst out laughing ; but he had controlled himself in the hope that his uncle would not remain. When he saw Olivier go out and the colonel take a seat in the middle of the room, he took courage, and was on the point of throwing off bedclothes and coverings ; he was also afraid that the girls might make a noise in the little closet. In order to distract the colonel's attention, he determined to speak to him ; and in order to broach the conversation, he uttered a plaintive groan.

"Aha !" exclaimed the colonel, "you are no longer asleep, M. Gustave ?"

"What ! is that you, uncle ?"

"Yes, nephew ; you scarcely expected me this

evening. I acknowledge that had it not been for Benoit, I should not have come here to look for you."

" Oh ! then it was Benoit who — told you."

" Yes ! after having received twenty blows in payment for his silence and the promise of as many more if he lied to me."

" Poor Benoit ! that's the only sort of wages he has received since he has been with me."

" It seems to me that you are no longer delirious, monsieur."

" Uncle, I feel better for the moment; tomorrow I shall have the honor to come to see you if I am able to walk."

" No, monsieur, you will come home this evening, either on foot or in a carriage ! I am not deceived by your illness, and — What's that I hear? One would say — "

" It's nothing, uncle; it's only Olivier's pug-dog."

" A pug-dog, a cat ! So you have all the animals here ? "

" Olivier is very fond of animals."

" The devil ! what a noise. Your dog must be badly out of sorts."

"Yes! the poor brute has drunk too much milk."

"But he seems to be under your bed."

"If you would get some sugar to burn, uncle ! "

" To burn on what? at the candle, doubtless ; but your friend is a long time coming."

" He won't have found anybody at home in the evening ! "

" Come, Gustave, get up and dress and follow me."

" I assure you, uncle, that I should not have the strength ; I can scarcely — "

" The devil ! I hear a noise again. It's in that closet."

The colonel approached the closet; to stop his uncle, Gustave sat up, forgetting that he was only half undressed. The colonel caught sight of Gustave's trousers and did not doubt that an attempt had been made to dupe him with fresh lies; to learn the truth, he ran to the closet, notwithstanding his nephew's entreaties, and tried to open it; but it was locked from inside.

" Aha ! " exclaimed the colonel, " That is probably M. Olivier's charwoman hunting for her reticule in the closet ! I am anxious to make the acquaintance of that poor Fanchette ; and, I'll answer for it, she won't go out without my seeing her, even if I have to stay here till tomorrow."

This threat terrified the young women, who were suffocating shut up in the little closet. Several times already, the little neighbor, who had emptied her bottle of eau de cologne while Lise was relieving her colic, had wanted to go out; but the little laundress had always restrained her companion by drawing a dreadful portrait of Gustave's uncle, and exaggerating the dangers they would run in exposing themselves to his anger. The shame of being discovered held back the little pearl embroideress, and fear fortified Lise's resolution. However, they were both exceedingly ill at ease when Gustave, who understood the discomfort of their situation, generously sacrificed himself for them.

He got up, and put on his coat, waistcoat and cravat in a moment; and approaching his uncle, announced that he was ready to follow him.

" Ah! you rogue," said the colonel, " so you are cured of your fever."

" Uncle, I expose myself to everything, to your anger, as you see; but it is for the sake of two interesting, charming and innocent women who cannot find it very amusing in that closet. I sacrifice myself for them; I attend you, uncle! "

" Before going away, I ought to lay the whip about those innocents who hide in the wardrobe of two young rascals; but I am willing to pardon them for this once. Come! march, monsieur! let us be off quickly; your little beauties must be as yellow as lemons and smoked like herrings! "

Gustave took his hat and left the apartment with the colonel, casting a last glance at the closet.

CHAPTER VIII

Too Long or Too Short. True Love. A Day of Annoyances

So Gustave is at home again with his uncle; he expects a dreadful lecture and severe reproaches with regard to his past and present conduct; and, my dear reader, you also undoubtedly expect the colonel to shout and swear and sermonize. Well! there was nothing of the sort. The colonel did not say a word to his nephew on any subject and Gustave was only too glad to escape for the present any kind of conversation with his uncle, so each retired to his own room without having exchanged a single word.

Whence arose this change in Colonel Moranval's conduct? Perhaps he wanted to save himself the trouble of useless talk; perhaps, like so many other people, he had so much to say that he did not know where to begin; perhaps, finally, and I think that this is the real reason, the colonel was afraid to give full vent to his anger lest his excitement should cause the gout to attack his stomach.

Gustave did not know what to think of his uncle's moderation; but he was resolved to render himself worthy of his indulgence, and to that end he stayed indoors for a week, leading a most exemplary life, rarely going out, working part of the day, and going to bed early.

The colonel did not open his lips, but he watched his nephew; he began to realize that a nature like Gustave's yields to gentleness and entreaty, but rebels against force and authority.

"So be it," said the colonel to himself, "I am only too willing to be gentle, and not scold so much. Gustave is a young man; he is a young rascal, but full of affectionate feeling; he is fond of women just as I was formerly, indeed, I should be fond of them still if only my gout and rheumatism would permit; before scolding others, let us call to mind what we ourselves have done. Let us merely try to prevent Gustave from forming evil acquaintance-ships, which is the ruin of young people, and get him married, if possible; because marriage is the tomb of folly and love and pleasure. Gustave will necessarily become reasonable and good and sedate when he hears his wife raising her voice, his servants quarrelling and his children crying; a small concert which is quite enough to put laughter and love-making to flight."

Gustave was beginning to suffocate with goodness; and, to pass the time away, he tried to make an ideal lackey out of Benoit, to whom, on returning to his uncle's house, he had administered a corrective in order to make him learn to play the

English jockey better. But Benoit had not been born to be a valet for a young man of wealth; he understood nothing about intrigue, and Gustave wasted his time and energy. One morning his uncle asked him to come into his study.

Gustave hastened to obey, and approached his uncle with all the respect and submission of a nephew who hasn't a cent left in his pocket.

"Gustave," began the colonel, "it seems to me that you are beginning to behave yourself. By this time you ought to be tired of the dissipated life you have been leading hitherto. For the complete ripening of your mind, I revert to my original idea, I want to get you married."

"Again, uncle! Do you mean to say that you have another wife in view for me?"

"No! listen; decidedly I wish to leave you free to choose, I think that you should be grateful to me for this consideration of your feelings."

"Yes, uncle; you are exceedingly kind. But where shall I choose a wife?"

"Most assuredly not in the society that you frequent with your Oliviers and your grisettes. You will accompany me into respectable houses; there you will see a pretty woman; you will become attached and you will get married."

"Very well, uncle! so be it!"

Gustave accompanied the colonel into several circles, where, indeed, he found women who pleased him, but whom he had no desire to marry. When

Colonel Moranval saw his nephew struck with a new beauty, playing the gallant and ogling the lady, he thought he had fallen in love, and, on returning home, he questioned him in regard to his feelings.

" Well, Gustave! so that tall blonde pleases you? "

" Yes, uncle! She is gay, amiable and witty."

" Would you care to marry her? "

" No! she's too pretentious; when talking to me, she was trying to make others listen to her, she talked loud to attract attention; in fact she is a coquette, and I don't mean to marry a coquette."

" And how about that little brunette to whom you were saying so many sweet things; what do you think of her? "

" Charming! she possesses grace and bearing and an expressive voice."

" Will you marry her? "

" No! she sang a duet with a young man and put all the expression into it. Uncle, a virgin couldn't have put so much expression into her singing of that piece."

" But the other one, so lively and full of gayety and who dances so well? "

" Ah! that one is extremely attractive! "

" You have fallen in love with her? "

" Why not? Her mischievous eyes say so many things, she laughs so prettily; and then her dancing, what lightness, what grace, what precision in her steps."

"Ah! so that's the one who will be your wife!"

"My wife? God forbid! she is too fond of dancing; she seeks the homage of the man who can make the best pirouette; and I don't want to conquer a heart by cutting capers."

"The devil! Gustave, you're awfully hard to please with a wife."

"Uncle! don't you agree with what I have said about those young ladies?"

"You think all women are coquettes!"

"More or less; but generally, all women are addicted to coquetry, a very natural leaning, and quite excusable in a sex which owes to its charms homage that is not always rendered to merit or virtue. Therefore, women should endeavor to please first of all, in order to assure their empire; that's what they do from the spring to the winter of their lives."

"They are quite right, by God! and we who deceive them in each of the four seasons of our lives — what do you call that?"

"That's seduction, uncle!"

"Ah! that's seduction! when you have six mistresses at the same time; when you fall to the first brunette who strikes your fancy; when at the same time you court the mother and the daughter, the mistress and the maid, the marquise and the seamstress, that's seduction! I think it's devilish like libertinism! Yes, nephew, men are all libertines, seducers, if you like, that's what you are even more

than the average man; so don't go setting yourself
up as a censor of women any more, and consider
yourself lucky if they are still willing to listen to
your nonsense and not laugh in your face when
you heave deep sighs."

" Uncle, I assure you that I never censure anybody."

" Enough of all this ! Are you going to marry ?
yes or no ? "

" Yes, uncle, when I find a perfect woman."

" You are mocking me ! Perfection does not
exist in nature; we are all born with faults that education may soften or teaching eradicate, but I do
not share the opinion of those who hold that we
come into the world as good as lambs and as sweet
as honey.   If that were so, should we see a two-
year-old infant stamping its foot and raging with
anger ? Is it its mother's caresses and its nurse's
care that makes a four-year-old child a liar and a
thief, gluttonous and obstinate ? We are born with
defects that develop into vices when education and
parental watchfulness do not correct them.   But it
does not follow from them that as we grow up we
are to be excused for giving way to our natural ten-
dencies, for then we have reason to enlighten and
guide us ; and so much the worse for us if we do
not listen to her counsels.   But if wisdom often
restrains us, human weakness sometimes prevails ;
it is therefore impossible to be perfect.   Where are
good men to be found who can command all their

passions? I have gone back in vain as far as the creation of the world without finding that Golden Age spoken of by the poets, and which every successive generation has called 'the good old times.' The first man has a coquette for a wife; and two sons, one of whom killed the other. The descendants of Cain and Abel behaved themselves so estimably that God was obliged to send the deluge. The descendants of Noah were constantly fighting with one another. Is the Golden Age to be placed in Asia in the days of Semiramis? What an assemblage of vices was contained in those famous cities, Nineveh, Babylon, Persepolis, Ecbatana! And that so highly vaunted Greece, which was composed merely of little states that were always ready to tear each other to pieces, always given over to tyrants or scoundrels! Aristocracy, democracy, oligarchy, factions, wars, treasons, slavery decorated with the pompous name of liberty; that's what Greece was! Is it among the Romans that we shall find perfection? if it is in their arts, it is far removed from their manners. Their republic offers a picture of nothing but battles and carnage, decemvirs, tribunes, revolutions, agrarian laws, perpetual dictatorships and proscriptions. The purple of the Cæsars shows us only one Titus to set against Tiberius, and the Neros, Caligulas and Caracallas.

"Was it under the pontiffs that the Romans were happy? I see the son of a poor vine-dresser attain the supreme dignity. Sixtus V takes his

seat on the pontifical throne and fills the world
with the sound of his greatness ; he embellishes
Rome and raises monuments; but he increases
the taxes and the people are unhappy and im-
poverished.   Sixtus V was more hated than admired.

" Is it the days of chivalry that were called the
Golden Age ?   Doubtless it was fine to break a
lance for one's fair lady, and to consecrate one's self
to the defence of the ladies ; but in these glorious
days, I see the serfs eaten up by the vassals, the
vassals by their lords, and the suzerains by the
monks.   I see a young bride forced to yield herself to a brutal chatelain ; and men called serfs
treated by other men as the prophet Elisha treated
poor little boys who called him bald.   Is it under
the good king Henri IV that the good time was
known?   It was in fact the desire of that great man
to make his people happy ; and if he alone had
been concerned the French would have known the
Golden Age.   But rebellions, civil wars, fanatics,
poisoners and assassins troubled the reign of Henri
IV, who perished like Henri III.

"After this good king, whither shall I go to look
for the good old days and the Golden Age, and
that perfection and constant wisdom that do not
exist ? "

" My dear uncle, you have forgotten Solomon,
called the Wise."

" Upon my word! a wisdom such as that would

just have suited you!—three hundred wives and seven hundred concubines. The devil! what a man that Solomon was! But this dissertation has led me further afield than I intended to go; and it's all your fault. You want a perfect woman! Then you won't marry?"

"Pardon, my dear uncle; it is sufficient for that if only I am in love; because the one we love is always perfect in our eyes."

"If you had only told me that sooner, my dear nephew, you would have spared me all this garrulity over perfection, the Golden Age and the good old days. Try to fall in love, then; it used to be so easy for you not long since."

"It is easy to find a mistress; but a wife! Ah! uncle!"

"Isn't a mistress sometimes a wife?"

"Yes, of course! but—"

"Don't you sleep with one as well as the other?"

"Without doubt!"

"Don't you have children by both?"

"Certainly, but—"

"Go along with your 'buts.' You haven't any common sense, my poor Gustave. These fellows who have turned so many heads, deceived so many husbands, and got so many girls into trouble, exhibit extreme severity in the choice of a spouse when one wants them to get married. Come! my dear boy, though you may be very learned in all the tricks of the ladies, your wife, if it so pleases her, will deceive you just like a man who knows nothing at all about the matter."

"I've never had the least doubt of that, uncle."

"Indeed! Well, in that case, let's go to bed."

One evening, as Gustave was returning alone from the theatre, his uncle having preferred to stay at home, he saw a woman sitting on the bench by the side of the porte cochère of the colonel's house. Without paying much attention to her, Gustave was about to go in. His hand was already on the knocker when a touching voice stopped him.

"It's you, M. Gustave, and you won't speak to me?"

"Great heavens! whose voice is that?"

"So you don't recognize me?"

"Can it be you, Suzon?"

"Yes, monsieur; it's I, the poor Suzon."

"And what are you doing in Paris?"

"I came to see you."

"To see me!"

"Certainly! I have been waiting for you here for two hours. They told me that you had gone out but would be sure to return; and I did not want to go far from your house."

"Dear Suzon! But I don't understand. With whom did you come to Paris?"

"Nobody."

"And your parents?"

"I didn't tell them I was coming."

"What! you have left them?"

" They were always wanting me to marry Nicholas and I didn't want to, because I was always thinking of you. Yesterday they set next Sunday for the wedding ; and this morning I ran away rather than marry Nicholas."

" How did you know my address?"

" Benoit gave me the street and number, and I hadn't forgotten it. Are you sorry to see me?"

" Poor Suzon ! sorry to see you, indeed ! I love you too much for that. But still, what are we going to do?"

" That's very easy, I'll stay with you."

" But you must be lodged and have a bed somewhere."

" I'll share yours. You remember when you were with us—"

" If I were alone that would be easy enough ; but I live with my uncle, and I am not my own master to do as I like."

" Ah, M. Gustave, I see that you no longer love me ! You turn me out and drive me away ; you still want me to marry Nicholas Toupet."

" Don't cry, Suzon, don't cry ! Do you think I'd send you away? No, my dearest. You did wrong to leave your family, but I was the cause of it, and certainly I shall not abandon you. Still, I should not like my uncle to know about all this. If only I could conceal you !"

" Oh, I will do anything you want. So long as I am with you only, I shall be satisfied."

" I'm going to knock ; I will leave the door half-
open. While I am talking to the porter, you must
slip in and gain the back of the courtyard. Then
we will see whether the servants have gone to bed.
Do you quite understand me ? "

" Oh, don't fear ! "

Gustave was afraid of the babbling of the porter,
who was Benoit's father and as stupid as his son.

Our young man knocked, went in and stood
in front of the porter's lodge ; the porter told him
that a young girl had been inquiring for him.
Meanwhile, Suzon slipped in and reached the
back of the courtyard. Gustave shut the door
and joined Suzon in the coach-house.

" Now you're in the house," he said, " I must
next get you up to my room ; let's hope we don't
meet anybody on the stairs ! "

He took her by the hand and mounted a flight
of stairs that led to his own and his uncle's rooms.

Having reached the landing, Gustave stopped
before his door ; he saw a light in the room leading to his bedroom ; so he told Suzon to go up
another flight and then went in. He found Benoit
asleep on a chair, waiting for his master.

Benoit awoke, and asked Gustave if he wanted
anything before going up to his attic chamber.
Since he would meet Suzon on the stairs, it was
necessary to make him go down first.

" Benoit ! I want some supper," said Gustave,
" go down to the larder and bring me something."

Benoit went downstairs, and, while he was gone, Suzon was smuggled into Gustave's bedroom. Benoit came back with a fowl and some wine; while he was placing it on the table, and Gustave was telling him to be quick about it, Suzon, who was in the dark, overturned a chair in trying to find a seat.

Benoit turned pale and let the fowl fall on the floor; he did not dare to raise his eyes; and Gustave did not know what to say.

"Did you hear that, monsieur?" the trembling Benoit asked at length.

"Yes, I thought I heard something."

"There are robbers in your room, and here I have been alone for a whole hour! Good God, if I had suspected that!"

"Nonsense, you are dreaming, Benoit."

"What, monsieur, was that noise made by itself?"

"Doubtless it was my uncle's dog."

"Fidéle was put to bed long ago, it must be robbers; I'm going to wake up everybody in the house!"

"Don't do anything of the sort; I forbid it! Go to bed, Benoit."

"What, monsieur, you want to stay here alone?"

"Go to bed, I tell you; and if you dare to wake anybody I'll discharge you tomorrow!"

"But, monsieur, do you want to be murdered?"

"You are a fool; go away and hold your tongue."

"Very well, good-night, monsieur. I'm going to load my gun; if you have any need of me, call me and I will fire it in the air, and that will awake the whole house."

"Benoit, do me the kindness not to touch your gun, unless you want my stick to make the acquaintance of your shoulders tomorrow. Go to bed and sleep!"

At last Benoit went away and Gustave was alone with Suzon; he could see her, talk to her and kiss her at his ease; he found her much improved in good looks and that her figure had developed since he had left the village. She allowed him to kiss and caress her. She was with Gustave again, and he had promised not to send her away; so she was quite happy and desired nothing more.

They had supper, and Suzon told Gustave all about her journey; she had come from Ermenonville to Paris on foot, she had walked the eleven leagues almost without a halt, for she was so afraid she might not arrive in time to catch her lover, and so she had blistered feet and aching limbs; but on the road she had not been conscious of fatigue, as love had doubled her courage and strength.

"Poor little one!" said Gustave, "She must love me very dearly."

He did not venture to say anything to her about the grief she was causing her parents; he strongly felt that she had done wrong in leaving them for the sake of coming to find him; but how could he reproach her when she was giving him so strong a proof of her love?

"Fate wills it thus," thought Gustave; "it was written that Suzon should not marry Nicholas, because I had been at Ermenonville. Come, then, let us enjoy the present and not worry about the future."

Gustave went to his bed and lay awake, wondering what he should do with Suzon and how to keep his uncle from knowing about her; his mind was not as easy as hers was. The colonel would be terribly angry if he should find the little peasant living with his nephew; and if he were to learn that this young girl had been seduced by Gustave and had abandoned her home and parents for him, that would be much worse still. So what was to be done to avoid all that? Send Suzon back to her parents, who perhaps would illtreat her? Gustave had not the courage to do that — Suzon being so sensitive and so sweet and pretty. Where was the heart that could voluntarily cast away such a treasure? — certainly not a youth of twenty.

"I will keep Suzon here," said Gustave, "and carefully conceal her, and try not to arouse my uncle's suspicions; and, on my faith! it shall last as long as it can."

It was late when Gustave awoke. Our hero gazed thoughtfully at the poor little one who, to find him again, had abandoned friends, parents and the village in which she was born. Involuntarily,

Gustave indulged in melancholy reflections; he was troubled with regard to Suzon's future.

There was a knock at the door of the anteroom. Gustave got up softly, so as not to awake Suzon, and went to answer it.

"Who's there?"

"It's I, monsieur," replied Benoit.

"What do you want?"

"Usually, monsieur gets up at eight o'clock; and now that it's nearly ten I was afraid the robbers might have killed monsieur; and then the colonel is waiting breakfast for you."

"All right! I'm coming down."

"Won't you give me your coat and boots?"

"Later on; leave me alone!"

Gustave went back to Suzon, who was still asleep. He did not know what to do; his uncle was waiting, and he must go to him. But what was to be done with Suzon? She could not spend the whole day in sleeping; she must have breakfast and dinner. And then, how was he to hide Suzon from Benoit, who made his master's bed and cleaned his room every day? If Benoit were not such a fool, he might be taken into confidence, and serve the young people; but there was no way of making use of him.

Benoit was not only stupid, but he was a gossip and very indiscreet; he couldn't keep anything from his father; and when once the porter learned anything, you might just as well have had the news announced by the town crier.

"The devil!" said Gustave, as he was dressing, "it is embarrassing — very embarrassing indeed! I suppose I had better go to my uncle first; but I will lock my bedroom door, and forbid Benoit to speak of the matter. I will see what can be done with Suzon later!"

Gustave, now being dressed, left a kiss on the lips of the young girl, who was still plunged in a deep sleep, double-locked the door of his bedroom, put the key in his pocket, and went to join the colonel. Outside his anteroom he found Benoit, who was waiting for him in the hall.

"Benoit, you are not to go into my room!"

"What?"

"I do not want you to put it into disorder. Besides, I have bought two doves that I want to tame, and you will frighten them."

"Oh, dear, no, monsieur! Oh, I know all about birds."

"I won't have you meddle with these."

"But your bed, monsieur, will you teach the doves to make that?"

"I will make it myself; it will amuse me."

"Oh, well, upon my word!"

"And I forbid you to speak about it to my uncle or anybody else in the house. If you do, you know Benoit that your ears can be easily pulled!"

"Oh, monsieur, I will not breathe a word of it! You are the master, and can make your own bed if it amuses you."

"That is very fortunate!"

"I shall simply have less to do, that's all! And if monsieur would like to brush his clothes and clean his boots —"

"Not at all; you can go into my anteroom; you will find everything there."

Gustave went to his uncle's apartments, where the latter was waiting breakfast for him. The colonel was in full dress. Gustave did not notice this at first; but, after breakfast, he was surprised to hear his uncle inquire if the horse were harnessed to the cabriolet.

"Are you going out, uncle?"

"Yes, Gustave, and you are going with me!"

"What? I?"

"Certainly you are going with me; I don't see anything in that to make you open your eyes in amazement!"

"But uncle! I wanted to work this morning on —"

"Bah! what a love for work you have; but you always have plenty of time. You can do tomorrow what you counted on doing today."

"Really, if you do not mind, I would rather —"

"Not at all, I wish you to go with me. Come along, the horse is ready; let us be off."

Gustave followed his uncle in a bad enough humor, but he hoped to get away after a few calls; during this time, Suzon would get thoroughly rested; and, as they had had a pretty fair supper the evening before, she could easily await his return.

They got into the cabriolet. The colonel drove, and Gustave noticed uneasily that they went through the city without stopping, and that they were aiming for the Barrière de l'Étoile.

"What are you doing, uncle?" he said impatiently. "Are you going out of Paris?"

"I know where I am going, nephew!"

"What! you are going to take me into the country?"

"I am going to take you to a delightful house, where you will enjoy yourself; I am very certain of that."

"As for me, well, I doubt it!"

"Well, we shall see! Besides, it isn't much for you to sacrifice one day to me."

"What! a whole day!"

"You will thank me for it this evening!"

"This evening! are you counting on keeping me until this evening?"

"Perhaps you may even spend the night at M. de Grancière's."

"Spend the whole day, perhaps the night? What? certainly not!"

Gustave stifled his vexation, impatience and disquietude; he wanted to jump out of the cabriolet and leave his uncle; however, wise reflections somewhat calmed him. He could not openly disoblige and cross his uncle. If he jumped out on the road

he might hurt himself and not get back to Paris
any the sooner ; he must then exercise patience and
wait for a favorable opportunity of making his
escape from M. de Grancière's.

"But Suzon! Poor Suzon ! what will you think?
How will you spend the day ? But I will tell her
all that has happened to me, and I will kiss her ;
she will easily forget all the past troubles, and she
will find in my arms compensation for the griefs
of the day."

Thus Gustave tried to console himself and to
have patience. The colonel related to him many
exploits of M. de Grancière, his old comrade and
companion in arms ; but all the eloquence which
Colonel Moranval used in painting pictures of the
battles, assaults and skirmishes in which he had
been with his friend were lost. Gustave heard nothing of what his uncle said to him ; he was only
thinking of Suzon, who, on his account, would have
to go without her dinner.

"Uncle, will it be long before we get there ? "
said Gustave, interrupting the colonel in the midst
of a lively recital.

"What? Good heavens ! is that all the interest
you take in my dangers, when I am surrounded by
enemies and wounded in the head ? "

"But, uncle, you are perfectly well ; we are no
longer on the field of battle ; and we have already
passed Courbevoie."

"What the devil is the matter with you today ?

I never saw you in such a hurry to get anywhere before."

" Uncle, I have a cramp in my leg; and the motion of the carriage makes me sick."

"If you had been as I have twelve hours wounded on the battlefield, surrounded by the dead and dying, you would not complain about cramps in the leg. You must certainly have the vapors. Come, calm yourself, here we are; that handsome house on the right is M. de Grancière's."

Gustave reckoned that they were about two and a half leagues from Paris; but with a good horse you can make this journey in less than an hour.

They alighted before a pretty country house. The groom started to lead the cabriolet into the yard.

" Don't unharness him," said Gustave.

"Certainly, certainly do so," said the colonel. "Good heavens! the horse will have plenty of time to rest."

Gustave bit his lips and followed his uncle in a rage.

They entered the drawing-room, where the uncle presented his nephew to his old friend. M. de Grancière was a very agreeable man and made many polite speeches to Gustave, to which the latter replied by some disconnected words spoken in an absent-minded manner.

" My friend," said the colonel to M. de Grancière, " I beg you to pardon my nephew; he has

days when he does not know what he is saying,
and, on my life, I have brought him to see you in
one of his bad humors."

This joke made Gustave blush; he tried to moderate his impatience, and resolved to try to conceal
his worry. At this moment a young woman, elegantly dressed and of a charming figure, entered
the drawing-room.

" This is my daughter," said M. de Grancière,
"my dear Eugénie, whom I present to you."

The colonel had to nudge Gustave, who was
then looking out into the garden, to make him
bow to the daughter of his friend. Gustave turned
around, and found himself face to face with a young
and pretty woman. One never likes to appear silly
and awkward before a person who seems to unite
good form with beauty and grace. Our hero became amiable, lively, gallant; he regained all these
advantages. The colonel smiled; he went up to
his nephew.

" Aha ! " he said to him, " are you still sorry
that you came with me ? "

Gustave made no reply; he admired the charming Eugénie; but he sighed and turned away as he
thought of poor Suzon.

Several neighbors came in ; Gustave noticed that
they carried bouquets which they presented to the
beautiful Eugénie.

" Is there a fête here ? " he asked his uncle.

" Yes, it is Madame Fonbelle's birthday."

" Who is Madame Fonbelle ? "

" M. de Grancière's daughter, Eugénie."

" Oh ! she is married ? "

" No, she is a widow and has fifteen thousand livres a year. Not only is she pretty, but she is wise and good and has mind and talents. What do you say to all that, Gustave ? "

" I say, uncle, that one must distrust the union of all these qualities in one person; I am certain that you are flattering the picture a little."

" You will soon see that it is far below the original."

" And why, my dear uncle, have you not presented me to Madame Fonbelle before ? "

" Because she was living in Touraine, and I did not wish to send you there for you to behave as you did at that poor De Berly's. Oh ! I know what you are capable of."

The company repaired to the garden before dinner. Gustave tried to find a good excuse to get away, but he couldn't think of any. Rudely to leave a house where he was received for the first time would be to defy all decent rules of society.

" It is certain that I shall have to dine here," he said to himself, " but after dinner I will feign illness, or an appointment, or perhaps I need say nothing at all, I will run away without being noticed. My uncle will scold and be angry, so much the worse. And Madame Fonbelle, what will she think of me ? that I am an original, an unconven-

tional and impolite man.   It is very disagreeable
to be judged in this way by a charming woman.
But my little Suzon is waiting for me; she has only
had for breakfast and dinner the remains of our
yesterday's chicken; only the carcass is left.   It is
true that Suzon adores me; and when one is in love,
one can live on memories and hope."

Gustave walked up and down a path in the garden while making these reflections.   Perceiving
Madame Fonbelle, he went up to her in the hope
of finding the time pass more quickly by talking
with the woman of whom his uncle had painted so
flattering a portrait; before leaving so brusquely
this evening, he would like to leave a few regrets
behind; vanity never sleeps.

M. de Grancière's daughter was very charming;
Eugénie was clever, elegant, sprightly, slightly coquettish and very romantic.   Gustave assured her
of the pleasure he would have in cultivating her
acquaintance.   Eugénie assured him that he would
always be welcome, either in Paris or in the country;
she accepted his compliments smilingly, but would
not accept his excuses for this evening.

"No, monsieur," she said, "you cannot leave us
like that.   No doubt you will miss some very pleasant appointment for this evening, but you will make
this sacrifice, and I shall be very much obliged to
you for doing so."

What can you say to a charming young woman
who detains you so pleasantly, and for whom you

already feel—what, love? What would you say? What would you have? That devil of a Gustave has a very inflammable heart; and Madame Fonbelle has many charms. But Suzon!—that poor Suzon who has left everything for him—oh, rest assured, reader, he still loves Suzon; he has not forgotten Julie; he still laughs with Lise; and pray don't believe that my hero is an imaginary being—almost all men are like him. We are no longer in that period—if it ever existed—when a man loved but one woman; we have made great progress in gallantry; we love the fair sex, generally speaking. Long live the French in order to make love! Let the Germans sigh, and walk about, and with their loved one admire in silence "the drop of dew falling on the last autumn leaf; the evening breeze murmuring among the rocks and carrying to the ear of a passionate heart the amorous sigh that escaped from burning lips, and the moon shedding upon the earth that sweet and melancholy glow that raises and transports an exalted and contemplative soul into the ethereal regions."

Let the Englishmen blow out their brains, or hang themselves, for their loved ones; let the Dutchmen smoke under the noses of their ladies and blow a cloud by way of compliment; let the Turks keep their little darlings locked up under the care of horrible eunuchs, always ready with the dagger or the cord; let the Spaniards spend half their lives in twanging the guitar and serenading;

let the Russians make love by means of the stick;
let the Scotchmen sell their women in the mar-
ket; let the Hindus take a wife at the age of ten;
let the Arabs hide their faces and show their
backs; let the Hottentots paint their bodies to be
attractive; let the Malays flatten their foreheads
and lengthen their ears; and let the Italians bring
down on their lovely country the fire that formerly
burned Sodom and Gomorrah, and which now, instead of falling from heaven, issues from the flanks
of Vesuvius.

Let us—let us leave all that, you are saying to
me, and return to Gustave, whom we left with
Eugénie. What is he doing now? He gave his
hand to Madame Fonbelle and went with all the
rest of the company to an arbor where the covers
had been laid. Either by accident or design, our
young man found himself next Eugénie, and the
repast did not seem long to him, although it lasted
nearly three hours, and it was dark when they went
into the drawing-room. Gustave glanced at the
clock. Oh, heavens! it is eight o'clock;—the time
he ought to be arriving in Paris! That poor Suzon
must be frightfully lonely! He must go! He
turned around; Eugénie was behind him; she took
his hand, and led him to the piano.

"I hear," she said to him, "that you sing with
taste, and that you love music; come, we will try a
very pretty nocturne together."

There was no way of refusing; he had to follow

Eugénie to the piano; they sang a nocturne, then a duet, and then a romance. Everybody applauded; the colonel seemed enchanted, Madame Fonbelle thanked Gustave, and her eyes had a tender expression! A man could spend his life admiring them. The clock began to strike. Ten o'clock! Gustave rose brusquely.

"Ten o'clock!" he said to himself, "and she has been waiting for me ever since the morning."

He gained the drawing-room door, went down to the yard, and asked for the cabriolet; but the horse was still in the stable. Gustave took him out, threw the first bridle he could find over him, and without stirrups or saddle, mounted him, urged him on, and dashed off towards Paris at full speed.

He arrived in the yard of the hotel in less than three-quarters of an hour. The horse fell against the porter's lodge; Father Benoit screamed; his son jumped to one side. Gustave was not hurt, but he got free of the horse, leaving him to the servants, and pushed Benoit towards the servant's offices.

"That poor horse," said Benoit, with a sigh, "he will never recover."

"Benoit, bring up at once a pie, a fowl, some wine and preserves."

"A pie, monsieur?"

"Go along, what is the matter? Haven't you heard what I said? How slow you are."

Benoit could not understand his master's appe-

tite; he quietly took up a fowl on a dish; Gustave was waiting for him at the door.

"What? Haven't you brought anything else?"

"Monsieur, as I did not want to break anything,
I am only bringing one plate at a time."

"Oh, you idiot! come with me."

Gustave put the fowl down in the vestibule and
went downstairs with Benoit to the larder. He
took all he could find, pasties, vegetables, fruits
and wine; he loaded Benoit up and carried several
dishes himself. Benoit looked at Gustave in astonishment.

"Monsieur seems to be hungry?"

"That is none of your business! Go along, you
cursed dawdler!"

"Take care, monsieur, you will make me break
something."

On the stairway a dog ran down past them with
a fowl in his jaw; it was Fidéle, who had smelled
the dish that Gustave had left before his door. Our
hero is furious; he stamps his foot and shouts after
Fidéle. The frightened dog runs away and gets
between Benoit's legs. Benoit falls on the steps
with all his dishes and daubs his face with cream
cheese.

Gustave was beside himself; he was desperate;
he didn't know what to do; finally he decided to
leave Benoit and the capon; and, contenting himself with the pie and some fruit, he went into his
rooms, shutting the door of his antechamber and

bolting it, and went into the bedroom where Suzon was awaiting him.

The little villager was sitting near the bed ; her handkerchief was on her knees, and her eyes were red and swollen ; as soon as she saw Gustave she gave a cry and rushed into his arms.

" Here I am, Suzon, here I am ! "

" Ah ! I thought I should never see you again ! "

" Ah, Suzon, you have been crying ! "

" Yes, nearly all day long ; but I assure you I have not made any noise."

" Poor little one ! and you had no dinner ? "

" Dinner ! Oh, I don't want any now. I was hungry this morning, but my appetite is gone."

" You believed, then, that I didn't love you any longer ? "

" Well, certainly, since you didn't come back to see me. You have been gone for a long time."

" Ah ! that was not my fault ; my uncle carried me off ; if you only knew how long the day seemed to me."

Gustave lied a little — perhaps ; but there are circumstances in which a white lie is necessary and even praiseworthy ; it would have been cruel to say to Suzon, " I have seen a charming woman, with whom I sang, and who made me forget how the time passed." That was the truth, however ; but then you know it is not always wise to speak the whole truth.

Gustave placed the pie, wine and fruit on the

table before Suzon, he pressed the little one to eat and she smiled upon her lover, for she saw by his solicitude and regrets that he loved her still; she therefore forgot about her wretched day and ate to please Gustave.

But while Suzon was taking her repast, Gustave reflected; he said to himself, "What has happened today may happen often again, and result in grave inconvenience; it will never do to let Suzon spend all her life in one room, without daring to speak loud, or move about, for fear of being heard; moreover, if she never goes out she will get ill, for nobody can change her manner of living with impunity; a young girl accustomed to run about in the country, to get up at sunrise, and to take a great deal of exercise, cannot support the thick and mephitic air of Paris condensed into a space of twenty square feet, which she cannot even renew without being seen by the servants of the house. And then Benoit, who would become suspicious through the extraordinary conduct of his master, might carry it to the colonel; and if he were to find Suzon!—Well, certainly she must not stay in the house; he must rent a little room and furnish it properly; there she could sing, talk, enjoy the fresh air and eat whenever it seemed good to her; and he would go to see her every day, both morning and evening."

"My dear child," said Gustave to Suzon, "I have thought of a way by which we can see each other without danger; tomorrow I will rent a pretty room on the boulevards and establish you there."

Suzon dropped her glass and her fork; she listened attentively to Gustave's recital of the pleasure she would have in her new dwelling; when he had finished, she still remained silent, but the tears fell from her eyes, and she threw herself at Gustave's knees with a supplicating look.

The latter, surprised by this action, begged her to speak and raised her up; but she persisted in kneeling and cried out sobbingly,—

"For mercy's sake, pray don't send me away from you, M. Gustave; I promise you that I will not make any noise. I will not cry again; you can go out whenever you please; but do not send me away from you!"

"What do you say, my dear one? I am not sending you away. It is to make you happier; you can go out with me."

"I would rather stay in your room!"

"I will come and see you every day."

"Oh! but when you had gone, I should be so afraid that I should never see you again; here at any rate, you have to come back to sleep."

"But if my uncle should find you?"

"Ah, well! it would be time enough to send me away then; but in Paris!—Ah! I should be lost if I did not live with you."

Gustave could only calm the young girl by promising to let her live in his room.

"As long as you wish it," he said to her, "you can stay here. I only hope that we shall not, both of us, ever repent of this resolution."

This promise restored Suzon's gayety; she kissed Gustave, ran about the room, jumped, and did a thousand foolish things; for she thought her happiness was now altogether assured. Gustave was not of the same opinion, but he did not wish to disturb her joy, regretting, perhaps for the first time, that reason had not triumphed over love.

CHAPTER IX

THE MYSTERIOUS ROOM. A CONJUGAL NIGHT

BEFORE eight o'clock the following morning
Benoit knocked at his master's door. Gustave got
up, and, without opening the door, asked who was
there and why he was disturbed at such an un-
earthly hour.

"Colonel Moranval wants to speak to you, monsieur," was Benoit's reply, who was much disappointed at not having a chance to see into the room.

Gustave expected a good scolding; he dressed
himself, locked his bedroom door, and went to find
his uncle. Benoit's curiosity was reawakened at
noticing that his master locked up his room as on
the previous day; but, nevertheless, he did not
dare to repeat his questions, and was forced to be
content with remaining in ignorance.

"The devil, monsieur!" exclaimed the colonel
when he saw his nephew, "kindly tell me what kind
of vertigo you were suffering from last evening.
You leave a house, where a thousand courtesies have
been extended to you, without paying homage to
the mistress of the establishment, whom you suddenly desert just as you are about to accompany
her in a sonata; you run away as if the devil were

at your heels, you mount a horse that has never been used except in harness — an excellent horse that cost me forty louis — and, to finish your exploits, you gallop the poor beast till he is broken-winded ; you plunge into the courtyard like a ball from a forty-eight pounder, breaking the windows of the porter's lodge, and terrify everybody ; you scare my porter almost out of his wits — and he had none too many to spare in the first place — and all this haste to get home was merely to get to the larder, to eat a pasty and a fowl, and to pillage the sideboard ! I can't understand it ; you certainly ate a pretty good dinner ! "

" Uncle, I was suddenly seized with a wolfish appetite ! "

" Good God ! eat as much as you want to, that's your affair ; but don't let your ravenous appetite founder my horses and turn my house upside down."

" Uncle, did Madame Fonbelle seem annoyed at my sudden departure ? "

" Oh, she is too good-natured ; she was the first to try to pacify me ; but you owe her an apology."

" Oh, I certainly will apologize, uncle ; I'll go and call upon her."

" And as for me, I've got to buy another horse. I must confess that I had an idea that some little love-affair took you away, and I thought that you had left us so unceremoniously to run after some pretty little face; but when I got home I was greatly astonished to hear that you had arrived at full

gallop for supper. The devil! What an appetite
you must have! Another time I beg you to put a
pasty and some cakes in your pockets so as not to
run the risk of playing me the same trick again."

Gustave retired. On his way back to his room,
he met Benoit, whose ears he boxed soundly to
teach him to carry tales of his behavior to his uncle.
Benoit shed bitter tears, protesting that Fidéle was
the sole culprit, because the dog had frisked around
the colonel, still holding in its mouth a portion of
the fowl that it had stolen on the landing.

After having kissed Suzon, Gustave hired a cab
and drove to the house of M. de Grancière. He
saw Eugénie and apologized for his sudden departure the day before. She accepted his excuses, but
joked about his appointment. Gustave thought
he noticed that Madame Fonbelle was piqued, and
it gave him a secret pleasure; he flattered himself
that already she was not indifferent to him, but notwithstanding the pleasure he took in her conversation, he shortened his visit and was back at the
house within four hours.

He hastened to rejoin Suzon and did not leave
her for the rest of the day. He had all that was
needed for her dinner brought up to the room.
Benoit had been too well punished to want to chatter any more; and besides, he never went further
than his master's anteroom.

Several days passed in this manner; Gustave
never went out of the house except to call upon

Madame Fonbelle, who had returned to Paris with her father, the season in the country having come to an end. With the exception of his visits to Eugénie, Gustave never left Suzon; he never left his room except to have breakfast with his uncle, and dinner when the latter dined at home.

The colonel was simply astonished at Gustave's good behavior; sometimes even he found fault with Gustave's unbounded love of work.

" My boy," he said to his nephew, " we ought never to run to extremes; hitherto you have been a young rascal and rover, playing the devil from morning till night; and now you shut yourself up in your room and never stir out of it; you are working too hard; you will make yourself ill; and the proof of that is that, notwithstanding your good behavior and regular hours, you are not putting on any flesh at all; on the contrary, your face grows longer and paler and your eyes more hollow and black-ringed; anyone would think that you spent your nights in running to the public balls and in love intrigues."

. " Uncle, close study is very fatiguing also."

" Well! don't do so much of it; that's what I am constantly repeating to you. Come with me into society; and don't shut yourself up in your room to wither away over books and papers."

Time was going to have far more effect than the colonel's admonitions; Gustave still spent much of his time with Suzon; but in order to pass the

hours that cannot be spent continually in love-
making — no matter how desirous the ladies may
be of its perpetuation — Gustave gave Suzon lessons in reading and writing, for she had had only
a few lessons from the Ermenonville schoolmaster
— who was not a man of great culture himself —
and to please him she studied all the time when
she was alone. These intervals of absence became
longer from day to day. Suzon was very gentle
and sweet and loving; but Gustave could see her
whenever he wanted to; he came home to her at
night and was overwhelmed with her caresses; and
when by her side, he often consulted his watch and
invented pretexts to go out. It was Madame de
Fonbelle whose presence he sought; there he found
the time all too short. Eugénie, however, only
accepted Gustave's homage jestingly; she laughed
when he sighed, and changed the conversation when
he began to talk sentiment; she mocked at him when
he assumed a sad and dreamy air. But, through
this somewhat coquettish behavior, Gustave noticed signs of sentiment and tenderness which she
tried to conceal from him, but which are not easily
hidden from the eye of a lover.

Suzon never reproached Gustave for his frequent
absences; she sighed when he went away and wept
when it was long before he returned; but when
she heard him enter the anteroom she hastened to
dry her eyes, drove back her tears and offered to
Gustave's gaze only a sweet and smiling face.

The colonel knew that his nephew paid frequent visits at M. de Grancière's house, and was joyful over Gustave's growing love for Eugénie. He had no doubt that this new passion was the cause of the happy change in his nephew's conduct. He had spoken to his friend of his desires and hopes; and M. de Grancière said that his daughter was entirely her own mistress to marry again as seemed good unto her. "After that," said the colonel, "things will go as I wish; for Gustave cannot fail to please Eugénie — he has every advantage for that ; and she will marry him, for she is too high-principled to be anything but his wife, and it is too troublesome to be forever refusing what our hearts are only too anxious to grant."

In accordance with Gustave's desire, Suzon had written a letter to her parents, full of expressions of regret for the sorrow that she must have caused them ; she attributed her fault to the repulsion she felt towards Nicholas, whom they wanted her to marry. She said she was settled in Paris, but she did not give any address to receive a reply, for she feared to be torn from the side of the man whom she never wanted to leave.

One morning when, contrary to his custom, the colonel was walking about in the courtyard, examining a horse that he had just bought, he thought he heard his nephew's name mentioned in the coach-house. He drew near and stopped where he could not be seen, and so heard the following conversation between Benoit and his father, who was cleaning the colonel's cabriolet.

" So, my boy, you say that M. Gustave won't let anybody go into his room ? "

" No ! certainly, papa, he won't allow anybody to go in ; he has expressly forbidden even me."

"Then who makes his bed, and cleans up his room ? "

" I'm sure I don't know; from what he tells me he has bought two doves and amuses himself in training them.   He plays all day with his doves, while the colonel thinks he is working."

" Bah ! taming doves at his age !   Then that's how it happens, Benoit, that I sometimes see shadows passing across his window curtains when he is out."

" Yes ! that must be it !   But these birds must eat an awful lot of food and drink wine, because M. Gustave's consumption of food and drink is something terrible — meat patties, and fowls, and fruit, and cake ! "

" But Benoit, don't you think that it's more likely to be a monkey that he is secretly training for a surprise for the colonel on his birthday ?"

"Ah ! that's quite possible ! Yes ! there must be one or even two monkeys, for sometimes I also hear chairs being moved, and on one occasion I thought it was a robber.   Most certainly no birds could have made that noise.   I should very much like to know exactly what it is !"

"So should I!"

"Well, I'll soon know all about it," soliloquized the colonel, as he quietly withdrew. "Monkeys that need fowls and wine! There's something underneath all this. And Gustave's extraordinary devotion to study! has he been duping me again? Let's see about it."

The colonel was not the kind of man to delay clearing up so singular a matter, which, moreover, filled his mind with a thousand suspicions. He went up to Gustave's rooms and tried to get in, but the door was locked.

"Aha!" he exclaimed, "Benoit was not lying; but I will find out what it is that they want to keep out of sight."

He went down and sent for his nephew's valet.

"Where is your master, Benoit?"

"Monsieur, he has gone out."

"Have you the key to his room? I need to go up and get something out of it."

"No, monsieur, I have not."

Benoit reddened with apprehension.

"Come, be calm!" said Colonel Moranval, "I know that you are never involved in my nephew's follies; he finds you too stupid to be taken into his confidence."

"That's true, Colonel Moranval."

"Go and fetch me a pair of pincers and a pick-lock!"

"Wouldn't you rather have a locksmith?"

"No! I can do without one; do what I tell you, and hold your tongue."

Benoit brought the colonel what he asked for, and followed him up to his nephew's room; but, when he reached the landing, the colonel turned round and ordered Benoit to go away. Benoit obeyed very regretfully, for he was curious to know what was in his master's bedroom.

The colonel knew how to break in a door better than how to pick a lock; however, he managed to turn the screw, and the bolt gave. He entered the mysterious room.

But he looked all around him in vain, he saw neither birds nor monkeys; however, some clothes that could not possibly belong to Gustave were lying on the foot of the bed.

"There is a woman here," said the colonel, "but where the devil has she gone?"

As he uttered these words, his eyes fell on a nook between the chimney and the window where Suzon was cowering behind an armchair. The colonel saw her: he stood motionless before the young woman, who, on her part, did not dare to raise her eyes.

"What the devil are you doing there, little one?" asked the colonel when at last he recovered his speech. But Suzon shut her eyes and would not move. The colonel pushed the armchair aside and took hold of the hand of the young peasant, who was trembling like a leaf.

"Come! don't be afraid; I'm not going to eat you. Answer my questions, little one, and above all, tell me the truth!"

"Yes, monsieur!"

"What are you doing in my nephew's room?"

"I'm living with him, monsieur."

"Oh! you're living with him?"

"Yes, monsieur."

"That's an excellent arrangement! And how long has this household been in existence, may I ask?"

"For six weeks, monsieur."

"What! you have been living in this room for six weeks and never gone out to get fresh air or exercise?"

"Oh, no, monsieur! I was too much afraid of being seen!"

"Then what do you do all day?"

"When he is here, I look at him, talk to him, and kiss him. When I am alone, I study reading and writing."

"But you must be often alone, for he has gone out a great deal during the last few days; doesn't this kind of life weary you?"

"No, monsieur, I am always thinking of him and always expecting him; and I know very well that he will return to me."

The colonel scrutinized Suzon; her grace and simplicity disarmed his anger; he returned to his interrogation.

"Where did you become acquainted with my nephew?"

"At Ermenonville, monsieur; he lodged at our house."

"Aha! he lodged with your parents; and, in return for their hospitality, he ruined and carried off their daughter."

"Oh, no! he did neither, monsieur; that all happened without premeditation. I happened to be in his room and we immediately fell in love with one another."

"So it seems that at Ermenonville, matters are arranged just as unceremoniously as they are in Paris. But why did you leave your home and family?"

"Ah! monsieur, they wanted to marry me to Nicholas Toupet, whom I can't bear. I should have been very unhappy; and then I was always thinking of M. Gustave and was dying with grief at being no longer able to see him."

"And suppose your mother died of the grief caused by your desertion! suppose your flight were to lead her to the tomb?"

"Oh! monsieur; don't say that."

Suzon began to sob. The colonel was greatly moved; he strode up and down the room, stamped his foot, looked at Suzon and then stopped and swore at his absent nephew.

Presently he came up to Suzon and took her by the hand.

"Come! my child, control yourself; stop crying and listen to me. I won't reproach you for your conduct; you evidently did not realize all the consequences; you simply followed the impulses of your own heart; and although people say that one should always be guided by that, yours has only led you to do foolish things. You cannot remain here; it's quite enough for you to have been here six weeks already. Come, now! don't cry like that, or I shall get angry! You are going to leave this house!"

"Oh! monsieur, let me be one of your servants; I will work for you and serve you —"

"Not for anything on earth! A nurse like you would soon get my household in a tangle. Moreover, do you think that M. Gustave would be pleased to see you mingling with my other servants? No, my dear child, you must leave this house; there is nothing more to be said on that point. Would you rather stay in Paris or return to your parents?"

"Ah, monsieur, don't send me back to the village, they will make me marry Nicholas as a punishment."

"The devil! how you do detest this Nicholas; and yet if you were like the Parisian women, that would not prevent you from — but that is not the question. I consent to your not returning to your home; but I must find some place for you to live, and you can write and tell your mother where you are. Let us see, where in the devil can I take you?"

"It is all the same to me, monsieur; since I cannot be with him any longer, I shall never be happy again."

"Bah! that is only childish talk. Love passes away, my dear; and if you had a little more experience you would feel that Gustave's is already — well, you cannot live upon love, and we must think about your future. My nephew is a heedless madcap to let you wither out your youth in this chamber, while he — Ah, good Lord! men don't deserve the tears that you women shed for them."

The colonel did not know what to decide upon; he tried to think what he should do with Suzon, whom he could not and would not keep in his house, but of whom he determined to take care, because he saw at once that, although she had been living in the room of a young man, this young village girl had had really less experience than many young girls who live with their parents. Suzon said nothing more; she glanced timidly at Colonel Moranval and waited until he decided her fate. The colonel went out of the bedroom and opened the door of the anteroom to call Benoit; but he might have saved himself the trouble, for the porter and his son were on the landing, burning with curiosity to see what strange creatures the colonel would bring out of the room. Colonel Moranval looked at them severely.

" What are you doing there?" he asked savagely.

"Colonel Moranval, we — we — are awaiting your orders," replied the porter.

" Say rather that you are waiting for me to come out of this apartment to go in yourselves, and see the monkey that my nephew is keeping there."

" Then it really is a monkey, colonel ? "

" Go down to your own lodging ! I don't like inquisitive people."

The colonel pushed the porter, who pushed his son, and both went downstairs, ashamed at having been caught and vexed at not having found out anything.

Colonel Moranval then went to see Madame Duval, the woman who had charge of the household linen, and who was neither inquisitive nor a gossip, and, moreover, had been in the colonel's service for ten years.

" Madame Duval," said the colonel, entering the room of the old workwoman, " I want to find a place for a young girl ; do you know of any shop where the business will not oblige her to be constantly running about the streets of Paris or listening to the doubtful jokes of the customers ? "

" Colonel Moranval," replied Madame Duval, after thinking a moment, " I only know Madame Henri, a silk-mercer in the Rue aux Ours ; she supplies me with all we need for this house, and it was only the other day that she asked me if I could not find somebody for her."

"And is your Madame Henri respectable?"

"Yes, monsieur; she is a widow; she is young, gay and goes to the play every Sunday; but, however, she is good and never receives doubtful characters."

"Well and good, I don't want to place this little girl in a convent nor with an ill-natured prude; I wish her to be occupied and amused at the same time; nothing could be better. Madame Duval, go and order a cab and get ready to accompany me to Madame Henri's."

"But, Colonel Moranval, she ought at least to be informed."

"That is not necessary. She knows you, doesn't she? She certainly knows me, at least by name, since she supplies my house with linen, and that ought to be enough. Go on, madame, have the cab drive into the yard and stop before the middle staircase."

Madame Duval went out. The colonel went upstairs to Suzon.

"Now, my dear, put everything that belongs to you in a bundle and get ready to go with me."

"What, monsieur, today?"

"At once."

"But I must say good-by to him!"

"Not at all; that would never do; on the contrary, you must go before he comes back."

"Ah, good heavens! what will he say when he doesn't find me here?"

" I will tell him that it was I who took you away."

" He will be very grieved.

" He will feel that I was right."

" He will be dreadfully angry."

" Good Lord ! I should like to see him."

Suzon wept and was in despair; she begged to be allowed to wait for Gustave. The colonel was inexorable.

" But at least, monsieur," she said, sobbing, " he will come and see me ? You will tell where I am ? "

" Yes," said the colonel, who did not wish to reduce her altogether to despair, " yes, my child, you shall see him if you are more reasonable, and if you behave yourself."

This assurance slightly assuaged Suzon's grief; she wiped her eyes, put all that Gustave had bought for her since she had been living with him into a bundle, and waited for M. de Moranval's orders.

A carriage drove into the yard and stopped at the stairway.

" Let us go down," said the colonel. He took Suzon by the hand ; she gave one more look round that room which to her was the whole universe, her bosom heaved and her knees trembled, but she kept back her tears for fear of irritating the colonel.

The cab is below, the door is open; the colonel leads the young girl in. He seats himself beside her and tells Madame Duval to sit on the other side. He shuts the windows and orders the coachman to drive to the Rue aux Ours. The cab drives away from the hotel. The two Benoits, father and son, are in the street opposite the gate; they lift their heads, craning their necks to see what is being carried off in the carriage, but Suzon is hidden by Madame Duval and the colonel, and their curiosity is rewarded by nothing but a splashing.

They arrived at Madame Henri's. The silk-mercer was very much surprised to see Colonel Moranval and Madame Duval enter her shop, bringing a young girl with red eyes, and who could hardly bear up.

"Madame," the colonel said, " you asked Madame Duval if she knew of a shopgirl, and I have brought you one. She is very unhappy, as you see, but she will tell you all about her little troubles ; you must console her first and then you can reason with her afterwards, and so, in time, everything will come right. I recommend Mademoiselle Suzon, in whom I take a very great interest. As she knows how to do nothing at present, you will have to take the trouble to teach her ; here are twenty-five louis for her board and lodging for the first year. Tell me, madame, if you agree to this ? "

"Monsieur," said Madame Henri, somewhat astonished at the great promptness with which the colonel did business, "certainly, your recommendation and that of Madame Duval are quite enough for me to take mademoiselle into my employ — if, however, she would like to remain."

"Yes, madame," said Suzon with a sigh, "I will do anything they wish."

"Very well, everything is settled then," said the colonel to Madame Henri; "I recommend once again to your care this child, who has but one fault, that of being too sensitive. Good-by, my dear; Madame Duval will often bring me news of you, and if you behave yourself well, I will continue to look after you. Good-by, again. Tomorrow your parents shall know that you are in a situation for which you have no cause to blush."

The colonel went away, leaving Suzon with Madame Henri. We shall return later to the little village girl; let us see in the mean time what Gustave was doing while they carried his roommate away.

Our hero had spent a part of the day at Madame Fonbelle's; when he returned to the hotel, the two Benoits, father and son, were paying a visit to his room. When they saw the cab drive off with the colonel, the two servants calculated that they would have time to go up to M. Gustave's apartment; they found the door of the mysterious chamber open, and they hunted in every corner, trying to find some clue that could aid them in learning what he had kept hidden in this room.

Gustave went upstairs, he was greatly astonished to find the door of his room open; he thought he must have forgotten to lock it. He entered; but, instead of Suzon, he saw the porter rummaging in

a large armoire and Benoit on his knees peeping
under the bed.

"What are you doing here?" cried Gustave.
"How did you get in? Are you going to answer
me, you scoundrels?"

The porter and his son could find no excuse, and
so they kept silent. Gustave took hold of Benoit's
ear and pulled it hard.

"Tell me, you idiot, where she is?"

"Where she is, monsieur?"

"Yes, what has become of her?"

"What has become of what? Monsieur, we
haven't seen your doves."

"I was hunting for them, monsieur," said the
porter, trembling.

"But tell me; who opened this door?"

"It was your uncle, but he came in all alone.
He called for a cab."

"And he took her away, then?"

"I suppose so, monsieur. He certainly took
away something, but we didn't see what it was."

"Get out of the room."

The porter and his son were only too delighted
to get away. Gustave hunted about to see if Suzon
had left any written message; but he found nothing. So it is all over, Suzon is lost to him. But
you will say that he loved her no longer, he was
even bored with her company, and he left her for
Eugénie. Yes, when he was with Suzon he no
longer felt those transports and that intoxication

so characteristic of love; he neglected her for a
part of every day, and as soon as he returned he
tried to find an excuse to get away again; but now
that she is gone, now that they have taken her away
from him, he feels his love return, he burns to see
her again, to speak to her, to kiss her. Such is
the contrariness of the human heart, and as a certain song aptly says,—

> Man wishes to have what he has not,
> And whatever he has pleases him no longer.

In despair at having lost Suzon, with whom he
was again in love now that she was no longer with
him, he went out of his apartment and down into
the court, ready to run all over the city to try to
discover the retreat to which the barbarous colonel
— for anyone who crosses us in our desires is always barbarous — had taken the young village girl.

But the city is very large; and when one does not
know in which direction to go, he is likely to try
many useless roads. Gustave had not gone a hundred steps before he stopped, looked around him
and wondered where he was going; as he could not
answer the question, he stood in the middle of the
pavement uncertain what to do, being jostled by
the passers-by, who were much annoyed to see a
young man standing motionless upon the pavement, and who, if he stayed there much longer,
doubtless would have attracted a crowd around him
to know why he stared vacantly in the air, where
he could see nothing; but in Paris most people are

idle and curious—two dogs fighting, a man whose
nose is bleeding, a lady who shows her garters when
she holds up her dress, a drunken man who falls
down, or a crying child, nothing more is required
to attract two hundred persons.

Gustave was suddenly called to himself by hearing his name called. This voice came from the
depths of a yellow cab, which was going as fast as
it could when drawn by two old horses, and driven
by a coachman who was paid by the hour.

"There it is," exclaimed Gustave, "a cab, and
I think Benoit said that it was yellow — a voice
calling my name, and in very familiar tones. It
must be Suzon, whom my uncle is taking away from
me! Come, let's follow the carriage! If it were
dark, I would get up behind, but I can't do that
in broad daylight; but never mind, I won't lose
sight of it! Still, I must not keep too close to it
for fear of attracting the colonel's attention!"

The cab left the city, and entered the Faubourg
du Temple. "That's it!" exclaimed Gustave, "he's
going to hide her in the country; perhaps even take
her back to Ermenonville! but most certainly those
two poor old horses won't be able to make the
journey; they will have to halt somewhere, and
then I shall find an opportunity to speak to
Suzon."

In fact, the carriage passed the barrier and went
up the Belleville high street; having arrived at the
village, it turned to the left, entered a street lead-

ing into the fields, and stopped in front of a rather
pretty little house. Gustave also came to a halt
about fifty paces away from the gate, and tried to
see, without himself being seen.

Two ladies and a young man got out and went
into the house. The ladies wore big hats that concealed their faces, and Gustave began to fear that
he had made a mistake, for though he could not
distinguish their features from that distance, yet
neither of them had Suzon's figure nor costume;
but still it was possible that the colonel might have
bought other clothes for her for the purpose of disguise. But then, the colonel was not in the carriage ; and who was that young man ? The little
peasant would not have been confided to his care ;
so Suzon was not one of those in the carriage, and
our hero had taken a fruitless journey from the
Rue Montmartre to the Près-Saint-Gervais.

It put Gustave into a very bad temper to have
lost his time in this manner. The ladies and the
young man had gone into the house ; the carriage
had gone away and our hero was left in the little
Rue des Champs in uncertainty as to what he
should do.

" Nevertheless, somebody called me by name, so
that one of those ladies knows me. Well ! there's
nothing astonishing in that, since I myself know
so many; and there are others whom I have forgotten. However, I should like to know who the
persons are who have entered that house."

As he said this, Gustave approached the house
and looked at the windows; he tried to discover
through the blinds the face of some acquaintance.
He thought he heard a window open, and then a
sweet voice again pronounced his name. This
voice was the same one that he had already heard.
There was no longer any doubt about it; one of
those ladies was acquainted with him; and most
certainly he would not return to Paris without seeing her. He had already reached the porte-cochère,
and was about to knock at the door, without knowing for whom to ask, when the same voice stopped
him.

"Don't knock!" it cried, "follow the wall along
and turn the corner to the left, and then wait before the little door."

"The devil! this is quite a mystery," said Gustave to himself. "A wall and a little door, it's like a
scene in a melodrama. Well, let me follow instructions; I'm going to find out who my heroine is."

Gustave went down the street and then turned
to the left, still following the wall, till at last he saw
a little door; and there he halted. He looked
above this wall, which extended quite a long distance, and saw only the tops of some fruit trees
and lilac bushes; so he concluded that these were
the gardens of the houses fronting the street that
were enclosed by this wall. He leaned against the
little door and impatiently waited to be admitted
into the garden. At last he heard the sound of

advancing footsteps; the person was walking fast; it must be a woman! Gustave even thought he could hear the rustle of her skirts. He felt his heart beat more quickly; but why this emotion? The advancing woman is perhaps old, or ugly, but then, again, perhaps she is pretty, and when there is a doubt, we like to dwell on the most pleasing idea; and then this mystery, that voice and all the circumstances produced a piquant effect that stimulated the imagination. And, indeed, in the most important circumstances of our lives, events affect us only in proportion to the situation in which they find us; the dreams of our imagination dispose our souls to love, joy or sorrow; there are moments when we ask for nothing but to shed tears, and others when everything looks rose-colored; and since at a masked ball people often become inflamed over a little domino whose features cannot be distinguished, Gustave might well feel his heart palpitating on account of her whose light feet he heard on the sandy path approaching the little door.

At last that little door was opened; Gustave entered the garden and pressed to his breast, not Suzon, but Madame de Berly.

The first moments were naturally given up to love; but after holding one another in a long and close embrace, Gustave and Julie had a thousand questions to ask. Our hero could not get over the astonishment caused by Julie's appearance.

"What, Gustave, you did not recognize my voice?" said Madame de Berly, with a sigh. "But, as a matter of fact, it is such a terribly long time since you saw me that you had forgotten me! Ingrate! and when I was thinking of you every moment of the day, your heart was occupied with another woman. The moments I passed in groans and sighs, you spent in courting others. Alas! so those are the oaths that should have been sacred. But what am I saying — have I any right to rely upon yours?"

Julie was shedding bitter tears; Gustave did not know how to excuse himself, for he felt that he was guilty, and yet the mere sight of Julie had again fired his heart with the sentiments that she had formerly inspired. But it is easy to console a woman who loves us. Madame de Berly was the first to attempt a reconciliation.

"Forgive me for my reproaches, dearest; it is unreasonable of me to indulge in them. Parted from me, how could I dare to hope that you would never love another? But you don't say a word to me; have you really completely forgotten me?"

"Oh, no! but I feel that I have been guilty of wrong-doing."

"Do you still love me, Gustave?"

"More than ever."

"Very well then, let us say no more about your misdeeds; a man's own self-reproach is harder to bear than the reproach of others."

"Julie, darling, how good you are! I am not at all worthy of such generosity."

"Don't feel under any obligation for that ; if I love you, it's entirely against my own will. I should far rather have overcome my feelings ; but love is like fortune, those who are least deserving are most often treated like spoiled children." Gustave took Julie in his arms and covered her charming throat and neck, which were exposed by a fluttering fichu, with kisses. His passion prompted him to make amends for a separation of several months ; but Julie restrained his ardor.

"Behave yourself; remember that we may be seen ! "

"Aren't you alone ? '

"Somebody might come at any moment; I am not even living in my own house. It's evident that you didn't recognize the lady who was with me."

"No! there's no doubt of that, since I didn't even recognize you. Who is the lady ? "

"Aurélie, my husband's niece, the lady who was to be your bride and who has been married now for six weeks to that tall young man who was in the carriage with us."

"Is it possible ? "

"I am staying with them; this place belongs to them. Occasionally, for the sake of civility, I come and spend a week with them ; and, moreover, whether I'm in town or in the country, it's all the same to me when you are not there. But I am afraid that Madame Frémont, or her husband, may notice my absence ; and if anyone were to see you with me—Aurélie has a malicious tongue—I should be lost."

" What's to be done ? I can't make up my mind to leave you. Is M. de Berly coming here this evening ? "

" No, he will stay in Paris until Sunday."

" This is Friday; so I can stay with you."

" My room is in that pavilion over there to the left ; you see it, there, in the middle of the garden."

"Good ! give me the key ? I'll hide in it and wait for you."

"Oh, Gustave; if—if Aurélie, or her husband—"

" So you don't love me as much as you used to, Julie ! "

" That's naughty of you ! Here, take this key, but be careful to avoid being seen."

" Rely on my prudence."

" I will return to the parlor now ; I will feign a headache and join you as soon as possible."

" Very well ; I'll wait for you."

Madame de Berly left Gustave and took a path leading to the house, while Gustave directed his steps towards the pavilion that had been pointed out to him. This building, which occupied an isolated spot in the middle of the garden, consisted of a groundfloor and a first floor, and was surmounted by a terrace, on which was a telescope for viewing the neighborhood.

Gustave reached the pavilion, but he had no need of the key which had been given to him, for the door was open. He reached a little entry, whence a flight of stairs led to the upper story and the terrace; close by these stairs, a door opened into the room on the groundfloor. .

"Does she sleep on the first or the groundfloor?" Gustave asked himself; "but, after all, it doesn't matter where I await her; she told me that her room was in this pavilion; and she is probably here alone, since she has the key of it. Let's go into the room on the groundfloor; I shall soon be able to see whether the room is made ready for her or not."

The key was in the door; Gustave opened it and saw a fine room, elegantly furnished and newly decorated. He went in, being satisfied that this was Madame de Berly's room that had been prepared to receive her. There was nothing lacking in effect in the apartment — an elegant bed, a sofa, mirrors, armchairs and double curtains — nothing had been forgotten to make this room a charming retreat. Gustave examined everything; he was astonished to see a mirror at the back of the alcove. "The devil!" he exclaimed, "what luxury and refinement! Formerly, Julie was not accustomed to all this. Certainly this room must be a boudoir; and it is an appropriate abode for a lovely woman. Without any doubt, Madame Frémont's apartment cannot compare with this. That prude of an Aurélie, who never raised her eyes and who looked black at the mildest pleasantries, must have very funny household arrangements. She certainly banishes from her room everything that may soften the senses or offend modesty. I pity her husband; there is nothing so annoying as a prude — at least in society; but I should like to know how the wedding-night was spent."

After having admired the apartment, Gustave shut the door and threw himself down in an armchair to rest while he awaited Julie's arrival. He went over the events of the day in his mind, and could not deny that it was not to spend the night with Julie that he had left home; and that he certainly would not find Suzon in Madame de Berly's rooms. Poor Suzon! were you already forgotten? No! Gustave faithfully promised himself to continue the search and discover the asylum whither the colonel had conducted Suzon; but the delay of a day or two would not have any effect on the result of his efforts, on the contrary, it would render success all the easier, since, when they saw that Gustave was making no attempt whatever to find Suzon, they would not keep such a close watch on her and she might possibly be able to communicate with her lover; at least, that is what our hero thought as he sat in Madame de Berly's bedroom. But, you will doubtless say, this was not the way he thought when he left his uncle's house and ran through the streets at random and followed

the carriage as far as Belleville. That is quite
possible, but

Other days, other cares !

It had long been dark and Gustave in his armchair was growing impatient for the coming of
Madame de Berly, when at last a light gleamed in
the garden and approached the pavilion. Soon a
confused sound of voices struck Gustave's ear ; he
got up in astonishment and listened attentively.

He recognized Aurélie's voice and a man's accents mingling with Julie's. Probably the newly-
married pair had wanted to accompany Madame de
Berly as far as the pavilion, but suppose they were
to carry politeness so far as to enter the room ! it
might happen. The voices came nearer, it was
necessary to meet the danger at all risks ; so, as
Gustave could not see any other hiding-place, he
crawled under the bed, where he hoped he would
not have to remain long.

They arrived at the foot of the stairs, and Gustave could hear what was said.

" What ! Aurélie ; are you going to sleep in this
pavilion ! "

" Yes, aunt ! I had it expressly put in order
last week."

" What foolishness ! you were so comfortable in
the room looking on the road ! "

" My wife forms many strange ideas like that;
she did this without consulting me."

"I hope, monsieur, that I have the right to sleep wherever it pleases me most!"

"Certainly, my dear wife, but —"

"But—but I tell you that we shall be much more comfortable here."

"But still, Aurélie, this pavilion is damp."

"But, aunt, you sleep here without any ill effects."

"Yes, but not on the groundfloor."

"I'm not at all afraid of damp, aunt. Come in and see how I have had the room furnished."

Without waiting for a reply, Aurélie opened the door and went in. Julie followed her with trembling knees, fearing that Gustave, whom she had not thought to tell that she slept upstairs on the first floor, might be waiting for her in the room downstairs. But one glance reassured her; he was not there.

"Very well, then, sleep here, since it suits you," she said; "I'm going to bed; I have a headache. I can see that it will be late before I am down tomorrow."

And Madame de Berly left Aurélie alone, being in a hurry to reach her own room, where she hoped to find Gustave.

But poor Gustave was exceedingly miserable under the bed where he had taken refuge; for the conversation had made him acquainted with the fact that he was in the bedroom of Monsieur and Madame Frémont. The couple shut the door and prepared to go to bed, so there was no means of escape. Gustave would be exceedingly lucky to escape detection; for what would be his excuse? To pass for a robber would not be possible, because Aurélie knew him; and in that case, Julie would be compromised. Well, the only thing to do was to stay under the bed and consider himself fortunate if he was not routed out.

Gustave stretched himself on his back and invoked Providence that neither Monsieur nor Madame Frémont might look under the bed before getting into it, as so many timorous people do, and waited in the deepest silence, without daring to move or scarcely to breathe, for chance or fate to help him to leave his hiding-place.

Madame Frémont put her hair in curl-papers, and her husband undressed. " Come, now! " said Gustave to himself, " I am going to be initiated into the mysteries of the matrimonial couch. I counted upon spending the night in love-making, and now I am to hear others engaged in it. That's an entirely different matter, but perhaps I shall gain some instruction from it; I must make up my mind to it."

The conversation of the married couple, however, did not exactly assume a sentimental tone.

" Be good enough to unlace me, monsieur! Oh, come now, how awkward you are! "

" My dear wife, there's a knot."

"Then cut the lace; you are easily embarrassed by a trifle."

"Ah! there it is."

"That's fortunate; I began to fear you would never finish it. What! are you putting on a cotton nightcap?"

"Certainly."

"How unbecoming it is to you. How ugly you look in it."

"It keeps me warm, and I don't want to catch cold in this room, which is said to be damp."

"Good heavens, you already act like an old man! Why don't you put on a flannel waistcoat?"

"That's just what I always wear, because it preserves me from many maladies."

"I hope you won't do anything of the sort, what foolishness! For my part, I don't want to sleep beside a bundle of flannel; it would scorify my skin."

"My dear wife, I am not completely clothed in it."

"That's a great pity."

Madame Frémont got into bed.

"The devil!" soliloquized Gustave, "what a woman. For a prude, it's very extraordinary that she should object to flannel waistcoats. What, that woman who constantly kept her eyes cast down when a man spoke to her! Then one must distrust appearances."

"Well, monsieur, will it be long before you have pottered about enough? Are you coming to bed tonight?"

"Here I am, dear; I was only seeing if the windows were tightly closed."

"Are you afraid of burglars?"

"No! but I am afraid of draughts; and in the country one can so easily catch a stiff neck."

"Good heavens! M. Frémont, if you had told me before we were married that you were afraid of draughts and stiff necks, I might have reflected. As a matter of fact, we are easily deceived by appearances. You played the blusterer, the roué, the indefatigable, the bully, and God knows what more!"

"Madame, I think that people select their partners in marriage on account of their solid qualities."

"Solid qualities, indeed! but where are yours, monsieur? Come, come, get into bed!"

Frémont blew out the candle and approached his better half.

"What's this, monsieur, you have blown out the candle?"

"Certainly, you know very well that I am not accustomed to keep a light burning while I am asleep."

"Asleep! ah, yes, that's very true, you are not in the habit —"

"What, my dear, are you annoyed at that?"

"How slow you are! Having a mirror put in my alcove was all lost labor."

"A mirror! I can't see how you should want to use one during the night!"

"Oh, no, with you I see it's of no use."

M. Frémont got into bed and his wife said no more. Gustave had great trouble in restraining the inclination to laugh that was caused by the above conjugal conversation. For five minutes the silence was not broken; but they were not asleep, for Gustave heard them frequently turning over. At last Aurélie's voice was again heard.

"Monsieur, are you going to sleep like that?"

"I don't think that there's anything astonishing in the fact that I should be sleepy. I was running about a great deal in Paris this morning, and am very tired."

"You are tired and that's all you have to say to me. I am not tired, monsieur, and I don't mean to let things go on like this."

"But, my dear wife, yesterday — "

"Yesterday, indeed! a fine thing to boast of! What, monsieur, after only six weeks of married life this is the way you behave! It's simply abominable! I shall seek a separation if this continues."

"In truth, madame, you astonish me; when I married you, I should never have believed that some day you would have indulged in such language; you, madame, who were so reserved in company, and so strict on all matters of propriety and decency! you who quarrelled with me when I sang the 'Sénateur' or the 'Grand Clerc à papa'; you, who couldn't understand how anybody could go to the Opéra-Comique to see 'Joconde' or the

'Femmes vengées,' and who had dismissed two chambermaids because their figures were too pronounced, and a cook because she dared to raise her eyes when she served the soup; it is you who now reproach me because I feel the need of a little rest."

"Well, monsieur, what has all that you have just said to do with marital duties? Yes, most certainly I like decency in public; but I also know very well why people marry. Religion teaches us to yield to the desires of our husbands, and even to anticipate them; it enables us to enjoy hymeneal pleasures and procreate beings after our own image and our own kind; you are a reprobate not to follow the commandments of the Lord!"

"Come now, madame! don't be angry! You know very well how tenderly I love you!"

"You say so, and that's all."

"Ah, I have given you many proofs of it. My dearest, let us embrace and make peace."

"Indeed, I give in too easily!"

Gustave could not distinguish the rest of the conversation.

CHAPTER X

Julie Loses Her Beauty and Gustave His Trousers. A Scene at La Courtille

THE conversation came to an end and Aurélie's voice no longer disturbed the silence of the night; there was no more restless tossing and tumbling about in the bed, and so Gustave concluded that the couple had fallen asleep. He was getting very tired of his cramped position under the bed, and determined to profit by this fortunate circumstance to make his escape, since he could not hope for a more favorable opportunity. If he were to wait till daylight to make his escape it would be much more difficult to avoid being seen by the servants; so he must take advantage of the sleep of the married pair and the darkness.

He crawled along very softly on his hands and knees and reached the middle of the room; then he got up and walked towards the door with out-stretched arms. He had almost reached it when he stumbled against a stool that his hands had not encountered; a wash-hand basin was on this stool, and it was kicked into the middle of the room, the basin was broken and the noise awakened the husband and wife.

" Who's there ? " cried M. Frémont. Gustave saw that there was no time to grope his way out; he had to escape. He reached the door, hurriedly opened it and mounted the stairs, while Aurélie screamed at the top of her voice, " Help ! help ! robbers ! " and Frémont ran to get his gun.

Gustave reached the first floor, knocked at the door and called Julie in low tones ; but there was no reply and Frémont came out of his room ; he was about to come upstairs and find Gustave, and, perhaps, put a ball through his head — which Gustave was very unwilling should happen. How was he to escape ? Our hero mounted the next flight and found the terrace door open, so he went through and shut the door behind him. He was now safe for a moment; but Frémont knew that he had taken refuge on the terrace, so he went downstairs and ran to assemble the servants, while his wife ran out into the garden in her night-dress.

But why had not Julie opened the door to Gustave ? Because, just at that moment, she was not in her room. And why was she not in her room in the middle of the night ? That is very easily explained.

When she went upstairs Madame de Berly quite expected to find Gustave there. What was her astonishment to find nobody. She hunted everywhere, in the presses and cabinets, and even in the bed, but no Gustave. Where could he be ? She went up to the terrace; he was not there, but where could he be? She had gone into her niece's room and knew that he wasn't there; so she could not understand what Gustave could be doing. She opened her window and looked out into the garden, listened attentively and coughed loudly, but nobody appeared.

"Well," she said to herself, "he must have grown tired of waiting and gone away. But no! Gustave would not have left me thus; perhaps he was afraid of being seen in the pavilion and preferred to wait for me in the garden; for he must be somewhere in the neighborhood. Let's visit the garden."

Julie took a light and went downstairs softly, so as not to awaken Monsieur and Madame Frémont, and searched every grove and clump, softly calling Gustave, who was then lying under Aurélie's bed.

The garden was a very large one, and Julie had not gone half over it when the cries of Frémont and his wife fell upon her ear. She stood still in terror, and said to herself, "He has been discovered; we are lost."

Madame de Berly hastened towards the pavilion; at the turn of a path Aurélie rushed into her arms.

"Oh, aunt, let us escape; there's a burglar in the house."

"A burglar?"

. "Yes, aunt! didn't you hear?"

"Of course! that's why I came out into the garden."

"It's very fortunate that you didn't meet him! He's now on the terrace."

"Are you sure of that?"

"Certainly; he hid under my bed. Good heavens! if I'd only known—but, aunt, don't go there; you are approaching the pavilion, and that man might fire at us from the terrace."

Madame de Berly would not listen to Aurélie, but kept on walking towards the pavilion. When she reached it, she mounted the stairs quickly, opened her door and uttered a loud cry when she saw a man who was black all over standing in the middle of her room; but her terror was soon dissipated, for this man was Gustave, who had been able to find no other way of reaching her and escaping from the terrace than by coming down the chimney.

"What! is it you? Poor Gustave! What a sight you are!"

"I was very lucky to find even that means of escaping them."

"But when they don't find you on the terrace, what will they think?"

"That I jumped off into the garden."

"Ah! an idea has just struck me! yes, I hear them coming."

Madame de Berly opened her window; Frémont had arrived with the gardener, his valet, and three or four neighbors, whom he had managed to wake up and who had consented to follow him to arrest the burglar.

These gentry all carried torches and guns; as they were about to mount the stairs to the terrace, Madame de Berly stopped them.

"The burglar has escaped; I saw him jump off the terrace into the garden and climb over that wall."

"Are you sure, aunt? The wall is very high and the espalier has not been injured."

"Those fellows are so nimble."

"Never mind, gentlemen," said Aurélie, "let us search the pavilion and terrace, nevertheless."

"On my word," said Gustave, "I hope they won't look for me here, especially when I am in your bed."

He hastily threw off his clothes and got into bed; Julie was about to do the same when hurried footsteps were heard descending the stairs and there was a loud knocking at the door.

"Open, aunt, open," cried M. Frémont.

"Why?"

"The burglar must be either in your room or in the chimney, we are certain that he came down that way; the chimney pot is broken."

"But, monsieur, I assure you that there is no one in my room; I should know it if there were."

"He is hiding, aunt; open quickly, or you are lost!"

"But, monsieur, I am undressed; wait a moment!"

Julie was, in fact, undressing, she quickly slipped

Gustave's clothes between the mattresses and then went to the door.

"Gentlemen, I am going to unlock the door, but please do not enter immediately; give me time to get into bed, I beg you."

"Yes, aunt; unlock the door!"

Julie did so, and hastened to get into bed beside Gustave, who made himself as small as possible and took refuge where people as a rule would not think of looking for a burglar.

Frémont with his servants and neighbors entered with guns to their shoulders; they looked into every corner and up the chimney, up which they fired two pistols.

"You see that he isn't here," said Madame de Berly; "he must have damaged the chimney when jumping off the terrace."

"But," suggested Aurélie, who had remained close by the door, "suppose he has taken refuge under my aunt's bed!"

They looked under the bed and found nobody.

"Didn't I tell you that I saw him scale the wall on the right?"

"But, aunt, there may be more than one!"

"Well, there aren't any here and I hope that I am to be allowed to go to sleep."

"Sleep! What, aunt, you can think of sleeping when we are surrounded by burglars!"

"Since I feel sure that there are none in the house now, I'm not afraid of anything!"

"Come, gentlemen," said Frémont to his neighbors, "let us make a thorough search of the gardens."

"But, monsieur," ventured the gardener, "if the robber climbed over the wall on the right, he must be on the premises of M. Courtaud, the schoolmaster."

"That's true; we must wake up M. Courtaud; perhaps we may succeed in arresting the villain."

They were about to depart when Aurélie stopped them.

"Gentlemen, are you going to abandon me? I don't want to stay all by myself on the ground-floor; they would only have to force the window-shutters."

"Come along with us, madame."

"In this condition? O heavens! I have been exposed to the gaze of these gentlemen far too much already. I will stay with my aunt; she has lots of courage, I shan't be afraid in her company. Aunt, will you allow me to sleep with you?"

"What nonsense!"

"Ah, please do, aunt. Go away, gentlemen, but leave us the gardener for a sentinel; he can remain below."

They went down and left the gardener on guard on the groundfloor with orders to fire on the first alarm, and then went to wake up M. Courtaud, leaving Aurélie in Madame de Berly's room.

Gustave was in a terrible situation; at any other

time he would have taken advantage of his position, but now, like another Tantalus, he could not taste the fruits within his reach. Our hero was not possessed with the virtue of St. Robert of Arbrissel, who slept between two maidens in order to mortify the flesh and thus defied the devil — who always ended by leaving him in peace. Gustave was possessed with the Evil Spirit and could not fight against him. Reader, I think if his case had been yours, you also might have fallen into temptation.

Julie was even more ill at ease than Gustave was ; she trembled as she watched Aurélie tying a handkerchief around her head and making her preparations to share her aunt's bed ; in another moment Madame Frémont would discover everything ; for the bed is close against the wall and there is no room for anybody to slide out on the other side. What is to be done? Well, heroic measures are needed ; sometimes we must risk all in order to preserve a part. Just when Aurélie was about to get into bed, Julie got up and took the candle that the former had set on the night table.

"Where are you going, aunt?"

" I thought I heard a noise ; I don't think that those gentlemen looked into that big wardrobe."

" Oh, aunt, you make me tremble ; don't go near it. Suppose someone were really inside."

" Well, we must make sure of that."

" Wait a moment while I call the gardener."

Aurélie opened the door and called the gardener. While her back was turned, Julie set fire to some papers at the bottom of the wardrobe and then came back to Madame Frémont. The gardener arrived all ready to fire at the robber.

"There's nobody there," said Madame de Berly, "I must have been mistaken."

"Never mind, aunt, let him make a thorough search everywhere."

The gardener came into the room and saw a thick smoke issuing from the wardrobe.

"Good heavens, ladies!" he cried, "there's certainly another one here; the robber has set fire to the place."

"Fire?"

"How unfortunate; it must have been I who dropped a spark in looking into that wardrobe."

"Let us escape, aunt, let us escape; I am already half suffocated with the smoke."

The smoke was beginning to fill up the room; Aurélie ran downstairs screaming at the top of her voice; the gardener dropped his gun and ran for some water. At last Julie was alone with Gustave, who jumped out of bed and threw his arms around her.

"Save yourself, my dearest! you haven't a moment to spare. Good God! what a night!"

"Darling Julie, and I am the sole cause of it!"

"Go immediately; we shall be suffocated with the smoke!"

"I must take my clothes, however, I can't go in this condition."

"Get out of this room at once, I implore you!"

"Leave you! I can no longer see anything. Ah, I have them, I believe."

"Go down; here is the key of the little door. Good-by, Gustave, make your escape!"

Julie pushed Gustave out of the room, that was now filled with smoke; but the gardener was just coming upstairs with two buckets of water, he saw a young man fleeing with a bundle and did not doubt that it was the robber they had been hunting for. Having no other weapon to fight with, he set down one of the buckets and emptied the other all over Gustave, who, thoroughly drenched, angrily pushed him aside. The gardener lost his balance and rolled down the stairs; Gustave jumped over him and made his escape from the unlucky pavilion. Fortunately, Aurélie had already disappeared, so he followed the path that led to the little door, opened it, and was in the country at last. For the second time he had to leap hedges, bushes and ditches almost in a state of nudity; and it was again on Julie's account that he found himself in this annoying situation.

"That's enough of it," said our hero through his chattering teeth, "I won't expose myself again to such an adventure. That woman costs too much."

When he had left M. Frémont's house a gunshot's distance behind him, Gustave stopped and began to put on his clothes; but here was a fresh misfortune; for instead of a pair of trousers he found a corset, a skirt instead of a waistcoat, and a robe instead of a coat; in fact, he had taken Julie's clothes instead of his own — a very natural error, since Julie had hidden his own between the mattresses of her bed and placed her own on the chair where his had been. In the thick smoke that obscured everything Gustave had seized what was on the chair, without noticing the change.

" They say there is a special god of lovers," said Gustave, as he tied around his waist a cambric skirt and a robe of gray taffeta; " but it seems to me as if the devil alone had mixed up with my affairs. Come then, let me be a woman, since I can't be anything else. I must confess that at the present moment this disguise scarcely suits me. When a fellow is drenched to the skin, a cambric petticoat, a taffeta robe and a little tulle bonnet are far from satisfactory substitutes for cloth coat and trousers. If it had even been summer time, but here we are in the month of March. What an idea to go down into the country at such a season. What an idiot. I was to follow that carriage. That was to teach me a lesson. What the devil do they do with all these cords? I must look like a merry-andrew, and, unluckily, the dawn is just beginning to break. What a night — to lie beside a charming woman 'and — to be bathed in her atmosphere, and then —

wrapped up in this way. Oh, dear uncle, if you could see me now, and Madame Fonbelle, to whom I swore every day that I was good and steady and constant. To the devil with these laces and ribbons. Now, let me be quick and get back to Paris before it is broad daylight; for if anybody saw me like this I should be carried before the prefect of police."

While our hero was proceeding with his novel toilet, sitting on the edge of a ditch between a patch of potatoes and a bed of pinks, Madame de Berly was exposing herself to the greatest dangers for his sake. Julie was behind Gustave when the gardener threw the bucket of water over him, and she saw him upset his adversary and gain the garden. " He has escaped," she said to herself, but very soon another thought occurred to moderate her joy; his clothes were hidden between the mattresses, could he have made a mistake? Had he mistaken a dress for a coat? Poor, unfortunate Gustave, in the condition in which he was left by the gardener, would certainly catch a bad cold if he couldn't very sbon get some warm clothes on his back. Thoughts like these thronged into Julie's mind, so she immediately formed a bold resolution; women do not calculate risks when it is a question of saving the object of their affection, and Madame de Berly was persuaded that Gustave would perish if he had only a robe and an underskirt to cover himself with.

She went up the stairs again; the flames were
already enveloping part of the room, but had not
yet attacked the bed. Julie shut her eyes and held
her breath and dashed into the room; she felt the
mattress and raised it, felt the clothes, dragged them
out. At last the precious objects are in her posses-
sion; she gropes for the door, but the smoke is
suffocating her and a whirlwind of flame reaches
her. Her hair, which is flying about her head in
disorder, soon catches fire and she loses courage
and falls down at the head of the stairs, exclaiming,
" Poor Gustave ! "

Julie would have perished if the gardener, who
had got up and somewhat recovered from the
stunned condition to which he had been reduced
by his fall, had not come to her rescue. The brave
fellow went up with his remaining bucket of water.
He saw Madame de Berly on the floor, took her
up in his arms, carried her down into the garden
and threw the water over her head to extinguish
the flames in her hair. At this moment help arrived from every direction; Aurélie had summoned
her husband. Frémont and his valet had aroused
M. Courtaud's entire household. The neighbors
hastened to the spot with water, they soon gained
mastery over the fire; the furniture of Julie's room
was burned and Gustave's clothes with it.

Madame de Berly came to herself, but she suffered horribly, her face was burned all over; she
would carry the marks of the wounds all her life.

Aurélie gave a cry of horror when she saw her aunt. Julie was resigned. " I shall be ugly," she said, " he will never love me again. My heart, however, is still the same ; but, at least, he will not run any more risks for me, and I will not fail in my duty."

Julie really lost all her beauty ; she was punished by her own sin. Just retribution of the things here below.

Gustave, with a bonnet over his ear, stays put on like a waistcoat and laced in front, a petticoat hanging down on one side and a dress trailing in the mud, walked through the Belleville high street with long strides. Day was breaking, and in this feminine costume he must avoid all adventures, particularly in La Courtille quarter, a common haunt of drunkards. Gustave congratulated himself on having passed the Ile-d'Amour ; he quickened his pace with great difficulty, holding up his dress with one hand and the petticoat with the other, and being frequently obliged to let go one or the other in order to hold on his bonnet, which the wind threatened to blow away.

Unfortunately for our hero, M. Favori, the savage from Calot's big hall and chorus-leader, known in the big assemblies of Kokoli, La Belle-en-Cuisse, the Salon de Flore, and others, for his talent on the big drum and his superb bass voice, had had a slight difference with Jean-Jean Courtepointe, a drummer in the cave of the Marronniers, on the subject of Mademoiselle Nanon Dur-a-Cuire, a mature maid who had long sold red-tinted eggs in front of the Grand-Saint-Morin, whose eyes set the hearts of all M. Desnoyer's customers aflame, but who rode a very high horse as to morals, and who stood as firm in her virtue as she was in her wooden shoes.

M. Favori, who had a fine gift of blarney, had a thousand ways of captivating the innocent beauties whom he considered worthy of his homage; with a fascinating grace he sang the romance of the "Pied de Mouton" or the plaintive song "The Sacrifice of Abraham." He went once a week to the Funambules to improve himself in pantomime; and every now and then to the café des Aveugles to pick up airs from the light operas.

Nanon loved the fine arts, especially music; she kept time on her heater when Favori hummed a romantic air, and contributed a second to the overture of "La Caravane" when the handsome savage played it on his big drums. Favori had taken care to foster Nanon's inclinations towards him; he flew to her in the entr'actes; he sat by her stall and taught her "O pescator del ondin fideli." This delightful air turned Nanon's head, and she hummed "O pescator" while shelling her hard eggs or cooking a herring.

M. Jean-Jean Courtepointe also cast his eyes upon the fair stall-keeper; the young drummer sang neither "O pescator" nor the songs of the

boulevards, but he carried himself gracefully while beating his drum ; he rolled the drumsticks with marvellous agility ; he made the little fifes strike up when they came down La Courtille, and often stopped in front of the red-egg stall to beat the retreat.

Nanon was virtuous, as I have already had the honor to tell you, but she was impressionable to gentlemanly manners and perhaps a little proud of having inspired love in the two handsomest men in the district. She smiled on the soldier, and kept eggs for him which she purposely colored yellow — a compliment that proves Nanon's candor and innocence. She would stop her work when the retreat passed, and Jean-Jean Courtepointe would never neglect to make his drumsticks dance.

Moreover, the young drummer was as good a dancer as Favori was a singer. Courtepointe had learned the allemande from a clown at the Acrobates, and he danced it to perfection, Sundays and Mondays, in Desnoyer's hall ; people thronged the place to see him go through his paces, and even the doorkeepers paid homage to his talent. Now Mademoiselle Nanon had a great liking for the allemande, a graceful dance, of the dangers of which her innocent heart was ignorant. M. Courtepointe had offered to give her lessons, she had accepted, and they practised every evening either at Calot's or at Desnoyer's till they had gained sufficient confidence to appear at the Ile-d'Amour.

You may easily imagine that M. Favori did not
regard Courtepointe's assiduities with a favorable
eye. He hung around his rival and watched him
with a jealous eye, he felt a strong inclination to
kick holes in his drum and to smash the sticks in
his face ; but Nanon, with a majestic glance, could
restrain the anger of her savage and calm by one
word the fury of his jealous transports.

"Favori," she would say to him, placing one
hand on her hip, "don't cast any doubts on my
virtue, or I will break off all singing and conversation; know that a girl of my character can dance
the allemande without making a false step."

Favori would look down, heave a sigh, take
Nanon's hand and kiss it, and leaning towards the
cheek of his fair one, would kiss that also, though
sometimes he would get a slap in reward for his
boldness, and then he would go away with a heart
less sore.

Jean-Jean also wished to attempt some liberties
while going through the steps of the dance, but
Mademoiselle Nanon had beak and claws, and did
not hesitate to use them ; one day she scratched
Courtepointe's nose, and thenceforward the drummer kept within the bounds of respect.

However, this state of things could not last;
the rivals darted menacing looks at one another,
sometimes, indeed, impolite words escaped from
their lips. Nanon restrained them with great difficulty, in vain she reminded them of her virtue

and morals, but without effect; these gentlemen were not quiet, for

It is not always a woman's goodness that is desired.

Favori and Jean-Jean knew each other to be terrible rakes who had overcome the virtue of several beauties who had been regarded as inaccessible; therefore, they did not put much trust in the protestations of the severe Nanon, for the most cruel heart has its moments of weakness, and all one has to do is to seize them. The flesh is weak, and the tempter, the demon, the devil, whatever you please to call him, greatly loves the flesh of young maidens and pretty girls; for it is with them that he turns souls away from the celestial path, to make them take that leading to perdition.

. One evening, while Favori was dressed up in his costume regaling the numerous spectators that filled Calot's big hall with a scene called "The Grief of a Carib, far from his Paternal Roof," M. Jean-Jean Courtepointe proposed to the fair Nanon that they should go and practise the allemande in one of M. Desnoyer's rooms. Nanon agreed; she was beginning to have some skill, and hoped on the following Sunday to exhibit her grace before a brilliant gathering. They went into a room on the first floor; and, faithful to her virtuous principles, Nanon opened the windows and door so that M. Jean-Jean might not attempt any liberties with her.

The drummer ordered up a bottle of white wine; Nanon accepted a glass—this had no effect, while Jean-Jean drank a draught with each new step.

Now, whether it was the effect of the wine or whether the drummer's passion had reached its height, he felt himself burning with extraordinary ardor; he invented charming figures and danced them in perfect style, and smiled on his fair one with a very amorous expression. Nanon, heated by the wine, electrified by her partner's talents, and wishing to do honor to her teacher, surpassed herself also and spun round like a teetotum in the arms of her drummer.

But the Tarpeian rock is near the Capitol, and Calot's large hall is opposite Desnoyer's. Favori, tormented by love and jealousy at the very moment of his triumph, perceives through the window Nanon whirling around with his rival. This sight makes him furious, he upsets three stools that represent the hut of a savage and a broom handle surmounted by a bunch of feathers which perfectly represents a palm tree; he jumps over his big drums, holding his club in his hand; he leaps over the benches and tables, breaking the glasses, upsetting an army pensioner taking a drink and two Auvergnats rubbing garlic on their bread; he runs ahead, upsetting everybody in his way, and runs downstairs several steps at a time. He crosses the street and flies into Desnoyer's like a madman. His false beard, that cost him forty-four sous, falls

off, but he does not notice that, and his knitted
trousers get torn across his stomach ; but nothing
stops him. He is determined to avenge himself
upon his odious rival. He goes upstairs, and finds
himself between Nanon and Courtepointe just as
the latter is performing a figure in which he has to
kiss his partner ; the drummer kissed Favori's
stomach just as the latter raises his redoubtable
club, rolling his eyes like the tyrant in a melodrama.

" Wretch, what are you going to do ? " said
Nanon, in a pathetic voice, seizing the arm of the
savage, who was about to strike his adversary.

" You have been pirouetting long enough with
this miserable drum-tapper. This must stop at
once, and he must feel the weight of my club."

Courtepointe was brave ; he pulled his shako
over his left ear, placed his right hand on the hilt
of his sword, retiring two feet and raising himself
on tiptoe so as to bring himself more on a level
with his adversary.

" Who are you calling drum-tapper, you miserable savage of the Rue Coquenard ? Do you think
you can frighten me with your Canadian get-up ?
Have I ever interrupted your singing lessons and
your pescator ? I will dance the allemande with
this lady as long as it is agreeable to her."

" You shall not dance with her any more."

" Yes, I will, Fifi ! "

The club was lifted, the sabre drawn, blood was
about to be shed. Nanon cried and screamed, but

they paid no attention to her; she threw herself
between the combatants, but they pushed her
away; she tore her hair and they let her do it; she
fainted on a chair, they took no notice of her; the
chair slipped, Nanon fell, her skirt caught and exposed her leg. The rivals stopped spontaneously.

"We must not settle our quarrel here," said
Courtepointe; "tomorrow, before it is light, I will
be on the exterior boulevard, outside the barrier."

"Agreed!" said Favori.

These gentlemen approached Nanon, they kissed
her skirt and placed her on a bench, threw a glass
of vinegar over her face and went away as soon as
she had recovered consciousness.

Now, whether Nanon had not entirely lost consciousness or whether she had divined the intentions of her two admirers, she appeared the next
day at the place of meeting just at the moment
when Favori and Jean-Jean, each armed with a
cudgel, were about to commence hostilities.

"Listen to me, first," said Nanon, advancing
towards the two champions, "you can fight after-
ward, if your minds are really set upon it. I am
the cause of your quarrels; it seems that I am not
to be allowed to dance with a drummer or warble
with a savage. You are both brave, that's well
known; your reputation is established and I want
to reëstablish my own, which has been compromised by your gallantry. I consent to marry one
of you, if you will lay down your arms."

"Good God!" cried Favori and Jean-Jean in the same breath, as they threw away their clubs; "choose! we are at your feet."

"One moment, gentlemen; first stand up, for the keeper of the barrier might draw evil conclusions from your positions. You are both handsome men, and both amiable and attractive, and I am wavering between the two; Fortune must decide the question. Here's a fifteen-sous piece, take it and toss, heads or tails; the winner shall receive my hand and the other must not bear me any malice."

"Let it be so!" exclaimed the two lovers. Favori took the coin and asked his rival to call.

"Heads!" cried Courtepointe. The coin spun in the air; Favori and Jean-Jean were on their knees devouring it with their eyes. "Heads!" cried Courtepointe; and he sprang up to cast himself at Nanon's feet.

Favori was in great consternation; but he played his part, and, as a man of honor, he approached the loving couple and himself joined the hands of Nanon and the drummer.

They all embraced and then started for the fine hall of the Grand-Saint-Martin to consecrate the morning to pleasure and to a copious breakfast. It was scarcely daylight, but La Courtille caterers are open at almost all hours. Courtepointe, who was standing treat, had ten casseroles put on the fire, besides ordering them to kill three rabbits, pluck six pigeons, and bring up enough wine for fifteen. They gave themselves up to gayety, and the future bride and groom were lavish in their mutual caresses. Favori was incapable of not keeping his engagements; but still, he had a heart, and every time Jean-Jean kissed Nanon's cheek he felt his poor heart failing. To distract his mind and drown his sorrow, he filled up bumpers for himself; but the wine did not extinguish his flame in the slightest; on the contrary, it increased and redoubled his amorous ardor. So what was he to do? Flee from the picture presented by the two happy lovers? That is what Favori did. He left the room, lighted his pipe in the kitchen, and went out to take the fresh air before the door.

A woman was coming along quickly from the direction of Belleville; she had somewhat of a cavalier stride, and her bonnet on the side of her head and her skirt lifted as high as her garters caught the fancy of the savage, who, as you know, was in a very tender mood. Favori admired a big but well-proportioned limb, a slim figure, and eyes that did not express timidity, and which the fumes of wine rendered provocative to him.

"There's my game!" said the savage, as he followed Gustave, whom you must have recognized by his gait and appearance.

"A word and a glass of wine," said Favori, approaching his charmer.

"Go away!"

"You are too attractive to be allowed to walk alone!"

"Go away; you annoy me!"

"I adore you; I have a crown to spend with you."

"Go to the devil!"

Favori would not be repulsed; he walked close beside Gustave and gave him a tender pinch; the latter turned round and slapped his face.

"Ho, ho!" said Favori, "severity! It's all the same to me; I must have you; I've set my mind on it and I won't play heads or tails with you, because it shan't be said that all the women have passed me by this morning. So now, not to waste any more words on you, I will carry you off."

Gustave struggled, but Favori, who had the frame of a Hercules, could have carried three of our hero; he tucked Gustave under his arm and started off with him on the run. Gustave cried out, but the street was still deserted; and, moreover, in the La Courtille quarter people were so accustomed to hear an outcry that they paid no attention to it.

The savage ran away with Gustave under his arm without heeding our hero's cries and protestations, telling Favori that he was laboring under a misapprehension. Favori was about to plunge into a little blind alley, at the end of which was his lodging, when two peasant women, mounted on their asses and bringing eggs and milk to Paris, turned into the street which Favori was about to enter. The savage, who hadn't seen them coming, collided heavily with the first ass he met, upset the peasant and spilled all her milk in the gutter. This accident allowed Gustave to escape for a moment from the arms of the savage; he gained his feet and took to flight. Favori ran after him, and as the second ass barred his passage, Gustave tried to jump over it. He hoped to clear the baskets without any trouble, but his legs got entangled in his robe and he fell heavily among the eggs intended for the inhabitants of the city. The terrified ass fell on its knees and the peasant rolled about with Gustave in a puddle of milk and broken eggs!

Favori now recognized that he had been mistaken in Gustave's sex. His ardor immediately cooled, and his sole thought was to escape so as to avoid paying the damage.

At length the peasants disentangled themselves from their asses, and shouted, "Help, thieves!" The savage was already some distance away, and Gustave was the only one left to pay for the spilled milk and broken eggs; but Gustave picked himself up, lifted his skirts high, and ran in the direction of the barrier. The angry peasants abandoned asses, baskets, eggs and milk in order to run after Gustave.

Our hero had a good start; he passed the barrier and went down the faubourg. The peasants ran after him, calling to the passers-by, " Arrest that thief of a woman, who owes us for eggs and milk!" A gaping crowd collected, looked at Gustave and then roared with laughter and made no attempt to stop him. Little ragamuffins ran along beside the peasants; it was now broad daylight, the crowd kept constantly increasing and had now reached the interior of the city. Gustave, in his dread of being arrested by the brutal populace and becoming the object of universal hooting, gained fresh courage and ran with surprising swiftness. He left the peasants and the crowd behind him, and took the first turning that came. He went down the Rue du Temple, turned to the right, went along the street again and then made several detours. Finally, exhausted with fatigue, he stopped. A young woman was just opening her shop; he darted in and threw himself on the first chair he saw before the astonished shopkeeper had time to ask him a single question.

GUSTAVE

Part II

CONTENTS
GUSTAVE — VOLUME II

CHAPTER I

Misapprehension. Suzon is Lost. Projects of Marriage

"Please, madame, for heaven's sake, save me; shelter me from the pursuit of all that riff-raff!" cried Gustave.

"But, really! madame — monsieur — I don't know what you are or where you may have come from!"

"I'm a madcap, madame; but that's all I am; and you may receive me into your house without any fear!"

"Good Lord! that voice! those features! yes, it is you. It's M. Nicholas Toupet, whom I met at the village wedding!"

"What, can this be Madame Henri, the pretty silk-mercer of the Rue aux Ours, who sat with me under the tree?"

"The very same, monsieur! What a singular meeting! But that poor little one! I must run quickly and tell her."

Madame Henri left Gustave in the shop and went up to the first floor, where she slept with the girl who had been left in her care. Suzon had been with Madame Henri only since the day before;

but two feeling hearts understood one another very
quickly.   Madame Henri was of an age and figure
to inspire love, and so she ought to be indulgent
towards the faults that that passion made others
commit.   These were not exactly Suzon's reflections, but after the departure of the colonel and the
housekeeper she had looked at Madame Henri and
then began to cry.   The little silk-mercer had consoled her by begging her to tell her all about her
troubles.   Madame Henri's gentle tones carried
confidence; when parted from a lover it is some
happiness to talk about him, and so Suzon had
naively related all her adventures.

Madame Henri had pitied Suzon, and then she
had uttered a cry of surprise at the name of Nicholas Toupet, whom the little one did not want to
marry.

"Why! I know that M. Nicholas; I met him
at a wedding at La Villette."

"Really! Isn't he ugly, and awkward, and
stupid?"

"On the contrary, he's a handsome fellow; he's
amiable and witty, and he dances divinely."

"Nicholas Toupet! he could never keep step;
he's heavy, and scarcely knows how to put one foot
before the other."

"You're joking; he was the best dancer at the
wedding."

"He's as timid as a hare."

"Timid? why he thrashed a cabinet-maker's

apprentice who picked a quarrel with him. He
would have fought the whole crowd if they had
allowed him."

" He's greatly changed then ; but was it really
Nicholas whom you saw ? "

" Certainly, Nicholas Toupet from Ermenonville, who was to marry the daughter of M. Lucas."

" Oh! that's the one ; but he will never marry
me. I would rather die than be his wife ! "

" Well ! I don't share your opinion ! and if he
were to love me, I would gladly marry him ! "

" Ah, madame, if you only knew M. Gustave,
Colonel Moranval's nephew, you would see what a
great difference there is between him and that vile
Nicholas."

" I have never seen the colonel's nephew ; he
may be very handsome; but I will never agree that
Nicholas is vile ! "

The two opinions remained at variance, though
in reality Madame Henri shared Suzon's opinion ;
but these ladies did not know Gustave's tricks.
Being somewhat calmer after having related her
adventures, Suzon had promised Madame Henri
to follow her advice and to be good and obedient.
They vowed mutual friendship and confidence.
Suzon tried to pluck up courage. She counted on
the colonel's promise that she should see Gustave
again. Nevertheless, she had spent the whole
night in tears ; it was the first night that she had
been parted from Gustave since leaving Ermenon-

ville. How interminable it seemed! how slowly time passes when away from one we love!

In the morning Madame Henri, who had heard Suzon's sobs, got up very quietly so as not to awaken the little one, who at last had fallen asleep from very fatigue. She went down alone to open the shop; and just at that moment Gustave hastily entered.

The silk-mercer thought she ought to tell Suzon of the arrival of the man whom she still took for Nicholas Toupet. She went upstairs and told the little one that he whom she detested was below.

"Oh, heavens!" exclaimed Suzon. "Ah, madame, I beg you not to tell him that I am in your house. Doubtless, he has come to hunt for me."

"I don't yet know what he is trying to do; he is disguised as a woman."

"A woman! that was so that I should not be frightened."

"Don't be afraid, I won't tell him that you are here; I merely warn you in order that you should not come down. Stay here. Why be afraid? I assure you that he shan't know anything."

Madame Henri went down again to Gustave, but Suzon was not reassured; Nicholas' arrival at the house of the silk-mercer was a proof in the eyes of the little one that the bridegroom elect still wanted to marry her. She got up, dressed, and in her anxiety she thought she heard Nicholas' footsteps on the stairs every moment. Her terror

was constantly increasing; she hastily made a bundle
of her clothes, opened the door very softly, and
went down the back staircase that led into the alley.
This alley opened into the street; Suzon crept
along the wall on the side of the street opposite to
the shop, and then took to her heels with the
bundle under her arms. She did not know where
she was going; but at least she hoped she might
escape Nicholas.

Gustave was resting in the shop without the least
suspicion that Suzon was so near him. He was
pleased to see that his pursuers had lost his trail.
Presently Madame Henri returned.

"Madame," said Gustave, "you must do me a
great favor, and that is to procure some man's clothes
for me, for I can't keep on wearing this costume."

"I should be pleased to accommodate you,"
said Madame Henri, "but I am still a young woman and have to consider my reputation. What
would the neighbors think of me if I were to bor-
row or buy a man's clothes? Moreover, monsieur,
you can't undress here!"

"Haven't you any back room?"

"Yes, but you could be seen from the shop;
somebody might come in at any moment, and there
would be a fine scandal."

"Do you sleep in another room?"

"You can't use it. The people on my floor have
very evil tongues; they might see you, and goodness knows what they might say."

"So, madame, you want me to depart thus strangely equipped, so that all the young ragamuffins may run after me and the guard arrest me."

"In the first place, I might ask you why you have assumed this disguise?"

"Ah, madame, we are the slaves of circumstances and the playthings of events. One man goes out to dine in the city, finds his friend dead, and attends the funeral; another goes to a ball, when he enters his own courtyard, a loose tile from the roof falls on his head and he is carried back to bed instead of attending the dance. Another man expects to spend the evening in agreeable company, dresses for the occasion, and is splashed by a cab; muddy from head to foot, he is forced to go back to change his clothes; he finds his wife did not expect him and she is playing écarté with a cousin; the gentleman is not very fond either of écarté or of the cousin, so he breaks out into a rage; the cousin goes away and then the wife raises a scene with her husband, calling him a monster and a tyrant and reproaching him with his jealousy; she becomes hysterical and the poor husband is obliged to run to the druggist's for ether and orange-flower water, and spends a whole evening on his wife that he expected to employ in playing cards and drinking punch. After that, what's the use of laying plans? For my part, madame, I assure you that when I left home yesterday I didn't expect to return in woman's clothes, but my own clothes were burned

up ; and although I do not present a very graceful appearance in these, I thought that it was better to cover myself with a dress than to go naked,
I sacrificed my self-esteem to a sense of decency ;
that's the reason I am disguised outside carnival
time.   Do I still meet with favor in your eyes ? "

" Doubtless, you have suffered somewhat in my
opinion.   Then you have not just arrived from
Ermenonville ? "

" Ermenonville, what should I be doing there ? "

" Don't you live with M. Lucas ? "

" M. Lucas ! Ah, I see the source of your error ; but I must correct it.   You will scold me,
doubtless, and consider me a sad rascal, but you
must know that I was never Nicholas Toupet."

" What, monsieur, you're not —"

" No, madame, I assumed that name, as I didn't
want to be known at the wedding to which I was
taken by M. Ledru."

" Is it possible ? Then that accounts for poor
Suzon insisting that Nicholas Toupet —"

" Suzon ! Suzon ! Ah, my dear Madame Henri,
do you happen to know her ? "

" Yes, monsieur, I know Suzon."

" Small, well-formed, fresh and pretty ?   Ah !
Madame Henri, I beg you to tell me where she
is. Have you seen her ? Do you know where they
have hidden her away ? "

" Good heavens, what vivacity ! what transports !
but since you are not Nicholas, who are you ? "

"I am he for whom Suzon has sacrificed everything, for whom she has deserted parents, friends and home — Gustave, the nephew of Colonel Moranval."

"You, Gustave! Ah, I ought to have guessed it."

"Is Suzon in your house? Yes, I'm sure of it; I can see it by your embarrassment. By letting me speak to her, you are afraid of my uncle's reproaches; but he won't know anything about it. Let me see her for only five minutes, and then I will go."

"Well, I can see very plainly that I must let you have your own way, or else you will be guilty of some fresh folly. Wait a moment and I'll tell her to come down."

Madame Henri went up to her room, and what was her astonishment to see no sign of Suzon. She went all through the house calling for her, and inquired of the neighbors, but it was all labor lost, for Suzon was already far away. Greatly disturbed, she returned to Gustave.

"Good heavens! here's another complication. Suzon is gone, she's no longer in the house."

"Gone! since I've been here?"

"I can imagine the reason of her flight, I went up to tell her of the arrival of him whom I thought to be Nicholas Toupet; she evidently believed that somebody had come for her, and ran away, so as not to go back to the man she detests."

" Poor Suzon ! I am again the cause of all her unhappiness. Where is she ? Without money and without resources, in a city with which she is unacquainted, what will become of her ? "

" Console yourself, M. Gustave, she will return here, I hope, and I promise to let you know."

" May you be right! Will you be good enough to send for a cab to take me home ? "

" What will your uncle say when he sees you in that costume ? "

" He'll make a row, fly into a passion, and finally end by calming himself. When I have changed my clothes, I will again start out to find Suzon, and I will answer for it that all the cabs in the city won't be able to turn me aside from my route."

Madame Henri went for a cab, Gustave hurried into it, thanked the compassionate silk-mercer and told the driver to take him home to the colonel's.

Gustave got out in the courtyard, ordered the porter to pay the cabman, and ran upstairs to his room. Benoit and his father stood gaping in front of the cab. Here was Gustave, who had not been seen since the day before, and who now appeared in female garb. Here was a fresh matter of conjecture for the servants. While the porter was paying the cabman, Benoit hastened to inform the colonel that his nephew had just returned in a muddy petticoat, a torn dress and a bonnet soaked with yolk of egg.

The colonel had not seen Gustave since his

interview with Suzon; he did not doubt that his
nephew had spent the night hunting for the young
peasant, and he had prepared a very severe lecture
by which he hoped to bring the youth to reason;
but he did not know what to think when he learned
that his nephew had returned disguised as a woman.
The colonel went upstairs to Gustave with the intention of rebuking him severely upon his disor-
derly conduct. Gustave was in bed; he had counted
on spending the day in searching for Suzon, but
fate had prevented him from accomplishing his
purpose; the gardener's bucket of water, his flight
through the fields in his shirt, his light robe of
taffeta and the race forced upon him from Belleville to the Rue aux Ours, had made our hero very
ill; he did not resemble the heroes sung of by
Homer, who were always victors because they were
invincible. O thou fiery Achilles, who wert mortal
only at the heel; thou savage Philoctetes, whose
arrows never failed in their aim; thou eloquent
Ulysses, who knew so well how to assume every
form; thou proud Agamemnon, who allowed thy
daughter to be strangled to make the gods favorable; thou charming Paris, protected by Venus;
and thou audacious Telemachus, whom Minerva
shrouded in a cloud when in the fray, I congratu-
late you all for having inspired the divine Homer.
In our day your bragging would be of no value;
to march to battle we have no longer any need of
talismans; moreover, we do not believe in them,

and our soldiers rush to the attack through a hail of bullets without invoking Mercury's caduceus or Minerva's shield.

Gustave listened to his uncle's sermon without interrupting him, for the fever had made him low-spirited; our frail machinery is indeed so subservient to the ills of life that the greatest genius when ill is rarely superior to them. Charles XII, the most courageous and the most enterprising man of his century, allowed himself to be carried away like a child from the field of Pultowa, not so much because he was defeated as because he was weakened by his wound; and the savage Cromwell, who made everybody about him tremble, became, it is said, very tractable when he had an attack of fever.

The colonel, perceiving his nephew's condition, forgot his anger and sent for a doctor. At the end of an hour, the doctor arrived. He examined Gustave, sounded him, looked at his tongue, examined his urine and said very gravely, that probably tomorrow the nature of the illness would declare itself.

On the next day the doctor recognized the disease and told the colonel that it was inflammation of the lungs. The colonel was in despair, for he loved his nephew, although he scolded him; he told the doctor that if his nephew died he would blow out his brains. The doctor bowed politely to the colonel and never returned to the house; he was afraid of causing a suicide.

M. Moranval called in other doctors and consulted half the medical faculty; at last, after six
weeks of danger, Gustave was saved, but his con-
valescence was slow. When he was strong enough
to remember all that had happened, and to look
about the room, Gustave thought of Suzon; he
told Benoit to beg his uncle to come and see him.

The colonel hastened immediately to comply
with his nephew's request.

"At last you are out of danger!" he exclaimed,
as he embraced Gustave.

"Yes, uncle; but where is she? What has become of her?"

"Whom do you mean by she?"

"Suzon, uncle; that poor little thing that I kept
hidden in this room and whom you took away to
the silk-mercer's. She ran away from Madame
Henri's because she mistook me for Nicholas
Toupet. What has become of her in this immense
city?"

"I have not the least idea; the disappearance of
that young girl has caused me a great deal of anxiety, but it is not my fault. Are you still in love
with that little peasant?"

"Yes, uncle, more than ever!"

"And Eugénie, Madame Fonbelle?"

"Oh, she is very amiable, but she does not love
me. Has she sent to inquire for me during my
illness?"

"Certainly, and very often, too."

"Indeed! Ah, if Suzon had known of it, she would have come to take care of me."

"Come, come; forget about Suzon, who cares no more about you, and think of Eugénie."

"Suzon not care for me! Oh, you judge her wrongly, uncle; she could never change!"

"You have said yourself that absence kills love."

"Yes, when it is light."

"And that women here are inconstant."

"Ah! but Suzon is not a Parisian."

"Was it to find her that you disguised yourself as a woman?"

"Uncle, six weeks in bed gives one time to think. I have compared all the women I have known. Suzon has the advantage over them all."

"Nevertheless, if you were married to Suzon, you would be unfaithful to her in a month."

"I don't think so, uncle."

"Well, I am sure of it; but make haste and get well; then, if you are sensible, you will renounce your past follies and get married, so that you may not be tempted to commit any more."

"Uncle, you are a terrible match-maker."

Gustave recovered slowly; every day Madame Fonbelle sent to inquire for the young invalid. Gustave was very appreciative of these attentions, and, little by little, the remembrance of Suzon was replaced by that of Eugénie.

Finally, Gustave was able to go out. His first visit was to Madame Henri.

"Have you seen Suzon?" he said as he entered the shop.

"Ah, monsieur, how you have changed."

"Tell me, Madame Henri, if you know what has become of Suzon?"

"No, monsieur, I have not seen her since you came into my shop disguised as a woman."

"Poor child! where can she be now?"

"At her parents, perhaps."

"Ah! I hope so; what did my uncle say to you?"

"He was angry; he scolded me; but I told him the whole truth, and he saw that it was not my fault."

Gustave went away very sad from Madame Henri's and called on Madame Fonbelle; Eugénie let him see all the pleasure she felt at his restored health, and evinced the tenderest interest in him. Gustave found Eugénie more charming than ever, and went home thinking seriously about his uncle's favorite project.

As he stepped out of the cab, he noticed that the porter was having a dispute with a little Savoyard of about fourteen or fifteen, who had placed his stool close to the gate of the house.

"What are you doing to this child?" said Gustave.

"Monsieur, he plants himself with his shoe-black's box close to the porte-cochère, and makes a mess. It is a great trouble to clean up, and this little rascal comes here to soil my pavement! Look how black he is! it seems that, not content with cleaning shoes, he also sweeps chimneys."

The little boy hung his head, and did not answer a word; Gustave felt compassionate.

"M. Benoit, why do you drive the child away if he finds that he can gain a livelihood here? The street is free to all. I wish him to stay here."

"But, monsieur!"

"Hold your tongue! Here, little boy, here is a crown for you; I hope it will bring you good luck."

Gustave threw a crown piece to the little boy and went in, leaving the Savoyard very happy and the porter very foolish.

Our hero recovered; with renewed health, he regained his vitality and amorous ardor. Eugénie was the object of his desires; he spent nearly all his time by her side; he courted her assiduously. Eugénie responded to Gustave's love, but she would not grant him a single favor, and grew very angry if he misbehaved. Moreover, to please Eugénie, Gustave had to break off with his old acquaintances. No more Lise, no more Olivier, no more infidelities and skittishness — such were the conditions that Eugénie imposed upon her lover. These might have seemed natural enough to anybody else, but to Gustave they were a little severe. However, our hero, who was getting more and more in love, had sworn to keep his promises, and Eugénie had promised her hand to Gustave.

" That woman is indeed a little exacting," Gustave said to himself sometimes on returning home. "She was cross this evening because I talked to a lady while she was playing; I certainly do not intend to remain in society without talking, or to pass for an idiot or a pedant! Eugénie is jealous; but that is a proof of love, and, therefore, I must forgive it."

The colonel was delighted to see that his nephew was going to marry; the day was fixed; the idea of the union was no longer a secret, and Gustave escorted Madame Fonbelle everywhere.

Whenever Gustave returned home, he always found the little Savoyard before the gate. The little boy would always take off his cap to him, and would never leave his place till he had seen him go in.

In three weeks, Gustave was to become Eugénie's husband; the colonel was making many plans for the future happiness of the couple; M. de Granci̇ère had a share in half of his friend's projects; Eugénie purchased dresses, materials and ribbons; and Gustave sighed and found the time long. Still three weeks! but how many events can happen in that space of time!

CHAPTER II

Woman's Intrigues. Jealousy. Fatal Meetings

"You must accompany me to Madame de Saint-Clair's entertainment this evening," said Eugénie one morning to Gustave; "there will be music; and, having heard that you have a good voice and know how to use it, for a long time they have wanted me to take you there so they could hear you sing."

"I don't like that Madame de Saint-Clair; that woman overwhelms you with demonstrations of friendship, protestations of affection and extravagant compliments. Do you really believe that she means what she says?"

"You know well enough, Gustave, that I value the ties of society for what they are worth; and to me Madame de Saint-Clair is a mere acquaintance. But her entertainments are brilliant; you enjoy yourself there, which is rare in large circles, because that severe etiquette and cold ceremony that kill gayety and banish pleasure in other houses do not exist in hers. Do come along; it will give so much pleasure to your uncle and my father and will please me."

"I will do whatever you wish, my dear Eugénie."

"Yes, I know that, while we are lovers; but when once we are married I shall have to be the one to yield to your will. Gustave, when I consider how marriage changes a man's conduct, ah! I tremble in advance. My friend, we ought not to get married!"

"What nonsense! you know how much I love you, and yet you think me capable of changing?"

"Oh, very capable! I am so happy now, why can't we stay as we are?"

"Certainly not, unless you will accord me all the rights of a husband."

"Ah, Gustave, you don't mean what you say! It is those very rights accorded to a husband that often cause the flight of love and pleasure. If, on the contrary, a husband had no more rights than a lover, marriage would preserve, despite the flight of time, all the charms of the first day."

"My dear Eugénie, you will never convert me; you will have to be my wife or my mistress."

"Sometimes a man loves neither; he keeps a mistress from habit and a wife from necessity. It is only a friend who can hope to be always a pleasure. I should like to be that only to you; but I love you passionately! That is a great pity."

"Between two persons of opposite sex one rarely sees ties that are only friendship unless that sentiment is the outgrowth of more intimate relations."

"Very well, I will be your wife, Gustave; but

I am jealous, and I do not want your love soon
to change to mere friendship.   I really am afraid
that I shall make you unhappy ; as the time draws
near, I feel that I am becoming more exacting and
uneasy."

"You don't seem to be ill-natured."

"No, but I love you too much, perhaps—and
that's a great fault.   Ah, my friend, how many
women there have been whose husbands have found
fault with them for this one crime ! "

"I shall not be one of those husbands."

"Till this evening, Gustave.   I must go and
think about my toilet."

Gustave went home.   On the way he thought
of Eugénie's reflections, he did not think he could
ever cease to love her, he did not fear that she
would ever make him unhappy ; but he was going
to be married !   Married !   He, who had so often
turned that bond into ridicule, who had made so
many jokes about husbands, who had played them
more than one trick and increased the sum of their
mishaps ; he must himself bear that name of husband, which he had despised and mocked a hundred
times.   The idea tormented him ; after having
frightened others, he trembled for himself; "par
pari refero," that axiom disturbed him.   Now,
ladies, that is an imitation of the evangelical moral,
do not do to others what you fear for yourself.   It
is by departing from this principle that among certain nations, particularly savages, they punish their

criminals only by the law of retaliation—"lex talionis"—a very wise law that ought to be in force among all civilized peoples.

So Gustave returned home, absorbed in his somewhat melancholy thoughts. He noticed that the little bootblack was seated on the curb before his gate, holding a handkerchief to his eyes and apparently overwhelmed with grief.

"What is the matter, my friend?" Gustave asked.

The boy did not answer but continued to sob.

"Monsieur," said Benoit, approaching his master, "I will tell you what the trouble is; a little while ago my father and I were talking, and we spoke of your coming marriage—of the wedding —of your wife—of the children you would have —of the breeches you would wear on that day—"

"Ah! you talked all that over with your father?"

"Yes, monsieur; because, as I want to do you honor, I must buy a second-hand sword to wear at my side when we go to the church—as I am young—if you wish me to look about for it—"

"Hurry up, Benoit, finish your foolishness, and above all do not think of wearing a sword."

"Ah, my father must also have his queue cut for the day of the ceremony, he must wear the Titus cut; you know perfectly well, monsieur, that he wears the pigeon-wings wig."

"Have you finished at last?"

"All right, monsieur, we were talking about the

costumes for your wedding. This boy stepped up familiarly and asked us who was the person who was going to get married. No sooner had I mentioned your name than he turned pale — yellow — red — that is to say, he was always black, but underneath the soot on his face I saw him change color, and ever since then he has been snivelling as you see him. Ah, I see what is the matter; he is afraid that your wife will think him too ugly to be allowed to stay at the gate."

"Benoit!"

"Monsieur!"

"You can go!"

Benoit withdrew, consigning to the devil the boy who stole some of his perquisites, for Gustave frequently charged the boy with commissions; the young bootblack always acquitted himself better than Benoit and always understood what Gustave said to him, although he received his orders with eyes on the ground and never spoke a word.

"What is the matter, my friend?" said Gustave, making a sign to his retainer to follow him into the courtyard. "Are you afraid that you will be sent away from here? Rest assured you shall stay; and when I take command of my house I will take you with me; you shall be my little page; will that suit you?"

The little boy made no reply, but he seized Gustave's hand, kissed it several times, and then suddenly ran away. Gustave was touched; he could not understand the grief and the affection that this poor boy had shown for him; but the thought of Eugénie and his marriage soon chased the boy from his mind.

It is now evening. Gustave goes to call for Eugénie and her father; the colonel does not wish to go out, for he has a slight attack of gout. They go to Madame de Saint-Clair's. The assembly was large; Gustave was welcomed with much politeness, but our hero thought that he could read the expression of malicious pleasure in Madame de Saint-Clair's eyes. That lady, though not pretty, had great pretensions. She had shown so many attentions and marked preferences to Gustave at M. de Grancière's entertainments that he had quickly divined her feelings; but Madame de Saint-Clair did not please him; he had feigned not to understand her, however, and he rightly dreaded her resentment; women will excuse a man they do not love from paying court to them, but they cannot pardon anyone whom they distinguish with attention for not responding to their love.

The brilliancy of the candles, the toilets, the music, in short, everything made the gathering seem a kind of fête. Gustave looked restlessly at the ladies seated around the room to see if he could find any of his acquaintances. Knowing already how jealous Eugénie was, he wished to avoid causing her unhappiness. Happily, he did not perceive any intimate friends. He was now more at ease.

Eugénie, whose lovely voice was well-known, was soon at the piano, and Gustave, who could not yet accompany her, took a vacant chair between an old dowager and a lady who wore a hat that concealed nearly her entire face. Eugénie saw where Gustave had seated himself and smiled on him tenderly.

"Come," he said, "she is satisfied; doubtless the lady in the big hat is ugly."

While Eugénie was singing, Gustave addressed to his neighbor a few of those insignificant words and phrases which are habitually exchanged in society and which fatigue neither the mind nor heart. However, the lady in the hat did not reply.

"This is singular," said Gustave to himself, "it is customary in society to reply to those who address us, and I have not said anything to this lady that could possibly offend her. Is she deaf? Is she also a grandmother?"

He leaned his head slightly forward and tried to look under the hat. She was a young woman, but she was not pretty; her face was blotched, and seemed cut up by seams and scars. Gustave retired, determined to say nothing more to his silent neighbor, when a sweet and very familiar voice came from under the large hat; it only said these words, "Is it true, Gustave, that you don't recognize me?" but these accents penetrated to the depths of his heart. He turned around suddenly and a cry escaped him; the same voice was again heard, "Take care, Gustave, eyes are upon us."

"What! this is no illusion? It is you, my dear Julie?"

"Yes, it is I — it is Julie — although I am hardly recognizable!"

"Ah! my friend, pardon me!"

"I have nothing to complain of, Gustave; why should I be angry? I know how I look now."

"But what has happened? What illness has overtaken you?"

"This was no illness. Do you remember that cruel night when I had so much trouble to save you in the pavilion? you know what means I employed; but you did not have your clothes; and the gardener threw a bucket of water over you. I went back to my room to look for your clothes, as soon as I had them I ran after you, but, stifled by smoke, I lost consciousness. My hair caught fire — I was saved — but I was never myself again."

"Dear Julie! and this was on my account! Oh, misery! I am the cause of all your misfortune."

"My friend, I never complain! I have done wrong, I deserve punishment."

"Ah, Julie! and to think of the women who are a hundred times more guilty than you and who have escaped!"

"I have lost your love, but I hope to keep your friendship."

"You have it, and for life."

"Then, Gustave, you must give me an immediate proof of it."

"Speak!"

"I want to preserve the little happiness that remains to me, and therefore my husband's peace must not be disturbed — he will be here in a few minutes."

"Here?"

"Yes; he has never met you since that fatal day. Ah, Gustave, I fear this meeting — I entreat you to avoid this trouble! — I now see the trap that was set for me. Madame de Saint-Clair knows M. Desjardins; she must have learned from him that you once came to see me."

"You are right, that woman has planned some unhappy scene; there is only one way to escape it — I will go."

"Ah, my friend, how I will thank you! I know that you are here with your future wife, and that it is hard for you to leave her — but this sacrifice is the last that you will make for me; you will go back to Eugénie, but Julie is lost to you forever."

"Dear Julie! only by great sacrifices could I prove that I am not unworthy of the attachment that you have shown for me! Good-by, I will go; may we meet again in a place where we may be free to give ourselves up to the feelings of our hearts!"

Gustave pressed Julie's hand tenderly and rose to move towards the drawing-room door.

Madame de Saint-Clair followed all Gustave's movements; she placed herself directly in front of him when he tried to leave the drawing-room.

"Why, monsieur," she exclaimed, loud enough for Eugénie to hear, "are you going to leave us already?"

"No, madame," replied Gustave, concealing his anger. "I am just going out to get a little fresh air."

During this colloquy, Eugénie, who was greatly disturbed, played and sang wrong notes, for she was watching Gustave. The latter was just about to get rid of Madame de Saint-Clair when two new arrivals entered the drawing-room and barred his passage. There was great surprise on the one side and embarrassment on the other; for these two personages were M. de Berly and M. Desjardins. Gustave stood stock-still. M. de Berly gave an exclamation which caused all eyes to be turned towards him; Desjardins opened his eyes wide in amazement and tried to speak; and Madame de Saint-Clair enjoyed Gustave's situation and Eugénie's wretchedness.

The scene soon changed. Julie had seen her husband enter before Gustave's departure, she feared an explanation and her strength gave way; she fainted and fell over on her neighbor, an old lady occupied in playing with her pug dog, the dog barked, the old lady was in despair, not on account of Julie's fainting, but because she feared her little dog was hurt. She gave piercing screams. Everybody rushed to Julie; only M. de Berly was not quite decided whether he should pay attention to

Gustave or to his wife. But our hero, who felt that his presence was more dangerous than ever, approached M. de Berly, "If you wish to speak to me, monsieur, I am at your service, and here is my address."

Having said these words, Gustave slipped his card into M. de Berly's hand, and left the room without giving him time to reply.

"That young man is still a little mad," M. de Berly remarked, as he approached his wife, who was recovering consciousness.

"Mad! monsieur," replied Madame de Saint-Clair; "he has never been anything of the sort."

"Pardon me, madame, pardon me! Oh, indeed he has, and very mad. Good heavens! I know all about it and so does my wife! Poor little wife! I am sure she became ill because she feared this meeting would result in a scene. I wanted to fight a duel with Saint-Réal; you know, Desjardins, that I said I should have killed him."

"Yes! I remember very well, even at that time."

"But, really, I do not want to fight with a madman! It is not worth while; moreover, my wife forbade me to do it."

"But, indeed, monsieur, you are certainly mistaken. My dear Eugénie, isn't it true that M. Gustave has all his wits about him?"

Madame Fonbelle could hardly speak. The sudden departure of Gustave, M. de Berly's words, and the fainting of his wife had brought trouble

and jealousy into her heart. She looked at Julie
very uneasily and could not understand the scene
that had taken place. To increase her anguish,
Madame de Saint-Clair asked her a thousand
questions, was sympathetic regarding her pallor,
and with perfidious attentions tried to redouble
Eugénie's embarrassment and augment her grief
and suspicion.

The day after this adventure Gustave went to
call on Eugénie very early. He expected reproaches, Madame Fonbelle made none. Her
manner was changed, she was no longer the same;
cold and reserved, she replied to the ardent Gustave, who could not understand this change. Hasty
and angry, he demanded, he exacted an explanation. She kept a sullen silence.

Gustave rose to take his departure.

" Monsieur," Eugénie said, finally, " I am going
this evening to the François theatre, would you
care to accompany me? "

" Willingly, madame, I will take great pleasure
in calling for you."

" What is the meaning of this caprice?" said
Gustave, as he returned to his uncle's, "she seemed
angry, yet she proposed that I should accompany
her to the play. Well, let us wait until this evening; perhaps I shall then learn the meaning of
this enigma."

" How goes the love affair? " asked the colonel;
" I hope the marriage will soon take place."

" On my soul, uncle, I can't tell you anything
about it; Eugénie is a strange woman. I believe
that somebody has set her against me. She is angry
about an occurrence that doesn't concern her in the
least, and if she is willing to believe perfidious words
that are retailed to her now, what will it be when
we are married ? "

" Bah ! all that is only a lover's quarrel. Tomorrow, or even this evening, you will think no
more about it."

After dinner Gustave called for Madame Fonbelle, who was waiting for him. They started for
the play, but they went in silence; Eugénie was
sad and seemed much preoccupied ; Gustave, vexed
at Eugénie's conduct, did not try to start a conversation.

They arrived and took their seats. The box
contained vacant places. Soon two ladies entered,
one was Madame de Saint-Clair, the other was a
young woman, quite pretty, and her face was not
altogether unknown to Gustave. He tried to recall her features, while Eugénie, seated in front,
chatted with Madame de Saint-Clair. The lady,
on her part, appeared surprised to see Gustave;
they looked at each other, they smiled and recognized each other. The person who accompanied
Madame de Saint-Clair was none other than Madame Dubourg, the one who spent the night waiting for her brother while her husband was on guard.

Eugénie appeared to be so busy talking to

Madame de Saint-Clair that Gustave thought he might venture to bow. Madame Dubourg did not seem to know that Gustave was with Eugénie; she had begun to address a few words to him when a gentleman entered the box. From his manner of speaking to Madame Dubourg, Gustave recognized the husband, the gentleman who always wore shirt frills and whom he threw into the gutter to escape from the patrol.

M. Dubourg was a tall man, and vain; he looked at the ladies through his opera-glasses, shaking his little finger on which was displayed a diamond ring; he expressed his opinion of the play, the actors and the audience in a very loud voice. He and Gustave soon engaged in conversation. Madame Dubourg no longer looked at Gustave. Eugénie was always serious, and Madame de Saint-Clair listened smilingly to everything that was said.

How in the devil, you will ask, perhaps, did this woman De Saint-Clair, who seemed to foment disunion between Gustave and Eugénie, know that Madame Dubourg knew our hero? How? Why, through her laundress, who, for the unhappiness of the future couple, happened to be little Lise of the Rue Charlot.

Lise was not wicked, but she loved to gossip and to take revenge when the occasion presented itself. Madame de Saint-Clair had learned that Mademoiselle Lise knew Gustave very well. Without any trouble she had induced her to talk of the

handsome young fellow who was such a bad lot;
a grisette will always make a parade of her connec-
tion with a young man in high society.

Madame de Saint-Clair had learned from Lise
the adventure of the night, Gustave's encounter
with the patrol and Madame Dubourg's morning
visit to the little laundress.

From the knowledge thus gained Madame de
Saint-Clair directed her batteries. She knew Monsieur and Madame de Berly, but that was not sufficient, she succeeded in forming an acquaintance
with Madame Dubourg. For a long time she
meditated upon her revenge, she planned meetings
and catastrophes, she wrote anonymous letters to
Eugénie, telling her of Suzon's sojourn at the Moranval house; a circumstance that she guessed from
what the elder Benoit told her, for he was not certain himself. Thus it was that Madame de Saint-
Clair destroyed Eugénie's peace of mind and
created suspicion and grief in the heart of a woman
already too much inclined to jealousy.

And why all this perfidy? To avenge herself
upon Gustave who had scorned her, and Eugénie
whom she detested.

If you wish to know how far the resources of the
imagination can go in destroying the happiness of
a rival, seek it in the heart of a vindictive woman.

But it was not sufficient to bring these people
together, some violent scene must be developed;
Madame de Saint-Clair succeeded. In order to do

this, she began a conversation with Gustave, at first
on indifferent subjects but soon she led it to other
topics.

"M. Saint-Réal," she said with a malicious glance
at Madame Dubourg, "I hope that when you are
married you won't make the patrol run after you
any more."

"What do you mean, madame?"

"I have lately heard of one of your follies —
which was quite pardonable in a youth. I laughed
heartily over it."

"What was that?" Eugénie inquired.

"A very amusing adventure; monsieur had a
nocturnal appointment with a lady, I think it was
in the Rue Charlot —"

"But, madame, this story concerns only myself,
and — "

"Good heavens! why be annoyed, M. Saint-
Réal? you are entirely master of your own actions.
Well, while monsieur was talking with his charmer,
who lived on the first floor, a patrol passed. The
husband was in the National Guard; he saw a young
man talking to his wife and gave chase to him."

"That's quite enough, madame. I don't know
what your motive is in relating this story, but I
declare that it is entirely false."

"False! Ah, monsieur, I must appeal to M. Dubourg; he lives in the Rue Charlot, and must
remember the noise you made that night by knocking at every door."

M. Dubourg had not opened his lips since the beginning of Madame de Saint-Clair's story, but he listened to it very attentively, and appeared to be greatly agitated. What monsieur feared more than anything else was to look like a fool and a laughing-stock. He thought he saw in this conversation between Madame de Saint-Clair and Gustave a scene purposely prepared to mystify him; from that moment he vowed to avenge himself for this affront, and, after darting a terrible glance at his wife, he touched Gustave's arm and invited him to follow him.

Madame Dubourg wept and was in despair as she saw her husband go out with Gustave; Madame de Saint-Clair feigned the greatest astonishment and asked what it all meant. Eugénie did not utter a word, but it was quite evident that she was suffering and trying to hide her feelings.

Meanwhile, Gustave followed Monsieur Dubourg out of the theatre. Finally he inquired, " May I ask, monsieur, what you have to say to me and why you are thus taking me out for a stroll? "

" You know very well, monsieur, that you have outraged me. There is no need for me to explain to you matters with which you are perfectly familiar, but I want you to know that you cannot mock me openly, to my face. It's bad enough to cuckold a husband, but, at least so long as he is kept in ignorance of it, he need not blush at it. To tell him of it in the presence of witnesses is carrying it somewhat too far, and I won't let it go by."

"Monsieur, I should like to remind you that I did not say a single word of all that,— in the first place because there is no truth in it, and secondly, because I am not such a coward as to compromise your wife in that manner. One may knock at your door at night without going upstairs. Consider also, monsieur, that a favored lover would not be likely to make a noise and awaken an entire neighborhood."

"Ah, so monsieur confesses that it was he!"

"Yes, monsieur, but I was not acquainted with your wife."

"Tell that to others. Monsieur, you have made a cuckold of me, that fact is perfectly clear; and you must answer for it to me."

"Monsieur, do you think that you ought to believe the scandalous tongue of a woman who is trying to create trouble in a household?"

"Madame de Saint-Clair is an honest woman, and incapable of saying what is untrue. Certainly, if she had known that I was the husband in the patrol she would not have related your adventure in my presence. These denials shall not deceive me, I am an abused husband; that's a misfortune that happens to many people of intelligence."

"But, monsieur—"

"I am a cuckold, monsieur, that's as clear as day."

" Well, monsieur, I will not contradict you, be one as much as you like ; it's no affair of mine."

" Monsieur ! so you add fresh outrages ; we must fight ! "

" Let us fight, monsieur, and put an end to the matter."

Gustave and M. Dubourg agreed to a hostile meeting on the following day.   The husband went back to the theatre and Gustave remained behind in the street, wondering whether he ought to return to Eugénie.   By going back to the box, he feared he might redouble the embarrassment of Madame Dubourg and the joy of the perfidious Saint-Clair, however, not to return for Eugénie, who had come alone with him to the play, would be a breach of good manners.   " Let us go back," said Gustave to himself.   " Poor Madame Dubourg!   It must be confessed that her husband is a singular man, he will insist on being a cuckold, and wants to hold me responsible for it.   I certainly am very unlucky ; I have deceived many men who have known nothing about it, and now it's a man whose wife I hardly know that forces me to draw my sword. Ah!   Madame Dubourg, if the opportunity ever presents itself, I will try to render your husband no longer a liar ! "

Gustave had the door of his box opened for him ; but the Dubourgs were no longer there.   Eugénie also had gone away, and Madame de Saint-Clair was left alone.   She turned around and looked at

Gustave; she did not say anything, but smiled; and her perfidious smile fully expressed all the feelings in her heart.

Gustave was about to break out, but he controlled his rage, the sight of which, he knew, would only increase the pleasure of the artful woman. He departed without giving vent to his anger and indignation against Madame de Saint-Clair. He remembered that she belonged to a sex that must be respected even though the individual is only worthy of contempt.

CHAPTER III

A DUEL. THE LITTLE SAVOYARD. A SPACE OF
THREE YEARS

GUSTAVE, after leaving the theatre, went to
Madame Fonbelle's house in the hope of pacify-
ing her and justifying himself; but the chamber-
maid told him that her mistress did not wish to
receive anybody and had given her orders that
she was not to be disturbed on any account whatever.

"What, not even her future husband?" cried
Gustave in astonishment.

"Nobody at all, monsieur. Those are madame's
orders."

"Ah!" exclaimed our hero, as he returned to
his uncle's house, "I am not married yet, it seems.
Eugénie is exceedingly jealous. The idea of getting angry about little things that happened before
we even became acquainted. That's being altogether too susceptible. I love her dearly, however,
and I feel that I should always be faithful to her;
that she does not believe because I have the reputation of being flighty, but I do not believe I am
quite so bad as my reputation and there is still some
good left in me."

Gustave did not say anything to his uncle about his last adventure, and the next day at dawn he got up to keep his appointment.

In order to avoid Benoit's gossip, Gustave decided not to take him. But, since fortune might be against him, and it is just as well to have somebody with you in case you have to be brought back home, Gustave made up his mind to take along with him the young messenger whose zeal in his service had never failed.

Gustave took his pistols and left his apartment. Everybody was still asleep in the house, the front gate of which was shut. It was necessary to awaken the porter, which was annoying to Gustave; however, he went and knocked on the window-pane, and asked to have the gate opened.

Instead of simply pulling the cord, the porter got up in his nightshirt, put his head out of the window, and looked to see who was leaving the house so early.

"What! that's you, M. Gustave?"

"Yes, it's I, M. Benoit; open the gate, if you please."

"Monsieur is going out very early this morning. Is Colonel Moranval indisposed? Has his gout returned? Is —"

"My uncle is asleep, I hope; and you weary me with your questions. Open quickly — hurry."

"But I don't see my son to accompany you, monsieur. Benoit! Benoit!"

"Devil take you! If I had needed your son, I should have waked him up myself. Open the gate, your chatter annoys me."

Gustave's tone was one that admitted of no reply. The porter opened the gate with profuse excuses. Now, being outside, Gustave at first fears lest the young bootblack may not yet have arrived as he looks at the spot he usually occupies ; but the little fellow is already seated at his post, eating a piece of bread and watering it with his tears. Gustave softly approaches him and touches him on the shoulder ; the bootblack, troubled at the sight of Gustave, hastened to dry his tears.

"What is it, my young friend ? I see you always crying, why don't you tell me what the trouble is ? If you are in want, or your parents are unfortunate, take this purse and don't stint yourself. I have often squandered money on follies, but I am not at all forward in aiding the unfortunate."

"I am not in need of anything," the little fellow answered in low tones, as he pushed aside the purse Gustave offered him.

The latter experienced a feeling that he could not define. The accents of the poor little fellow were as gentle as those of a woman, and echoed in the very depths of Gustave's heart; he tried to recall at what period of his life so sweet a voice had already made his heart palpitate.

But time was flying, and he must not make M. Dubourg wait.

" Follow me," said Gustave, " I need your services."

He got up immediately and followed our hero, who went in the direction of the Allée des Veuves in the Champs-Elysées, where he was to meet M. Dubourg. In fact, Gustave soon caught him strolling along the path. He made his little companion stop about a hundred paces from M. Dubourg, and ordered him to stay there till he was sent for. He did as he was told, and Gustave advanced towards M. Dubourg.

" I am exceedingly sorry, monsieur, to have kept you waiting."

" There is no harm done, monsieur, I have only just arrived. Have you your pistols?"

" Yes, but let us go a little farther on, I beg you, I am anxious that that child who has followed me shall not see us."

" Just as you please, monsieur."

They went a few steps farther into another alley. Gustave stopped and the two adversaries took up position.

" Fire, monsieur!" cried Gustave, " you consider yourself the injured one, and so it's for you to begin."

M. Dubourg did not wait to be entreated, he took aim at Gustave and hit him in the right side. He fell and M. Dubourg ran up to him.

" Well, monsieur, will you acknowledge at last that you have made a cuckold of me?"

"No, monsieur, no, I will never confess to a thing that is not true, and at the point of death I again tell you that you are mistaken."

"In that case, monsieur, I am very sorry for what has occurred. I will send a carriage and your little attendant to you."

M. Dubourg went away and found the boy very anxious ; he had heard the report of the pistol and was about to go and try to find Gustave when M. Dubourg came and told him that his master was wounded. The poor boy flew to the place where Gustave was lying on the ground covered with blood. He went up and wanted to aid him, but his strength failed and he fell fainting beside the wounded man.

"On my word!" exclaimed Gustave, "that was a fine idea of mine to bring this child with me when he is overcome by the sight of a wound. I wish I could revive him, but I have nothing about me. I feel that I can't walk, and nobody is in sight. It's very early, if M. Dubourg can't find a carriage to send to me, we shall be a long time without help."

Gustave shouted, but nobody appeared ; he tried to walk and summon assistance, but himself fell unconscious beside the boy.

Fortunately for our hero and his companion, M. Benoit, the house-porter, was as inquisitive as talkative. After opening his gate, he had immediately called his son, who had just got up. The latter hastened to his father and found him excitedly walking up and down the yard and then from time to time looking through the window of his lodge that opened on the street.

" What is the matter, papa? "

" Some mystery, my boy, something suspicious in M. Gustave's behavior. He has just gone out of the house like a madman, without deigning to reply to me. Look, there he is, talking to the little messenger boy."

" Ah, yes, he's a favorite of his, you know that well enough."

" Wait, he's going away and the boy is following him. Benoit, he's your master and you also ought to follow him, but at a distance."

" I haven't a hat here."

" Take my black silk cap. Go quickly, don't lose sight of them. You will tell me all that you have been able to learn."

" Set your mind at ease."

So Benoit had followed at a distance. When his master had made the boy stop, he had done the same, he had heard the pistol-shot, had seen M. Dubourg going away, and had run after him to ask if his master was wounded. On receiving an affirmative reply, he had gone to get a carriage, and arrived on the field of battle a few moments after Gustave had lost consciousness.

With the help of the coachman, Benoit placed his master in the carriage, got in beside him and told the coachman ·to drive on, without troubling about the boy, whom he left unaided. M. Benoit was vindictive, it was very easy for him to revenge himself upon one whom he disliked. Fools are generally spiteful, it belongs only to great minds to pardon offences and return good for evil.

They arrived at the house. Gustave recovered consciousness and was received by his uncle. The latter was walking up and down his room in considerable anxiety on his nephew's account — for the porter had taken care to inform him of all the events of the morning with amplifications — and swearing at his gout that prevented him from going out.

Fortunately Gustave's wound was a slight one and there was no cause for anxiety. It was not till after receiving this assurance that the colonel scolded his nephew. The latter was telling his uncle all that had happened the night before when a letter was brought to him from Madame de Fonbelle. Gustave read it and passed it on to his uncle.

" Is it a reconciliation ? " asked the colonel.

" Read it, uncle, you will see that it is impossible to get me married."

The colonel read the following letter,—

GUSTAVE : — I do not wish to make either you or myself unhappy by marrying you. I feel that I love you too much to be happy with you. Your light and fickle nature would constantly put my heart to the most cruel suffering. Two days ago, I

received proofs of your inconstancy ; and the past makes me
tremble for the future. Adieu! The Julies, Dubourgs, Lises,
and village girls will console you for the loss of

EUGÉNIE.

" May the devil fly away with all women, lovers,
intrigues and marriages!" cried the colonel, as he
threw away the letter, "but still, it's your own fault;
you are continually guilty of some fresh foolishness."

" My dear uncle, this time, allow me to tell you,
I am not in the least guilty; a malicious woman has
done it all. Madame de Saint-Clair has brought
about all the scenes that have taken place. She
has been trying for a long time to make me lose
Eugénie's heart, and she has succeeded at last.
But if, before becoming my wife, Madame Fonbelle is willing to believe everything that people
say about me, I ought not to regret the loss of her
hand. In order to live happily together, people
ought not to keep secrets from one another; and,
more especially, they ought not to lend their ear
to the tales of others who may try to disturb their
repose."

" If you were really in love with Eugénie you
would not reason as coldly as that. Well, I see
that it is written that you are to die a bachelor."

" No, uncle, no — I shall marry, I wish to give
you that satisfaction; and since I can't find here a
woman who wants me, as soon as my wound is
healed I will travel. I will go to Switzerland,

where they say that women are sincere; to England, where they love with passion; I will visit the
four quarters of the globe, if I must; and perhaps
I may end in finding a woman who is not afraid to
marry a bad lot.   But, by the way, I don't see —
Benoit! Benoit!"

"Here I am, monsieur."

"Was it you who found me unconscious in the
Champs-Élysées?"

"Yes, monsieur."

"Then you must have noticed beside me a little
messenger-boy; the poor boy who fainted when
he found me wounded."

"Ah! the boy on the corner?"

"Exactly!   Answer me; what did you do with
him?"

"I?   Nothing at all, monsieur."

"What! you idiot; did you abandon the little
fellow without giving him any assistance?"

"Monsieur, he ran away as soon as he saw me."

"Ran away! when he was in a swoon!"

"Oh, pardon me, monsieur, he was singing when
I arrived with the carriage."

"Singing! instead of fetching help for me!
Benoit, you're trying to impose on me."

"Monsieur has only to ask my father and he
will learn that I have been properly brought up,
and that—"

"Benoit, if that boy does not appear again in
front of the house today, I will discharge you."

" But, monsieur — "

Benoit was trying to exculpate himself when a
noise was heard in the courtyard; a servant came
up to say that the little bootblack had just arrived
at the house, and was insistent on being allowed
to see M. Gustave.

"Let him come in," said Gustave.

The little fellow came running into the room
and threw himself down on his knees beside the
bed of the wounded youth, seized his hand and
covered it with tears, unable to say a word on account of his emotion.

"Oh, the little dissembler !" said Benoit to himself, " how he plays the hypocrite; and all that
because he wants to try to be my master's valet and
jockey !"

Gustave reassured the boy as to his health,
told him of the extent of his injuries and questioned
him to find out whether Benoit had told the truth
about what happened.

While Gustave was interrogating the lad, and
Benoit was trying to think of some way to excuse
himself to his master, the colonel was scrutinizing
the little fellow and seemed to be deeply preoccupied.

M. Benoit was scolded; the bootblack was rewarded for his attachment to Gustave; and the sick
man was left to get a little repose, which we may
be sure he stood in need of.

At the end of ten days Gustave's wound was

healed. During this time the colonel had found out what Madame Fonbelle was doing; with difficulty, he learned that she had gone down to one of her country seats. This news deprived him of all hope of renewing the engagement between his nephew and Eugénie, for Gustave was not the kind of man to run after a woman who seemed to be trying to avoid him.

As soon as Gustave was well he began to make preparations for his travels; he had decided to go away for a time from France, where there was now nothing to hold him. For the sake of pleasing Madame Fonbelle he had given up all his old acquaintances; Julie had said farewell to all intrigues; the opera-dancers had lost all attraction for our hero; little Lise had just married a hatter and was satisfied with maddening her husband; Suzon had disappeared; Olivier, continuing to gamble instead of going to his office, had lost his place, and his conduct was so irregular that Gustave, who preserved his self-respect even in his follies, could no longer frequent the society of a man who only ran after the girls and went to low resorts. So Gustave had nothing left to keep him in Paris. He told the colonel of his resolve, and the latter approved, in the hope that travel would ripen his nephew's mind.

Gustave made all his preparations and consented to take Benoit with him, in order to prove to his uncle that he had no intention of plunging into fresh intrigues — for Benoit's reputation was made; it was well-known that he was good for nothing but to wait at table and groom a horse.

Benoit was delighted to follow Gustave, for at first he had been afraid that his master might be inclined to take the little messenger boy with him. In his delight he talked to his father constantly about his approaching travels, and took care that his conversation should reach the ears of the little fellow outside, because he saw that it troubled him. Benoit was naturally fond of teasing.

The day of the departure arrives. The colonel wants to accompany his nephew as far as Saint-Germain. He has his carriage made ready and Benoit is sent on in advance with horses, for Gustave wants to travel on horseback; and, in truth, that is the most agreeable way to get a good knowledge of the country through which we travel.

On getting into the carriage Gustave looked about for his friend the bootblack, whom he wanted to leave with some token of his generosity; but he was not in his customary place, neither was his box there nor his little bench. Gustave was astonished at the absence of the little fellow, and was sorry to leave without having seen him.

The carriage started, and they arrived at Saint-Germain in two hours. The colonel drove to the inn where Benoit had been appointed to meet them; they were nearly there when a country cart, going like the wind, collided with the colonel's carriage, which had no time to avoid it. The awkward driver upset the light carriage and then whipped up his own horses to escape from the colonel's anger.

Gustave and his uncle fell to the ground ; the colonel got up swearing and was not much hurt. Gustave had a sprained ankle. But plaintive cries were heard behind them, a crowd immediately gathered around the carriage ; the colonel went to see if anybody had been hurt by the upsetting of his carriage, and saw a little bootblack being picked up and carried into the inn. Gustave uttered an exclamation of surprise ; he recognized his little messenger boy and learned from the bystanders that he was riding behind the carriage when it was upset.

" For heaven's sake, uncle," cried Gustave, " get them to give that poor boy all possible attention while I go and get my foot bandaged."

The colonel complied with his nephew's wish and followed the boy in. Gustave, whose ankle was paining him greatly, was taken into another room and Benoit fetched a barber-surgeon who undertook to cure sprained ankles in twenty-four hours.

Gustave, forced to remain in a room without moving, grew impatient at his uncle's delay in returning; he was anxious for news of the little bootblack. He was about to send Benoit to look for him when Colonel Moranval entered the room. The colonel's face was pale and troubled ; his features showed such agitation that Gustave was frightened.

"What's the matter with you, uncle? What has happened? Is that poor boy mortally injured?"

"No, no, his injuries are very slight; they won't amount to anything."

"Then what is the cause of your agitation?"

"Our tumble might easily upset a man's nerves."

"But you weren't in that condition before you went to look after the boy; you are hiding something; in heaven's name, tell me what it is."

"I'm not hiding anything from you; what the devil do you expect me to tell you? The little bootblack is scarcely hurt at all; but he is slightly dazed with fright; he'll have got over it tomorrow."

"How did he happen to be up behind our carriage?"

"Apparently he had run after us."

"Run after us! with what intention?"

"The devil! with the intention of stealing a ride, doubtless. Don't you know that it is customary for little rascals to get up behind carriages?"

"Nevertheless, uncle—"

"Come, now, that's enough with regard to the boy; I tell you there's scarcely anything the matter with him; I have given him some money to pay for his remedies, and now don't worry about him any more. As for yourself, since a sprain is not dangerous, you can set out on your way tomorrow. Good-by, I'm going back to Paris."

"What, uncle! are you going to leave me all by myself in this inn? What is it that's so pressing? You can return to Paris just as well tomorrow."

"I tell you that I must start at once; probably I have private reasons for returning home; you can surely remain alone in an inn for one day; since you are going all through Europe, it is to be presumed that that will sometimes happen to you. Adieu; embrace me, Gustave; you have money and letters of recommendation for various countries; and moreover you know that you may draw on me at need, I will honor your drafts if you behave yourself well. Travel and try to be guilty of no more indiscretions; and if you come across a good, gentle and faithful woman, bring her back with you and she shall be your wife; but remember that I insist on these three qualities."

The colonel tenderly embraced his nephew and left him. A few moments later Gustave heard the sound of the wheels as the carriage departed.

Gustave fancied that there was something extraordinary in the colonel's behavior; his visible emotion on his return to speak to his nephew and his sudden resolve to depart immediately when there was nothing to call him back to Paris seemed to cover some hidden mystery. Gustave tried to fathom it, but he vainly racked his brains to discover the motive of this prompt departure. He hoped he might be more successful on the morrow, when he would question the little bootblack.

After dinner Gustave ordered Benoit to go and find out how the little wounded boy was. The servant went and soon returned.

"Well, Benoit, how is the poor boy?"

"Well, monsieur, it would seem that he is pretty well, since he has gone away."

"Gone away! the injured lad has gone away! Come! that's not possible!"

"Monsieur, I merely repeat what they told me; I am also greatly astonished."

"You are mad, Benoit!"

"But, monsieur, what is stranger still is that the maid of the inn assured me that your uncle took him away in his carriage."

"My uncle took the bootblack with him?"

"Yes, monsieur, yes! He took every possible care of him; he would not allow anybody but himself to help the boy into the carriage; that little blackguard must certainly be a sorcerer to make friends with the colonel like that."

Gustave was greatly astonished at his uncle's conduct; but he attributed this last action to the colonel's goodness; for under a somewhat harsh exterior was hidden a kind and compassionate heart.

Two days later our hero found himself well enough to mount his horse; so he left Saint-Germain to begin his travels.

Instead of following the road to Italy, which he had intended to take, Gustave turned aside and went towards Ermenonville.

Benoit, who did not know the road, was very curious to know where his master was going. He was a little less timid than he was on his first journey with Gustave; he willingly brought his horse up close to that of our young traveller, but he did not as yet dare to ask any questions.

At last they arrived in the village. Benoit recognized the château, the little bridge, and Father Lucas' house, before which Gustave stopped; he could not resist the desire to know what they were going to do here.

" Monsieur, are we going to stay here again ? "

" You will see."

" Monsieur, are we going to turn the house upside down again, make the cows run away and the old woman yell? "

" Benoit, I will do as I please. If you ask me any more questions, I will send you back to Paris."

" I will not speak again, monsieur."

Gustave entered the courtyard of the house; a peasant girl gave a cry on perceiving the young man; it was Marie-Jeanne, who had recognized Gustave. The latter was very glad before seeing the Lucas family to learn from the young peasant how he would be received, so he beckoned to the fat girl to come and speak to him.

" What, is that you, monsieur? Ah, I never expected to see you again. Why, it is nearly a year since you were here, yes, it will be a year in three months, it was about prune time —"

"Tell me, my dear Marie-Jeanne, how they all are? Are they as happy and gay as ever?"

"Oh, monsieur, there has been a great change, but of course you have not heard of it. Mamzelle Suzon has left us. But come in, monsieur, my mistress will tell you all about it."

Gustave saw by Marie-Jeanne's discourse that they were ignorant of the true cause of Suzon's flight. He went into the house, where he found Father and Mother Lucas.

The peasants received him with friendliness. Father Lucas did not talk as much as formerly, but his wife was as voluble as ever, and she told Gustave all about the disappearance of her daughter. Mother Lucas wept while talking of Suzon, and the tears of the good woman fell on Gustave's heart, for he knew that he was the cause of them. If he had never stayed in Lucas' house the young girl would have remained in the village. Peaceful in her parent's home, she would never have dreamed of other pleasures, and her heart would have rejected any thought of separation from them; but the presence of Gustave had changed everything, and Mother Lucas never suspected that she was talking to the very one who had turned the head of her little Suzon. Gustave was astonished when he learned that for the last two months Suzon had written to her parents frequently, though without giving them her Paris address, because she always feared that they would force her to marry Nicholas.

"She is entirely wrong, the dear child," added Mother Lucas. "Good heavens, Nicholas Toupet is married, he doesn't think any more about her. As for us, I was very grieved and very angry when she first went away, but since she has written us such tender letters and begged our forgiveness for what she has done—ah, upon my word, I am quite ready to forgive her, and I hope that she will soon come back."

"She is still in Paris," said Gustave to himself, "and she has never tried to see me since she ran away from the silk-mercer's! Well, Suzon does not love me any longer. Suzon is like all the rest, she has listened to the proposals of some libertine; I must think no more about her. I was a great fool to think that so pretty a girl would have remained faithful to me, I must forget her. May she be happy."

The young man left the cottage after having given Marie-Jeanne some tokens of his liberality; he withdrew from Ermenonville, but he promised himself to come back on his return from his travels, to learn if Suzon had returned to her parents.

Gustave went directly to Italy without any remarkable adventures on the way. He arrived in the city of the Cæsars, he visited the capitol, the basilica of St. Peter's, the tombs of the popes, he found the remains of Roman grandeur still among the ruins of the temples and palaces; but he sought in vain among the inhabitants for traces of that proud and warlike people, he saw only beggars and monks where consuls and patricians once lived.

"And these are the Romans!" said Gustave to himself, as he regarded those wan and dirty men that swarmed in the streets of the city, where many spend their whole lives with no other lodging save a niche in the wall, no other covering save a dirty and ragged cloak, no other food save macaroni boiled in water.

"Indeed, I am almost sorry that I came to Rome. I have lost here some of the illusions of my youth, and I begin to think that the sole benefit you derive from your travels is to appreciate the difference that exists between the past and the present, between dreams of the imagination and reality. It is doubtless on that account that travels make you wiser and develop your reason. I realize, indeed, that everything one sees can give rise to very philosophical reflections; a church where a circus once stood; a lottery office near the Tarpeian rock, and a Punch and Judy on the spot where the sons of Brutus perished. What would that savage republican have said if some one had predicted to him that his country would one day be that of jugglers, clowns and marionnettes?"

Gustave left Rome without regret; Benoit regretted the parades that he enjoyed as he walked about the town. Our hero visited a part of Italy, and then he travelled to Spain, Portugal, Germany, Poland and England.

Our young man had adventures everywhere; but the recital of his love affairs, which were alike wherever he went, would not interest the reader. Where the heart is not concerned, amorous relations are very monotonous. Gustave found that it was hardly necessary among the Italians to make a declaration, for those ladies saved him the trouble of doing so; and whatever may be said of the gallantry and coquetry of the Frenchwomen and of the looseness of the morals of the Parisian women, they cannot be compared to the facility with which the Italian women enter into an intrigue.

However, Gustave had the glory or perhaps the misfortune to inspire some violent passions; he carried away from Italy several stabs of the stiletto, and Benoit several declarations and proposals, which he made up his mind to ask his dear papa to explain to him on his return.

In Spain, Gustave twanged the guitar and made love through little lattices. He went to hear sermons so that he might admire the pretty women and exchange glances; he offered them holy water at the door, and the old shrews whom they call duennas and whom we call here by a very different name, followed him to his lodgings and brought him love-letters. In Spain there is more luxury and more beggary even than in Italy; extremes, nearly always meet.

Benoit, who did not know that in this country mendacity is a profession and that here beggars are

people who must be answered respectfully, was
unfortunate enough one day to repulse somewhat
roughly a señor beggar who was asking for " caris-
tade " ; immediately a crowd of beggars assailed
Benoit, he was beaten, rolled about and maltreated.
Gustave, seeing his valet in the clutches of a crowd
of beggars, flew at them with blows of his cane ; then
the affair became serious. To thrash beggars ! That
is an attack upon the customs, manners and privi-
leges of the Spanish, and these people will not listen to reason about anything that touches their
pride ; they introduce arrogance into meannesses,
self-love into child's play, and stubbornness into
puerilities.

The "alguazils " arrived ; they took Gustave,
Benoit and the beggars before his honor the cor-
régidor. His honor decided that the proud rabble
was in the right, and found it very hard that a one-
armed man had received two blows of the stick,
and he paid no attention to Benoit's broken teeth
and torn ears. Gustave swore and got into a terrible passion, and his honor was about to put
him in prison with his valet, but happily his wife's
duenna arrived. She recognized Gustave as the
handsome young fellow to whom she had rendered
many services and who had paid her liberally for
them. She protected him and saved him, and
Gustave left Spain, disgusted with a country whose
laws are made by inquisitors, monks and beggars.

In Germany our hero found the women very

amiable and their husbands great smokers. He lodged at the house of a handsome German woman who was passionately fond of waltzing, and invented a new figure every day — for in Germany when they waltz they are not satisfied with merely turning round, as we do in France. Gustave's hostess never got tired of it; she was even worse than Jean Courtepointe. Her husband played while she danced, and Benoit took lessons on the flute from the daughter of the house, a jolly fat girl who played on every instrument and could take her part in a quartet.

But the waltz tired Gustave and the flute made Benoit thin. Our hero left Germany convinced that the women excel in the dance, while Benoit was satisfied at having become a musician.

" That is a nice country," he said to his master, " without knowing any German, the women understood you at once; and as for the men! just say to them Haydn and Mozart, and they will talk to you for hours without giving you time to reply."

" Who taught you that ? "

" The fat girl who showed me how to play the flute. Those are the only German words that I have learned, and even now I don't know what they mean; but when you were waltzing with the hostess, my flute-player would say to the husband, ' Haydn and Mozart'; oh, then he would take his violin and he would stop for nothing but a drink. Ah, he was a terrible musician ! "

Gustave embarked for England. Benoit had himself bound to a plank during the voyage so as to be certain of keeping afloat in case of shipwreck; but they arrived without experiencing a storm. Benoit got off with having to vomit for four days in succession; when he left the ship he declared that his tongue had grown two inches longer.

A stay in great Britain is only enjoyable to a man whose chief pleasures are horse-racing, cock-fighting, betting, punch and plum puddings. A Frenchman finds it very singular to see all the women rise from the table after dessert and the men give themselves up to the gross gayety inspired by burned brandy, without regretting the departure of the fair sex, which is, on the contrary, the signal for giving themselves up to folly, if, however, the pleasure of drinking till you fall under the table can be called folly.

The young traveller thought the selection of English walks very dismal, for they have a preference for taking the fresh air and refreshing themselves from work and business in the cemeteries; in truth their cemeteries are very beautiful, and one may read on the tombstones very touching and often very original inscriptions. But you must be an Englishman to be able to take such a promenade without feeling melancholy; and that is a sentiment which is sometimes pleasant to experience, but which is dangerous to indulge in often.

Gustave noticed to what point this thoughtful

people carry their attention to little things, and the exacting usages of society.

In a brilliant circle, the young Frenchman was laughed at because, when he drank his hot tea, he poured the contents of the cup into his saucer, and because he did not put his spoon into the cup when he did not want to drink any more.

"If great geniuses are remarkable in little things," said Gustave, "then it is very certain that the English are a profound race. But I am surprised that, in the history of the Athenians and Spartans and all those Grecian people renowned for their intellect and valor, we are not told how a stranger should hold the cup that is handed to him."

Benoit quickly got used to the customs of England; he ate five meals a day, drank tea at all hours and punch as soon as it was night. He began to see his chest swell, and he learned with grief that his master wanted to leave a country where people lived so well.

The young misses were beautiful, and in England the young ladies have a great deal of liberty; they can go out alone with a young man into the country, to the play, or even to a ball without being considered improper;. but once they are married — what a difference! They never leave their houses without their husbands, and they give themselves up entirely to the care of their households.

However, the society of the young Englishwomen could not make Gustave forget France.

"Do you know," he said to Benoit one day,
"that we have been away for three years?"

"Three years, monsieur? My God! how tall,
stout and improved my papa will find me!"

"Oh, indeed, he will not recognize you!"

"Travel has polished me very much?"

"We stayed eight months in Italy, six in Spain,
a year in Germany, three months in Poland, and
now for two months we have been eating beef-
steaks and roast beef! I have had enough of this
already. Add to this the time we have taken up
in travelling, oh, indeed, we have been gone longer
than three years. Pack up our boxes, Benoit; I
want to go home to my uncle."

"What a pity! I am beginning to like punch
so well."

During his travels, Gustave had frequently received letters from his uncle. The colonel had
had a severe illness from which he had finally recovered. He always kept asking his nephew if he
had found a wife; he questioned Gustave on this
subject in every letter, but in this last he assured
him of the pleasure he would have in seeing him
again, and Gustave did not wish to defer his return
any longer. Moreover, our hero was tired of running about the world. Gustave was no longer that
bad lot who jumped out of windows, woke up a
whole quarter and fought with the guard; he was
more poised, more reasonable, and more reflective
than formerly, and without ceasing to love pleasure

and beautiful women, he felt the necessity of choosing his acquaintances.

"Let us go," said Gustave to Benoit, "let us return to France. I will go back to my uncle without presenting to him the woman of my choice, but, on my life, I must confess that during my travels I haven't tried very hard to find one. Decidedly I prefer a Frenchwoman to any other. The Italians are too fiery, the Spanish too jealous, the Germans too fond of waltzing, and the English too sentimental."

"This is true, monsieur, and I declare that with the exception of the flute, the marionettes and the plum pudding, I have not seen anything remarkable in the towns that we have visited."

Gustave bade farewell to the banks of the Thames. He went on board the steam packet and soon arrived at Calais. He smiled with delight on once more setting foot on his native soil, he was wild to see his uncle and his old friends again, and Benoit was impatient to relate to his father all that he had heard, seen and admired, and very probably a great deal more besides.

CHAPTER IV

Had You Guessed It?

An announcement of Gustave's return had already been sent to his uncle; the latter had sent a tall boy of good appearance to meet him, who was dressed like a postilion and who carried a letter in his hand as he approached our hero.

"Pardon me, monsieur, but are you not M. Gustave de Saint-Réal, of Paris, the nephew of Colonel Moranval?"

"Yes, my friend; what do you want with me?" asked Gustave.

"I have been watching for your arrival, monsieur, I am sent by your uncle, Colonel Moranval; I must first give you this letter, which he commissioned me to hand to you."

"A letter from my dear uncle? Give it to me quickly."

Gustave took it and read,—

My Dear Gustave:—You must be very tired from your journey and anxious to get to Paris; in order to see you the sooner, I send Germain, my new groom, with a comfortable post-chaise. Germain will drive you, and I hope to embrace you soon.

Colonel Moranval.

"Nothing could be better," said Gustave, "and

my uncle is extremely obliging; I am tired of horseback, and, moreover, my own horse died in Germany; at least, I shall arrive in Paris like a lord. So, Germain, you have a post-chaise, then?"

"Yes, monsieur, and it is quite ready."

"That is delightful; we will start as soon as I shall have dined."

Gustave was taken by Germain to the inn where the post-chaise was, and after he had dined well he got into the carriage with Benoit, and ordered Germain to drive quickly.

"Upon my word, monsieur," said Benoit, who sat opposite to his master, "it was very kind of your uncle to send us such a nice carriage and driver. We are very comfortable and shall arrive fresh in Paris."

Gustave did not reply to Benoit; he was buried in thought, he was thinking of all the persons he had left in France, and wondering what changes three years might have wrought everywhere.

The first day the travellers only stopped for meals and to change horses. Gustave was very satisfied with Germain, who drove like the wind. The second day was drawing towards its close, it was beginning to get dark, and Gustave thought with joy that they could not be far from Paris. He put his head out of the window. It did not seem to him that they were on the high road.

"Germain, where are we?"

"About six leagues from Paris, monsieur; we are getting near Montmorency."

"Are you sure that you have taken the right road?"

"Oh, yes, monsieur. I have taken a short cut which will save us a great deal."

"Suppose he should make us lose our way, monsieur!" said Benoit, anxiously.

"Why, idiot, are you frightened?"

"Damn it, monsieur! it is night — I do not see a single house."

"Do you always see houses from the high road?"

"But you said that we were no longer on the high road."

"Go to sleep, or hold your tongue!"

"Monsieur, I cannot sleep when I am frightened."

Germain drove slower; soon he stopped suddenly to speak to his master.

"Monsieur, I believe you are right, I have lost my way; I don't know this road!"

"I was sure of it!" said Gustave.

"Have we got to spend the night in the fields?" cried Benoit.

"Go along, Germain, and ask your way at the first house we come to."

"But, monsieur, the devil is in it all! One of my horses has lost a shoe, he can hardly trot, and if I continue to gallop him he will be injured."

"Good heavens!" muttered Benoit to himself, "what a fool he must be to let his horses lose their shoes. We are in a nice fix!"

Gustave did not know what to do. Germain proposed to go on a voyage of discovery; he thought he saw a light on the left, and he wanted to go and ask his way.

"If it is a house where they will take us in," said Gustave, "we will spend the night there, in case you cannot get your horse shod."

Germain went away, and soon came back to Gustave. The light that he had seen came from a very nice-looking house, where they had willingly consented to lodge the travellers.

"Let us go then and ask for their hospitality," said Gustave; "but you, Germain, you must try to get to the next village and bring back a blacksmith. I will not give up the hope of reaching Paris tonight."

"Yes, monsieur, you may depend on my best efforts."

Gustave got out of the carriage and, followed by Benoit, took his way towards the hospitable dwelling where people would be kind enough to receive them. He found a pretty house which evidently belonged to wealthy people. He knocked at the door, an old woman came to open it.

"I have been told, madame, that the master of the house is kind enough to permit me to stay here for a few moments while my carriage is repaired."

"Yes, monsieur, yes, you can enter. I will show you the way."

The servant took Gustave and Benoit upstairs

to the first floor, and opened the door of an elegantly furnished drawing-room. The master and the valet looked all around them and did not see anyone. The servant invited Gustave to sit down, and, leaving the light, went away.

"Monsieur," said Benoit, after examining each piece of furniture separately, "we are in the home of some distinguished person."

"I hope that we shall soon see the master of this dwelling, I want to thank him."

The servant returned with refreshments.

"Shall I have the pleasure of saluting your master?" Gustave asked her.

"Monsieur, it is a lady who lives in this house with her servants, she is very willing to give a lodging to travellers, but she never speaks to them nor sees them."

"What, shall I not be able to thank your mistress?"

"Oh, that is unnecessary, monsieur."

"Nor see her?"

"She does not wish to see anybody."

"That is very singular."

"Monsieur, there is some mystery in all this," Benoit whispered to his master.

Gustave was about to risk some more questions when a great noise was heard outside. Benoit gave a jump, the servant went downstairs to see what it was. Soon Germain appeared and came up to Gustave tremblingly.

" What is the matter now, Germain ? "

" Ah, monsieur, you will scold me, I am very awkward. Happily it didn't happen when you were inside. After all, it wasn't my fault."

" Well, explain yourself, then."

" It was a cursed rut that I didn't see, I was leading one of my horses, and just then — crack ! — the post-chaise rolled over on one side."

" What, the carriage ? "

" Oh, my God, monsieur, it is ruined. A wheel gone, the axle-tree broken."

" Now we are in a nice mess," said Benoit, stamping his foot, while Gustave laughed.

" What, monsieur, does this make you laugh ? "

" I was thinking of the idea my uncle had in sending Germain with a carriage in order to see me the sooner ; on my life, it succeeded well. But, notwithstanding all that, where shall I spend the night ? "

" Here, monsieur," said the old servant, who had been present during Germain's recital. "Your carriage will have to be repaired, you cannot continue your journey. But in this house you will lack nothing, and it will not inconvenience my mistress in the least ; she charged me to tell you that you can stay here as long as you please."

" Upon my honor, your mistress is too good. Since she gives permission, I will accept her kind hospitality for the night."

" I will go to prepare your room, monsieur, and

those for your servants. You will be served with supper very soon."

The servant withdrew, and Germain followed her to put up his horses and carriage, for it was too late to go to the next village to look for workmen.

"Don't you think, Benoit, that the lady of this house is very kind?" said Gustave, as he threw himself into an armchair.

"On my life, monsieur, we are very fortunate to be in the home of such an obliging person. However, I think there is an air of mystery here."

"Which excites my curiosity, I confess. This lady who receives strangers so hospitably, and will not show herself."

"That is because she is ugly, monsieur."

"You think so? Well, I find something, I can't say just what, rather romantic in her behavior. If I were still in Italy I would see in this a love adventure. Truly we are very strange; when something is hidden from our vision, we burn to see it. I should be enchanted to see this mysterious lady."

"Wait, monsieur, somebody is coming upstairs. I can see — Ah, nothing could be better!"

"What is it, then, a beautiful woman?"

"No, monsieur, it is the supper which they have served in the next room."

"Plague on the glutton, with his supper!"

The servant entered to tell Gustave that supper

awaited him. Gustave passed into the dining-room
and seated himself at a table that was elegantly
served.

During supper he addressed new questions to
the servant, but the latter did not seem to be a
gossip; all that he could draw from her was that
the mistress of the house was young and had a
child.

When supper was over, the servant conducted
Gustave into a pretty bedroom, and told him that
his servants were sleeping just underneath him, and
that he could easily call them if he had need of
them.

Gustave was alone. After two days spent in a
post-chaise, he should have need of rest. However, he did not feel the slightest desire to sleep.
The evening was beautiful; he opened his window.
The moon was just rising, and every object could
be distinguished. Gustave saw from the window
a portion of the gardens that belonged to the house.
On the right was the main building, in which he
perceived a light; doubtless these are the apartments of the lady who will not be thanked for her
touching hospitality. While his glance was fastened
upon the lighted window, our young man wished
that he could see into the interior of the rooms,
but soon he felt ashamed of his curiosity.

"What," said Gustave, "because a lady does not
wish to see a stranger, I lose my head. I have
created a thousand chimeras. She is a beauty! She

is a marvel! And, my God, she is probably a very ordinary woman who likes to be useful, and does not care to mix with people whom chance brings to her house. There is nothing very mysterious in that. And for a man who has just been all through Europe I am astonished at a very little matter — I who now pretend to be reasonable. Let us go to bed, that will be better than gazing at the moon and the apartments of that lady."

Gustave had just closed his window when the sound of a harp reached his ear. His curiosity gained the upper hand; he went to the window again and listened attentively. Somebody played a prelude with taste. The person who played had not very much strength perhaps, she did not surmount difficulties that astonish without charming, but she put taste and sentiment into her execution; soon a voice mingled with the sounds of the instrument, somebody sang a romance. Gustave experienced an extreme pleasure in listening to this unknown lady, for certainly it must be she, it could not be any one else, since the servant said her mistress lived in this house alone. But, alas, the song ceased, voice and harp were mute. Gustave listened again, he would have liked to have heard it forever. Never before had music aroused in him such sweet sensations.

After having listened in vain for an hour, in the hope of hearing some tones again, Gustave went to bed at last, but he was determined to know the

person who sang so well, and he went to sleep thinking of his mysterious hostess.

The next morning Gustave woke up early ; he
went downstairs and met the servant.

" My good woman, may I walk through the
garden ? "

"Yes, monsieur. Oh, you may go wherever you
please."

" Is my carriage being repaired ? "

" Yes, monsieur, but it will not be ready today."

" But I cannot allow myself to remain here any
longer."

" Why not, monsieur ? "

" It would be abusing your mistress' kindness—"

" Not at all, monsieur, she told me to beg you
to stay until your carriage was in thorough repair."

" I am afraid of inconveniencing her. And since
she will not receive me —"

" Ah, monsieur, there is nothing in that. It will
give pleasure to madame. I will go and get your
breakfast ready."

The servant went away.

" What a curious house," said Gustave, as he
entered the garden ; "you are treated perfectly, and
yet they won't see you. Well, I may as well stay
another day. Luck may come to my aid and allow
me to meet this lady."

As he was walking by a flower-bed full of lovely
blossoms, Gustave saw a little girl hardly three

years old; she was as pretty as a cupid and was running about in the garden all alone, gathering flowers as if for a bouquet.

"What are you doing, my dear little friend?" said Gustave, giving her a kiss.

"I am gathering flowers for mamma," replied the child, smiling.

"Where is your mamma?"

"In the house."

"Do you love her very much?"

"Yes, and my papa, too."

And her father, too! The devil! There was a reply that upset all Gustave's ideas; her father was alive, then. Why was he not with his wife? Perhaps it was on account of his absence that the lady would not receive anybody.

Gustave tried to make the child tell him more, but she was too young to express herself clearly; without replying, she escaped and regained the house.

Gustave went in to breakfast, he thought of this little girl whose charming features brought back confused memories, and of the mother's voice which had penetrated to the depths of his soul. He was sad and dreamful, he did not touch the breakfast. Benoit tried in vain to distract his master and make him talk; Benoit was forced to eat for two, but he acquitted himself well, for he had brought back from England the habit of eating all day long.

"How can I manage to see her?" finally cried Gustave, rising from the table.

"Who, monsieur?"

"Why, good heavens! the lady of the house?"

"Ah, good Lord! I have seen her, I, monsieur."

"You have seen her, you scoundrel, and you never told me?"

"Ah, when I say that I have seen her, I mean I saw her back in passing through the vestibule, and heard her tell the old woman to carry her harp into the little pavilion in the garden."

"She said that?"

"Yes, monsieur, oh, she said that."

"Good heavens! then I shall see her."

Gustave had noticed a pavilion at the end of the garden. This building had only a groundfloor, and you could see into the interior through the venetian blinds that shielded the windows. Our young man walked down the garden, he approached the pavilion and listened; nobody was there yet, but in order not to frighten the young lady by his presence he withdrew a slight distance and sat down behind a thick hedge.

Soon he heard footsteps, he parted the hedge carefully and saw through it a lady holding the little girl by the hand; but a thick veil covered part of her face, and she entered the pavilion without his having been able to distinguish her features.

Gustave went up to the pavilion, the key was in the door, it would be inconsiderate to enter, since this lady receives no one; but at least it is permissible to listen, and this is what Gustave did.

The harp sounded, a melancholy prelude was heard, then she sang a romance whose words described the sufferings of a heart far away from the loved one. Gustave listened attentively, he tried to recall where he had heard that voice that charmed him so much.

He walked all around the pavilion, he tried in vain to look through the venetian blinds, but all the windows were hung with curtains. But, oh, joy! she stopped singing to open one of the windows. Gustave went nearer, he gently parted the blinds, and his glance finally penetrated into the interior of the pavilion.

However, he was not entirely satisfied; the young lady was seated opposite to him, but her back was turned to the window, and from where he was he could not see her face.

The little girl was on her mother's knees, playing with her hair.

"Mamma, you are not singing any more; you are unhappy; you are always crying."

The young lady only replied to the little one by covering her face with kisses; then she put her handkerchief to her eyes.

Gustave is trembling, he can scarcely breathe; it seems to him that it is he who has caused the tears of this young woman.

The little girl jumped off her mother's lap.

"Wait! wait!" she said; "you know how I can always stop your crying."

The child went to get a large frame that was standing on a chair and which Gustave had not noticed before; the little girl could scarcely carry this picture, because it was nearly as large as she was; however, she placed it before her mother and covered it with kisses. The young woman caught up her little girl, kissed her and made her kneel down before the portrait.

"Pray to Heaven," she said to her, "that your father may still love me, and that some day he may return to us."

Gustave was no longer master of his feelings; that voice was well-known to him; he climbed up on the window-sill in order to see the portrait also. He recognized the striking likeness; his knees shook, his tears fell. It was himself, it was indeed himself who was represented on that canvas. But, this woman!—this child! He entered the pavilion and approached, scarcely believing his eyes. It was Suzon who was before him, and who threw herself into his arms and presented him with his daughter.

He fell overwhelmed into the chair on which she had been sitting. His heart had no longer the strength to support all the emotions he was feeling.

The door of a small room opened, and Colonel Moranval appeared.

"My dear Gustave," he said, advancing gayly to his nephew, "you did well to return alone, for I have been keeping your wife and child for you."

Gustave could not speak ; he held Suzon and his daughter in his arms and covered them with kisses.

"There—calm yourself," said the colonel, smiling. "You must be very impatient to know how it happens that your little peasant girl, whom you lost in Paris, should have become the lady who possesses the accomplishments and manners of good society. A few words will tell you everything. The little bootblack who established himself before the gate of my hotel was Suzon!"

"Suzon!" cried Gustave, "and I did not recognize you!"

"Ah, my dear, I was so disguised, so blackened that you could not recognize me ; and I was careful to speak very little in your presence."

"And why this disguise?"

"In order to be near you, to see you every day, not to leave you—"

"Poor Suzon! how many griefs I caused you."

"It was when running away from Madame Henri's that I formed that plan ; I sold and exchanged everything I possessed for the outfit of a bootblack. Alas! I was a mother. I bore within me the fruit of our affection and whenever you passed by me, I longed to throw myself into your arms and confess everything to you, but the fear of being separated from you prevented me from yielding to the impulses of my heart."

"The poor little one was afraid of me," said the

colonel; "however, I am not as terrible as I seem.
Suzon followed us when we left Paris ; she got up
behind our carriage which was overturned at Saint-
Germain. You remember, Gustave, that in order
to please you I went to see how the little bootblack
was. Imagine my astonishment when in the child I
recognized the young girl who had interested me.
I calmed Suzon's grief, for she wanted to die because you were going without her; I consoled her
by giving her hope that she would see you again
and I promised faithfully never to abandon her.
Meanwhile, I took care to keep you out of the
matter, and went back to Paris taking the little
bootblack with me.

"I confess that Suzon's devotion, the strength
and sincerity of her affection, her candor and youth
had already made me attached to the girl. I established her in my house and looked after her
education. She learned with astonishing facility,
and her sole pleasure consisted in talking sometimes
to me about you. She brought into the world this
little girl whom I soon learned to love like her
mother, for she already possessed all her sweetness
and beauty. Meanwhile Suzon learned that her
mother was ill, so she left everything to go to her,
and I approved of her conduct. Madame Lucas
died, pardoning her daughter for the fault that love
had led her to commit. Suzon remained at Ermenonville; she was unwilling to leave her father,
who had only her to console him. She spent eight

months in her native village; at the end of that time a malignant fever carried off the old man. I went to Ermenonville and compelled Suzon to return home with me; I had some trouble to induce her to do so, as she did not want to leave the village and her parents' tomb; but I talked to her again about you and her love prevailed.

"Finally, my dear Gustave, I appreciated more every day the virtues and amiable qualities of her whom I had taken under my protection. A severe illness would have carried me off but for Suzon's care and help. So much devotion touched my heart, and I began to wish that in your travels you might not meet with a woman who completely captivated you. I confided my views to Suzon; and you may judge of her joy. Nevertheless, she begged me not to say a word to you about her, as she wanted to leave you entirely the master of your own heart. But you may imagine with what anxiety she listened to your letters, from which she ceaselessly feared to learn that you had made a choice.

"At last you announced to me your return, and I sent Germain to meet you, instructing him to bring you here. I wanted to pique your curiosity; I know your heart, Gustave, but I tried to move it deeply so that you might appreciate all the more the great happiness that I have reserved for you. Be happy, my dear boy, I 'give you a charming child and an adorable wife, by whose side you won't find time pass slowly; in the first place, because she possesses talents that embellish domestic life, and in the second, because, possessing a cultivated mind, you can converse with her on other subjects than love. Love is a charming conversation, my children, but in order always to have something to say on that subject, it must not be exhausted in the first place—and that's what you were doing during Suzon's first residence in my house."

" My dear uncle," cried Gustave, throwing his arms around the colonel's neck, " I will be constant henceforth. By the side of Suzon, yourself and my daughter I shall find the happiness I have vainly sought in the whirl of intrigue and folly."

" My boy, youth must run its course ; you have sown your wild oats, so much the better, that reassures me regarding your future."

" Ah, Gustave," said Suzon, taking her lover's hand, " I could never have believed that I should be so happy. Who could have imagined when you came to the village that I should be your wife ? "

" My dear child," said the colonel, as he joined the hands of the two lovers, " you have proved to me that virtue, sweetness, wit and beauty can take the place of birth and fortune."